the
natural

BERNARD MALAMUD

the natural

With an Introduction
by Roger Angell

TIME Reading Program Special Edition
Time-Life Books Inc., Alexandria, Virginia

Time-Life Books Inc.
is a wholly owned subsidiary of
TIME INCORPORATED

TIME Reading Program: *Editor*, Max Gissen

Library of Congress CIP data following page 241.

For information about any Time-Life book, please write:
Reader Information, Time-Life Books,
541 North Fairbanks Court, Chicago, Illinois 60611

For My Father

BERNARD MALAMUD

editors' preface

At a time when many authors are scrutinizing the sad condition of alienated man, Bernard Malamud has chosen to celebrate life. In 1959, when he received the National Book Award for his first volume of short stories, *The Magic Barrel*, Malamud said that the writer's chief task is to recapture man's image as human being "as each of us in his secret heart knows it to be, and as history and literature have from the beginning revealed it." Malamud is fascinated with the choices that men turn from or grasp in life; by facing up to those choices, he tells us, we learn to understand and to accept ourselves as human beings. In much of Malamud's writing, self-discovery brings a spiritual rebirth, and with it a chance to make new choices for a better second life.

This is the outstanding quality of Malamud's hugely successful second novel, *The Assistant* (1957). In that story, the troubled thief Frank, who robbed an old, saintly grocer, returns to the shop to work and, in serving his penance, to be reborn. Similarly, the hero of Malamud's third novel, appropriately titled *A New Life* (1961), is a chronic failure who tries to rediscover himself; his choices in the end are uncertain, and neither he nor the reader can be quite sure that he will get another chance.

Roy Hobbs, the hero of *The Natural*, Malamud's first novel (1952), is a reborn man, too, but he is a special case. In fact, *The Natural* is a wonderfully special book altogether. First off, it is quite possibly the zaniest baseball yarn ever written—"a book of magic," as Roger Angell puts it in his new introduction to this special edition. It is almost as if Malamud decided to pluck from baseball lore every oddball character, every sudden-death play, every tattered cliché of the sports pages, every outrageous lump-in-the-throat plot device of pulp baseball fiction, and concoct from all this a kind of Marx Brothers extravaganza that even the earliest one-reeler moviemakers could not have imagined.

There is Roy, the taciturn, Gary Cooper-ish country boy, who makes it to the big leagues carrying his hand-hewn bat in a bassoon case. His first time at the plate, Roy follows orders and literally wallops the cover off the ball. Eventually he brings his team from last place to the first division. Here too you will find the malevolent sportswriter; the aged manager; the muscular, insufferable stars of the team; the nasty gambler; the crooked owner (a judge in wig and green eyeshade) who tries to sell out his own team; a beautiful girl who gets her kicks by murdering current sports heroes; and finally, the cruelly insatiable fans—demanding, whacky, worshipful—among whom none is so cruel or so insatiable as the strange, foul-mouthed, horn-blasting dwarf, Otto Zipp. (Wait till you see how Roy pays his respects to Mr. Zipp.)

While there is plenty to laugh about in *The Natural*, there is also much to ponder, for Malamud throws a pitch that is much more than a satiric knuckleball. Within the baseball framework is a close-up view of the American mythic hero, illustrated at times with a lyrical quality that raises language to literature. The problem for Roy Hobbs, as critic Leslie Fiedler writes, "is the proper and pious use of his gift, that natural (or magical) talent which has its meaning only in its free exercise, the gratuitous, poetic act. For the fans, which is to say for *us*, the problem is our relationship to the hero and the question of whether he can survive our bribes and adulation, make the singular, representative act which alone can fulfill us, before we corrupt him into our own sterile image."

For an example of how the crowd corrupts its heroes, Malamud presents an afternoon at the stadium when the fans have declared a familiar ritual. It is "Roy Hobbs Day," and the lovers of the game have showered Roy with the symbols of their gratitude:

Two television sets, a baby tractor, five hundred feet of pink plastic garden hose, a nanny goat, a lifetime pass to the Paramount, one dozen hand-painted neckties offering different views of the Grand Canyon, six aluminum traveling cases, and a credit for seventy-five taxi rides in Philadelphia. Also three hundred pounds of a New Jersey brand Swiss cheese, a set of andirons and tongs, forty gallons of pistachio ice cream, six crates of lemons, a frozen side of hog, hunting knife, bearskin rug, snowshoes, four burner electric range, deed to a lot in Florida, twelve pairs of monogrammed blue shorts, movie camera and projector, a Chris-Craft motor boat —and, because everybody thought the Judge . . . was too cheap to live—a certified check for thirty-six hundred dollars. Although the committee had tried to keep out all oddball contributions, a few slipped in, including a smelly package of Limburger cheese, one human skull, bundle of comic books, can of rat exterminator, and a package of dull razor blades, this last with a card attached in the crabbed handwriting of Otto Zipp: "Here, cut your throat."

Besides drawing humor like that out of the blight of materialism, Malamud has also created a hero who is a haunted man, groping despondently among his own personal demons for a clue to his own being. Iris, the woman who loves him, says, "Without heroes we're all plain people and don't know how far we can go . . . it's their function to be the best and for the rest of us to understand what they represent and guide ourselves accordingly." Roy comes to understand this, but he makes the wrong choices, and so the myth fails. At the end, a fan says of him, "He coulda been a king," and a newsboy pleads with him—in a line straight out of baseball's book of legends— "Say it ain't true, Roy."

It is worth mentioning that in tackling a serious subject in a comic vein, Malamud built his story on a classical underpinning, the legend of the Holy Grail. The league pennant itself is Roy Hobbs's Grail; Pop Fisher, the manager, is the Fisher King of the Grail stories; the name of the baseball club, the Knights, is an obvious reference to the Arthurian Legend; Roy's bat, Wonderboy, fashioned from a lightning-struck tree, is King Arthur's Excalibur.

Malamud was probably at home with the mystique of baseball long before he ever heard of the mysteries of the Holy Grail. He was born in Brooklyn, where the Dodgers were the Knights of their day. After attending public high school, Malamud got a Bachelor of Arts degree at the College of the City of New York and his Master's at Columbia University. For nine years he taught English at evening high school classes, and in 1949, at the age of 35, became an assistant professor at Oregon State College. He stayed there for 12 years, drawing on that scene for the background to A New Life. Since 1961, he has been teaching writing and literature at Bennington College in Vermont. In 1963 he published his second collection of short stories, *Idiots First*.

Those who have discovered Malamud in his other novels and stories are likely to agree with the growing number of critics who see in him a man of generous literary dimensions; those who rediscover him in this special edition of *The Natural* are certain to be convinced of that. With a deceptive effortlessness wreathed in comedy, Malamud has shown us how to make the right choice when we get a second chance. He has also fixed things so that we will never again be able to flick through the baseball pages of the newspapers without thinking of Roy Hobbs and Wonderboy.

—THE EDITORS

ⓇⓉⓅ introduction

Roger Angell is a writer and fiction editor on the staff of *The New Yorker*. His contributions to the magazine, in addition to fiction and humor, include reports on baseball for "The Sporting Scene" department. He is the author of a book of stories, *The Stone Arbor*, and two baseball books, *The Summer Game* and *Five Seasons*.

The literature of baseball is famously skimpy. One starts with those celebrated antiques, the Ring Lardner stories, and concludes almost at once with three pleasing, Lardner-touched novels by Mark Harris—*The Southpaw, Bang the Drum Slowly* and *A Ticket for a Seamstitch*. The intervening prairie is occupied only by a few fictional ballplayers like Nebraska Crane in Thomas Wolfe's *You Can't Go Home Again*, a handful of short stories and a gentle, marvelous poem by Rolfe Humphries called *Polo Grounds*. (Some of Hemingway's males talk about baseball from time to time, but I have never quite trusted them; Hemingway misspelled Frank Frisch's name in *The Sun Also Rises*.) This surprising sparsity becomes explicable only if one reads the second-rate baseball novels—there are two or three of these every year—and notices that most of them founder on the identical reef. Almost without exception they are literal, documentary, implacably insidey. Their authors, awed by living big-league ballplayers and real big-league teams, seem to conclude that their first task is to create a fictional ball team that can go out and beat the Cardinals tomorrow afternoon. These books are worse than unlikely, they are dull; if one is forced to choose between Willie Mays and Dusty Appleton, the kid shortstop who is batting .485 for the Goliaths, the decision will always be to grab one's sunglasses and head for the ball park. Most baseball novels are distinguishable by that final, fatal stab at verisimilitude, the fictional box score. It is as if Thoreau, despairing of his pen, had arranged to have a black-eyed Susan placed in each copy of *Walden*.

The Natural, which is our best baseball novel, got off to a terribly slow start, selling only about 3,000 copies in its first decade. I think it must have puzzled and disappointed the traditionalists who made up its initial audience, for while the book seems to be about baseball, it is not the same baseball that is reported in the morning newspapers. It contains no sensible strategy, no box scores, not even the happy, convincing sound of a solid bat meeting an official ball. The ballplayers in *The Natural* seem gigantic but insubstantial. They are described in a style left over from ancient sports pages and boys' books, and they talk an odd, hyperbolic, old-fashioned lingo. We have seen and heard them before, but never in a television interview. They are ballplayers remembered, phantoms from our boyhood past, heroes reborn in a dream. The ball they swing at and pursue can fly like a bird, bang in a glove like a firecracker, explode like a 21-gun salute or vanish altogether. Watching its flight, we understand: this is not just a baseball novel, it is a book of magic.

What obsesses Bernard Malamud in *The Natural* is the magic of time, the awful mystery of the passage of an instant. To penetrate the sporting disguise of the book and to appreciate the genius of Malamud's choice of setting, it is necessary to think for a moment about the very special nature of time on the baseball field. The most subtle tension of our national game derives from the fact that it is literally possible to halt time on the ballfield. The passage of each game is marked not by a clock but by the ticking off of balls and strikes, the counting of outs. Hit a single, get a walk, gain a base on an error, and you keep the game as young as before, you have postponed its end. In baseball talk, you have "won a life." Yet baseball is implacable, for the using up of its time is never casual or unnoticed. Records are kept and responsibilities assigned. No baseball joy is without sadness, for every success is also a failure; the slugger's homer is the pitcher's gopher ball. It is somebody's fault that we lose, even somebody's fault that we cannot sustain the big rally forever and thus defeat time itself. Released by the pitcher, the ball pursues its sudden course and finishes as a statistic. Is becomes was, action becomes history, and we file out of every ball park stricken with an evening sadness.

Most of the characters in this novel have a confused, anguished consciousness of awful injuries inflicted upon them by time. Whammer Wambold, flailing at a pitch, realizes with sadness that "the ball he had expected to hit had long since become part of the past," and he becomes an old man. Roy Hobbs—the "natural," the rookie who possesses the apparently invulnerable talisman of strength and youth—is magically cut down by a silver bullet and transformed into an old rookie of 34. Iris Lemon, his counterpart and true love, is a grandmother at 33—a reality that Roy cannot bear and that drives him back to his endless, unsatisfying dream of Memo Paris. Only Iris has the courage to accept time as a reality and thus to defeat it. "I was tied to time [she writes]—not so much to the past—nor to the expectation of the future, which was really too far away—only to here and now, day after day, until suddenly the years unrolled and a change came—more a reward of standing it so long than any sudden magic."

For the ballplayers, especially for Roy, time is squashed out of shape and is capable of any sorcery. Roy does not merely take the place of the great slugger Bump Baily when Bump is killed, he *becomes* Bump; the crowds barely notice the difference. (Remember how easy it was for us to transform Babe Ruth into Joe DiMaggio? Remember how we then turned DiMadge into Mickey Mantle?) Only in Roy's moments of youth can he defy time—injure it, in fact: "In the second game at Ebbets Field, he took hold of himself, gripped Wonderboy, and bashed the first pitch into the clock on the right field wall. The clock spattered minutes all over the place, and after that the

Dodgers never knew what time it was." These prodigious moments leave us gasping with laughter and relief—the same astonished laughter that greets the triumphant swirl of silk at the conclusion of the magician's famous trick. But time, of course, always recovers. In the end, it brings batting slumps, doubt, and the exhaustion that comes with conscious effort. This is called experience, and everyone knows there is no magic in experience. The last pitcher Roy bats against—the one who gets him out for good—is a 20-year-old rookie named Herman Youngberry.

The Natural is a first novel, and at times it demands considerable tolerance. Malamud, perhaps made careless by the freedom of a tall story, occasionally overreaches himself, especially when the story leaves the diamond. Too many objects in the book have double lives. Arrows and messages are scribbled all over the scenery during Roy's long, tortured pursuit of his Memo, as if the author were afraid we might lose our way. The smudgy multiple explication of sexual meaning becomes pretentious and, much worse, tiresome; but I don't believe it does any permanent damage to the book unless the reader makes the mistake of taking it too seriously. Malamud *almost* writes another kind of box score into his novel—one listing the lineups for the Myths vs. Symbols game—but he thinks better of it in the end, and so should we. A magic show requires a willing, gentle audience, and all is not destroyed if we sometimes glimpse the black thread that supports the floating golden ball.

What especially illuminates this small classic is the confidence and simple exuberance that Bernard Malamud so clearly feels inside a ball park. If there is such a thing as a natural fan, he is it. His knowledge, his flair for the game, his plain joy at being there burst out again and again in passages of wild comedy. Baseball is an outdoor spectacle, after all, and the best part of it comes when we can leap to our feet and roar with joy for the triumph of our boys and the discomfiture of our foolish enemies. Malamud is a marvelous companion at the park, constantly noticing, pointing, chattering, whistling encouragement. His guffaws, snickers, horselaughs and cheers sail raucously up from the field and bounce about in the upper stands. He is never too serious to enjoy himself. Moments before the final calamity, he is gleefully encouraging Roy Hobbs's mad effort to demolish the unappeasable spectator, Otto P. Zipp, with a bombardment of foul balls.

The Natural is incomprehensible to an outsider; everyone who reads it must be, to some degree, a baseball fan. Malamud makes no attempt to win over his demanding, expert audience with pages of baseball detail. Sensing from the outset that he cannot invent heroics that will match the real thing—the true, evergreen memories and moments that every fan carries about in his head—the author simply throws the problem out the window and appropriates those memories for his own story. This is Malamud's coup—the making of the book. The tall doings and Bunyanesque ballplayers in the story are no longer rivals to the chronicles and heroes of Cooperstown; they are frequently the same. The work is full of echoes, half-remembered legends and ghostlike recognitions, and toward the end we sense, with increasing apprehension, the repetition of a tragedy, the Black Sox scandal, which the whole country once knew by heart. This rustling of yellowed newspapers, the momentary relighting of long-faded afternoons, seems to disconcert and puzzle the principals in the novel. Roy Hobbs, the hero, wants to break all the records in the book; he has to be another Babe Ruth. At moments, without knowing it, he *is* the Bambino —an orphan, a man who can smash a ball between the pitcher's legs and over the center fielder's head, the victim of a million-dollar bellyache. Yet the effort of these heroics fills Roy with foreboding and exhaustion. He struggles dazedly with time, attempting to save himself, and yet becomes, in the end, another famous ghost, one forever shamed and lost.

Bernard Malamud finished *The Natural* in 1952, and time, unappeased by his tribute, has gnawed slowly at the work. Roy Hobbs has receded a little into the baseball past. He remains to the end a country ballplayer, and now we have run out of country. No more rookies ride into view on a Pullman car, with a homemade bat tucked under their seat; nowadays, they drive to spring-training camp in the convertibles they have bought with their bonus money. Our new baseball heroes, never ill at ease, conduct mass interviews after a World Series game, speaking before microphones and television cameras and fielding questions like the Secretary of State. They think about stock options and golf scores while riding to work from their suburban homes; more and more, they resemble each other—and ourselves. It's sad.

Baseball has changed more in the last few years than in all its previous history, but I think the biggest change is not the coming of television, nor the smoothing-out of the players, nor the million-watt night glare over the shiny new stadiums. It is, rather, the disillusionment of the fans themselves—a blunting and cooling of the game's ancient loyalties. Nothing escapes the fans (we are all Otto P. Zipps), and in recent years they have watched the owners of the game engage in a careless, greedy and wholly cynical scramble for new revenues and franchises that has strained and perhaps severed a good many of the tough, subtly wound cables that have always tied baseball to the American heart. The suspicion is growing that we in the stands, entranced and childlike as we are, understand baseball and love it more than those in command. We know that only a cold eye—the kind that sees baseball simply as a kind of show business—can destroy the summer spell of our old game. Malamud knows this, too. There is nothing dated or metaphorical about his villain in *The Natural*—the sanctimonious, nickel-pinching, perfidious Judge Goodwill Banner. Apprehensively, we lift our gaze from the sunlit ballfield to the dark window in the tower where the owner stands.

—ROGER ANGELL

the
natural

pre-game

Roy Hobbs pawed at the glass before thinking to prick a match with his thumbnail and hold the spurting flame in his cupped palm close to the lower berth window, but by then he had figured it was a tunnel they were passing through and was no longer surprised at the bright sight of himself holding a yellow light over his head, peering back in. As the train yanked its long tail out of the thundering tunnel, the kneeling reflection dissolved and he felt a splurge of freedom at the view of the moon-hazed Western hills bulked against night broken by sprays of summer lightning, although the season was early spring. Lying back, elbowed up on his long side, sleepless still despite the lulling train, he watched the land flowing and waited with suppressed expectancy for a sight of the Mississippi, a thousand miles away.

Having no timepiece he appraised the night and decided it was moving toward dawn. As he was looking, there flowed along this bone-white farmhouse with sagging skeletal porch, alone in untold miles of moonlight, and before it this white-faced, long-boned boy whipped with train-whistle yowl a glowing ball to someone hidden under a dark oak, who shot it back without thought, and the kid once more wound and returned. Roy shut his eyes to the sight because if it wasn't real it was a way he sometimes had of observing himself, just as in this dream he could never shake off—that had hours ago waked him out of sound sleep—of him standing at night in a strange field with a golden baseball in his palm that all the time grew heavier as he sweated to settle whether to hold on or fling it away. But when he had made his decision it was too heavy to lift or let fall (who wanted a hole that deep?) so he changed his mind to keep it and the thing grew fluffy light, a white rose breaking out of its hide, and all but soared off by itself, but he had already sworn to hang on forever.

As dawn tilted the night, a gust of windblown rain blinded him—no, there was a window—but the sliding drops made him thirsty and from thirst sprang hunger.

3

He reached into the hammock for his underwear to be first at breakfast in the dining car and make his blunders of ordering and eating more or less in private, since it was doubtful Sam would be up to tell him what to do. Roy peeled his gray sweatshirt and bunched down the white ducks he was wearing for pajamas in case there was a wreck and he didn't have time to dress. He acrobated into a shirt, pulled up the pants of his good suit, arching to draw them high, but he had crammed both feet into one leg and was trapped so tight wriggling got him nowhere. He worried because here he was straitjacketed in the berth without much room to twist around in and might bust his pants or have to buzz the porter, which he dreaded. Grunting, he contorted himself this way and that till he was at last able to grab and pull down the cuff and with a gasp loosened his feet and got the caught one where it belonged. Sitting up, he gartered his socks, tied laces, got on a necktie and even squirmed into a suit coat so that when he parted the curtains to step out he was fully dressed.

Dropping to all fours, he peered under the berth for his bassoon case. Though it was there he thought he had better open it and did but quickly snapped it shut as Eddie, the porter, came walking by.

"Morning, maestro, what's the tune today?"

"It ain't a musical instrument." Roy explained it was something he had made himself.

"Animal, vegetable, or mineral?"

"Just a practical thing."

"A pogo stick?"

"No."

"Foolproof lance?"

"No."

"Lemme guess," Eddie said, covering his eyes with his long-fingered hand and pawing the air with the other. "I have it—combination fishing rod, gun, and shovel."

4

Roy laughed. "How far to Chicago, Eddie?"

"Chi? Oh, a long, long ways. I wouldn't walk."

"I don't intend to."

"Why Chi?" Eddie asked. "Why not New Orleans? That's a lush and Frenchy city."

"Never been there."

"Or that hot and hilly town, San Francisco?"

Roy shook his head.

"Why not New York, colossus of colossuses?"

"Some day I'll visit there."

"Where have you visited?"

Roy was embarrassed. "Boise."

"That dusty sandstone quarry."

"Portland too when I was small."

"In Maine?"

"No, Oregon—where they hold the Festival of Roses."

"Oregon—where the refugees from Minnesota and the Dakotas go?"

"I wouldn't know," Roy said. "I'm going to Chicago, where the Cubs are."

"Lions and tigers in the zoo?"

"No, the ballplayers."

"Oh, the ball—" Eddie clapped a hand to his mouth. "Are you one of them?"

"I hope to be."

The porter bowed low. "My hero. Let me kiss your hand."

Roy couldn't help but smile yet the porter annoyed and worried him a little. He had forgotten to ask Sam when to tip him, morning or night, and how much? Roy had made it a point, since their funds were so low, not to ask for anything at all but last night Eddie had insisted on fixing a pillow behind his back, and once when he was trying to locate the men's room Eddie practically took him by the hand and led him to it. Did you hand him a dime after that or grunt a foolish thanks as he had done? He'd personally be glad when the trip was over, though he certainly hated to be left alone in a place like Chicago. Without Sam he'd feel shaky-kneed and unable to say or do simple things like ask for directions or know where to go once you had dropped a nickel into the subway.

After a troublesome shave in which he twice drew blood he used one thin towel to dry his hands, face, and neck, clean his razor and wipe up the wet of his toothbrush so as not to have to ask for another and this way keep the bill down. From the flaring sky out the window it looked around half-past five, but he couldn't be sure because somewhere near they left Mountain Time and lost—no, picked up—yes, it was lost an hour, what Sam called the twenty-three hour day. He packed his razor, toothbrush, and pocket comb into a chamois drawstring bag, rolled it up small and kept it handy in his coat pocket. Passing through the long sleeper, he entered the diner and would gladly have sat down to breakfast, for his stomach had contracted into a bean at the smell of food, but the shirt-sleeved waiters in stocking caps were joshing around as they gobbled fried kippers and potatoes. Roy hurried through the large-windowed club car, empty for once, through several sleepers, coaches, a lounge and another long line of coaches, till he came to the last one, where amid the gloom of drawn shades and sleeping people tossed every which way, Sam Simpson also slept although Roy had last night begged him to take the berth but the soft-voiced Sam had insisted, "You take the bed, kiddo, you're the one that has to show what you have got on the ball when we pull into the city. It don't matter where I sleep."

Sam lay very still on his back, looking as if the breath of life had departed from him except that it was audible in the ripe snore that could be chased without waking him, Roy had discovered, if you hissed scat. His lean head was held up by a folded pillow and his scrawny legs, shoeless, hung limp over the arm of the double seat he had managed to acquire, for he had started out with a seat partner. He was an expert conniver where his comfort was concerned, and since that revolved mostly around the filled flat bottle his ability to raise them up was this side of amazing. He often said he would not die of thirst though he never failed to add, in Roy's presence, that he wished for nobody the drunkard's death. He seemed now to be dreaming, and his sharp nose was pointed in the direction of a scent that led perhaps to the perfumed presence of Dame Fortune, long past due in his bed. With dry lips puckered, he smiled in expectation of a spectacular kiss though he looked less like a lover than an old scarecrow with his comical, seamed face sprouting prickly stubble in the dark glow of the expiring bulb overhead. A trainman passed who, seeing Sam sniff in his sleep, pretended it was at his own reek and humorously held his nose. Roy frowned, but Sam, who had a moment before been getting in good licks against fate, saw in his sleep, and his expression changed. A tear broke from his eye and slowly slid down his cheek. Roy concluded not to wake Sam and left.

He returned to the vacant club car and sat there with a magazine on his knee, worrying whether the trip wasn't a mistake, when a puzzled Eddie came into the car and handed him a pair of red dice.

"Mate them," he said. "I can't believe my eyes."

Roy paired the dice. "They mate."

"Now roll them."

He rolled past his shoe. "Snake eyes."

"Try again," said Eddie, interested.

Roy rattled the red cubes. "Snake eyes once more."

"Amazing. Again, please."

Again he rolled on the rug. Roy whistled. "Holy cow, three in a row."

"Fantastic."

"Did they do the same for you?"

"No, for me they did sevens."

"Are they loaded?"

"Bewitched," Eddie muttered. "I found them in the washroom and I'm gonna get rid of them pronto."

"Why?—if you could win all the time?"

"I don't crave any outside assistance in games of chance."

The train had begun to slow down.

"Oh oh, duty," Eddie hurried out.

Watching through the double-paned glass, Roy saw the porter swing himself off the train and jog along with it a few paces as it pulled to a stop. The morning was high and bright but the desolate station—wherever they were —gave up a single passenger, a girl in a dressy black dress, who despite the morning chill waited with a coat over her arm, and two suitcases and a zippered golf bag at her feet. Hatless, too, her hair a froth of dark curls, she held by a loose cord a shiny black hat box which she wouldn't let Eddie touch when he gathered up her things. Her face was striking, a little drawn and pale, and when she stepped up into the train her nyloned legs made Roy's pulses dance. When he could no longer see her, he watched Eddie set down her bags, take the red dice out of his pocket, spit on them and fling them over the depot roof. He hurriedly grabbed the bags and hopped on the moving train.

The girl entered the club car and directed Eddie to carry her suitcases to her compartment and she would stay and have a cigarette. He mentioned the hat box again but she giggled nervously and said no.

"Never lost a female hat yet," Eddie muttered.

"Thank you but I'll carry it myself."

He shrugged and left.

She had dropped a flower. Roy thought it was a gardenia but it turned out to be a white rose she had worn pinned to her dress.

When he handed it to her, her eyes widened with fascination, as if she had recognized him from somewhere, but when she found she hadn't, to his horror her expression changed instantly to one of boredom. Sitting across the aisle from him she fished out of her purse a pack of cigarettes and a lighter. She lit up, and crossing her heartbreaking legs, began to flip through a copy of *Life*.

He figured she was his own age, maybe a year or so older. She looked to him like one of those high-class college girls, only with more zip than most of them, and dressed for 6 A.M. as the girls back home never would. He was marvelously interested in her, so much had her first glance into his eyes meant to him, and already felt a great longing in his life. Anxious to get acquainted, he was flabbergasted how to begin. If she hadn't yet eaten breakfast and he could work up the nerve, he could talk to her in the diner —only he didn't dare.

People were sitting around now and the steward came out and said first call for breakfast.

She snubbed out her cigarette with a wriggling motion of the wrist—her bracelets tinkled—picked up the hat box and went into the diner. Her crumpled white rose lay in the ashtray. He took it out and quickly stuck it in his pants pocket. Though his hunger bit sharp he waited till everyone was maybe served, and then he entered.

Although he had tried to avoid it, for fear she would see how unsure he was of these things, he was put at the same table with her and her black hat box, which now occupied a seat of its own. She glanced up furtively when he sat down but went wordlessly back to her coffee. When the waiter handed Roy the pad, he absently printed his name and date of birth but the waiter imperceptibly nudged him (hey, hayseed) and indicated it was for ordering. He pointed on the menu with his yellow pencil (this is the buck breakfast) but the blushing ballplayer, squinting through the blur, could only think he was sitting on the lone four-bit piece he had in his back pocket. He tried to squelch the impulse but something forced him to look up at her as he attempted to pour water into his ice-filled (this'll kill the fever) glass, spilling some on the tablecloth (whose diapers you wetting, boy?), then all thumbs and butter fingers, the pitcher thumped the pitcher down, fished the fifty cents out of his pants, and after scratching out the vital statistics on the pad, plunked the coin down on the table.

"That's for you," he told the (what did I do to deserve this?) waiter, and though the silver-eyed mermaid was about to speak, he did not stay to listen but beat it fast out of the accursed car.

Tramping highways and byways, wandering everywhere bird dogging the sandlots for months without spotting so much as a fifth-rater he could telegraph about to the head scout of the Cubs, and maybe pick up a hundred bucks in the mail as a token of their appreciation, with also a word of thanks for his good bird dogging and maybe they would sometime again employ him as a scout on the regular pay-roll—well, after a disheartening long time in which he was not able to roust up a single specimen worthy to be called by the name of ballplayer, Sam had one day lost his way along a dusty country road and when he finally found out where he was, too weary to turn back, he crossed over to an old, dry barn and sat against the haypile in front, to drown his sorrows with a swig. On the verge of dozing he heard these shouts and opened his eyes, shielding them from the hot sun, and as he lived, a game of ball was being played in a pasture by twelve blond-bearded players, six on each side, and even from where Sam sat he could tell they were terrific the way they smacked the pill—one blow banging it so far out the fielder had to run a mile before he could jump high and snag it smack in his bare hand. Sam's mouth popped open, he got up whoozy and watched, finding it hard to believe his eyes, as the teams changed sides and the first hitter that batted the ball did so for a far-reaching distance before it was caught, and the same with the second, a wicked clout, but then the third came up, the one who had made the bare-handed catch, and he really laid on and powdered the pellet a thundering crack so that even the one who ran for it, his beard parted in the wind, before long looked like a pygmy chasing it and quit running, seeing the thing was a speck on the horizon.

Sweating and shivering by turns, Sam muttered if I could ketch the whole twelve of them—and staggered out on the field to cry out the good news but when they saw him they gathered bats and balls and ran in a dozen directions, and though Sam was smart enough to hang on to the fellow who had banged the sphere out to the horizon, frantically shouting to him, "Whoa—whoa," his lungs bursting with the effort to call a giant—he wouldn't stop so Sam never caught him.

He woke with a sob in his throat but swallowed before he could sound it, for by then Roy had come to mind and he mumbled, "Got someone just as good," so that for once waking was better than dreaming.

He yawned. His mouth felt unholy dry and his underclothes were crawling. Reaching down his battered valise from the rack, he pulled out a used bath towel and cake of white soap, and to the surprise of those who saw him go out that way, went through the baggage cars to the car between them and the tender. Once inside there, he peeled to the skin and stepped into the shower stall, where he enjoyed himself for ten minutes, soaping and resoaping his bony body under warm water. But then a trainman happened to come through and after sniffing around Sam's clothes yelled in to him, "Hey, bud, come outa there."

Sam stopped off the shower and poked out his head. "What's that?"

"I said come outa there, that's only for the train crew."

"Excuse me," Sam said, and he began quickly to rub himself dry.

"You don't have to hurry. Just wanted you to know you made a mistake."

"Thought it went with the ticket."

"Not in the coaches it don't."

Sam sat on a metal stool and laced up his high brown shoes. Pointing to the cracked mirror on the wall, he said, "Mind if I use your glass?"

"Go ahead."

He parted his sandy hair, combed behind the ears, and managed to work in a shave and brushing of his yellow teeth before he apologized again to the trainman and left.

Going up a few cars to the lounge, he ordered a cup of hot coffee and a sandwich, ate quickly, and made for the club car. It was semi-officially out of bounds for coach travelers but Sam had told the passenger agent last night that he had a nephew riding on a sleeper, and the passenger agent had mentioned to the conductor not to bother him.

When he entered the club car, after making sure Roy was elsewhere Sam headed for the bar, already in a fluid state for the train was moving through wet territory, but then he changed his mind and sat down to size up the congregation over a newspaper and spot who looked par-

ticularly amiable. The headlines caught his eye at the same
time as they did this short, somewhat popeyed gent's
sitting next to him, who had just been greedily question-
ing the husky, massive-shouldered man on his right, who
was wearing sun glasses. Popeyes nudged the big one and
they all three stared at Sam's paper.

WEST COAST OLYMPIC ATHLETE SHOT
FOLLOWS 24 HOURS AFTER SLAYING OF
ALL-AMERICAN FOOTBALL ACE

The article went on to relate that both of these men had
been shot under mysterious circumstances with silver bullets from a .22 caliber pistol by an unknown woman that
police were on the hunt for.

"That makes the second sucker," the short man said.

"But why with silver bullets, Max?"

"Beats me. Maybe she set out after a ghost but couldn't
find him."

The other fingered his tie knot. "Why do you suppose
she goes around pickin' on atheletes for?"

"Not only athletes but also the cream of the crop. She's
knocked off a crack football boy, and now an Olympic runner. Better watch out, Whammer, she may be heading for
a baseball player for the third victim." Max chuckled.

Sam looked up and almost hopped out of his seat as he
recognized them both.

Hiding his hesitation, he touched the short one on the
arm. "Excuse me, mister, but ain't you Max Mercy, the
sportswriter? I know your face from your photo in the articles you write."

But the sportswriter, who wore a comical mustache and
dressed in stripes that crisscrossed three ways—suit, shirt,
and tie—a nervous man with voracious eyes, also had a
sharp sense of smell and despite Sam's shower and tooth-

brushing nosed out an alcoholic fragrance that slowed his usual speedy response in acknowledging the spread of his fame.

"That's right," he finally said.

"Well, I'm happy to have the chance to say a few words to you. You're maybe a little after my time, but I am Sam Simpson—Bub Simpson, that is—who played for the St. Louis Browns in the seasons of 1919 to 1921."

Sam spoke with a grin though his insides were afry at the mention of his professional baseball career.

"Believe I've heard the name," Mercy said nervously. After a minute he nodded toward the man Sam knew all along as the leading hitter of the American League, three times winner of the Most Valuable Player award, and announced, "This is Walter (the Whammer) Wambold." It had been in the papers that he was a holdout for $75,000 and was coming East to squeeze it out of his boss.

"Howdy," Sam said. "You sure look different in street clothes."

The Whammer, whose yellow hair was slicked flat, with tie and socks to match, grunted.

Sam's ears reddened. He laughed embarrassedly and then remarked sideways to Mercy that he was traveling with a slambang young pitcher who'd soon be laying them low in the big leagues. "Spoke to you because I thought you might want to know about him."

"What's his name?"

"Roy Hobbs."

"Where'd he play?"

"Well, he's not exactly been in organized baseball."

"Where'd he learn to pitch?"

"His daddy taught him years ago—he was once a semi-pro—and I have been polishin' him up."

"Where's he been pitching?"

"Well, like I said, he's young, but he certainly mowed

them down in the Northwest High School League last year. Thought you might of heard of his eight no-hitters."

"Class D is as far down as I go," Mercy laughed. He lit one of the cigars Sam had been looking at in his breast pocket.

"I'm personally taking him to Clarence Mulligan of the Cubs for a tryout. They will probably pay me a few grand for uncovering the coming pitcher of the century but the condition is—and Roy is backing me on this because he is more devoted to me than a son—that I am to go back as a regular scout, like I was in 1925."

Roy popped his head into the car and searched around for the girl with the black hat box (Miss Harriet Bird, Eddie had gratuitously told him, making a black fluttering of wings), and seeing her seated near the card tables restlessly thumbing through a magazine, popped out.

"That's him," said Sam. "Wait'll I bring him back." He got up and chased after Roy.

"Who's the gabber?" said the Whammer.

"Guy named Simpson who once caught for the Brownies. Funny thing, last night I was doing a Sunday piece on drunks in baseball and I had occasion to look up his record. He was in the game three years, batted .340, .260, and .198, but his catching was terrific—not one error listed."

"Get rid of him, he jaws too much."

"Sh, here he comes."

Sam returned with Roy in tow, gazing uncomfortably ahead.

"Max," said Sam, "this is Roy Hobbs that I mentioned to you. Say hello to Max Mercy, the syndicated sportswriter, kiddo."

"Hello," Roy nodded.

"This is the Whammer," Max said.

Roy extended his hand but the Whammer looked through him with no expression whatsoever. Seeing he had his eye hooked on Harriet, Roy conceived a strong dislike for the guy.

The Whammer got up. "Come on, Max, I wanna play cards."

Max rose. "Well, hang onto the water wagon, Bub," he said to Sam.

Sam turned red.

Roy shot the sportswriter a dirty look.

"Keep up with the no-hitters, kid," Max laughed.

Roy didn't answer. He took the Whammer's chair and Sam sat where he was, brooding.

"What'll it be?" they heard Mercy ask as he shuffled the cards. They had joined two men at one of the card tables.

The Whammer, who looked to Sam like an overgrown side of beef wrapped in gabardine, said, "Hearts." He stared at Harriet until she looked up from her magazine, and after a moment of doubt, smiled.

The Whammer fingered his necktie knot. As he scooped up the cards his diamond ring glinted in the sunlight.

"Goddamned millionaire," Sam thought.

"The hell with her," thought Roy.

"I dealt rummy," Max said, and though no one had called him, Sam promptly looked around.

Toward late afternoon the Whammer, droning on about his deeds on the playing field, got very chummy with Harriet Bird and before long had slipped his fat fingers around the back of her chair so Roy left the club car and sat in the sleeper, looking out of the window, across the aisle from where Eddie slept sitting up. Gosh, the size of the forest. He thought they had left it for good yesterday and here it still was. As he watched, the trees flowed together and so did the hills and clouds. He felt a kind of sadness, because he had lost the feeling of a particular place. Yesterday he had come from somewhere, a place he knew was there, but today it had thinned away in space—how vast he could not have guessed—and he felt like he would never see it again.

The forest stayed with them, climbing hills like an army, shooting down like waterfalls. As the train skirted close in, the trees leveled out and he could see within the woodland the only place he had been truly intimate with in his wanderings, a green world shot through with weird light and strange bird cries, muffled in silence that made the privacy so complete his inmost self had no shame of anything he thought there, and it eased the body-shaking beat of his ambitions. Then he thought of here and now and for the thousandth time wondered why they had come so far and for what. Did Sam really know what he was doing? Sometimes Roy had his doubts. Sometimes he wanted to turn around and go back home, where he could at least predict what tomorrow would be like. Remembering the white rose in his pants pocket, he decided to get rid of it. But then the pine trees flowed away from the train and slowly swerved behind blue hills; all at once there was this beaten gold, snow-capped mountain in the distance, and on the plain several miles from its base lay a small city gleaming in the rays of the declining sun. Approaching it, the long train slowly pulled to a stop.

Eddie woke with a jump and stared out the window.

"Oh oh, trouble, we never stop here."

He looked again and called Roy.

"What do you make out of that?"

About a hundred yards ahead, where two dirt roads crossed, a moth-eaten model-T Ford was parked on the farther side of the road from town, and a fat old man wearing a broad-brimmed black hat and cowboy boots, who they could see was carrying a squat doctor's satchel, climbed down from it. To the conductor, who had impatiently swung off the train with a lit red lamp, he flourished a yellow telegram. They argued a minute, then the conductor, snapping open his watch, beckoned him along and they boarded the train. When they passed through Eddie's car the conductor's face was sizzling with irritation but the doctor was unruffled. Before disappearing through the door, the conductor called to Eddie, "Half hour."

"Half hour," Eddie yodeled and he got out the stool and set it outside the car so that anyone who wanted to stretch, could.

Only about a dozen passengers got off the train, including Harriet Bird, still hanging on to her precious hat box, the Whammer, and Max Mercy, all as thick as thieves. Roy hunted up the bassoon case just if the train should decide to take off without him, and when he had located Sam they both got off.

"Well, I'll be jiggered." Sam pointed down about a block beyond where the locomotive had halted. There, sprawled out at the outskirts of the city, a carnival was on. It was made up of try-your-skill booths, kiddie rides, a freak show and a gigantic Ferris wheel that looked like a stopped clock. Though there was still plenty of daylight, the carnival was lit up by twisted ropes of blinking bulbs, and many banners streamed in the breeze as the calliope played.

"Come on," said Roy, and they went along with the people from the train who were going toward the tents.

Once they had got there and fooled around a while, Sam stopped to have a crushed cocoanut drink which he privately spiked with a shot from a new bottle, while Roy wandered over to a place where you could throw three baseballs for a dime at three wooden pins, shaped like pint-size milk bottles and set in pyramids of one on top of two, on small raised platforms about twenty feet back from the counter. He changed the fifty-cent piece Sam had slipped him on leaving the train, and this pretty girl in yellow, a little hefty but with a sweet face and nice ways, who with her peanut of a father was waiting on trade, handed him three balls. Lobbing one of them, Roy easily knocked off the pyramid and won himself a naked kewpie doll. Enjoying the game, he laid down another dime, again clattering the pins to the floor in a single shot and now collecting an alarm clock. With the other three dimes he won a brand-new boxed baseball, a washboard, and baby potty, which he traded in for a six-inch harmonica. A few kids came over to watch and Sam, wandering by, indulgently changed another half into dimes for Roy. And Roy won a fine leather cigar case for Sam, a "God Bless America" banner, a flashlight, can of coffee, and a two-pound box of sweets. To the kids' delight, Sam, after a slight hesitation, flipped Roy another half dollar, but this time the little man behind the counter nudged his daughter and she asked Roy if he would now take a kiss for every three pins he tumbled.

Roy glanced at her breasts and she blushed. He got embarrassed too. "What do you say, Sam, it's your four bits?"

Sam bowed low to the girl. "Ma'am," he said, "now you see how dang foolish it is to be a young feller."

The girl laughed and Roy began to throw for kisses, flushing each pyramid in a shot or two while the girl counted aloud the kisses she owed him.

Some of the people from the train passed by and stayed to watch when they learned from the mocking kids what Roy was throwing for.

The girl, pretending to be unconcerned, tolled off the third and fourth kisses.

As Roy fingered the ball for the last throw the Whammer came by holding over his shoulder a Louisville Slugger that he had won for himself in the batting cage down a way. Harriet, her pretty face flushed, had a kewpie doll, and Max Mercy carried a box of cigars. The Whammer had discarded his sun glasses and all but strutted over his performance and the prizes he had won.

Roy raised his arm to throw for the fifth kiss and a clean sweep when the Whammer called out to him in a loud voice, "Pitch it here, busher, and I will knock it into the moon."

Roy shot for the last kiss and missed. He missed with the second and third balls. The crowd oohed its disappointment.

"Only four," said the girl in yellow as if she mourned the fifth.

Angered at what had happened, Sam hoarsely piped, "I got ten dollars that says he can strike you out with three pitched balls, Wambold."

The Whammer looked at Sam with contempt.

"What d'ye say, Max?" he said.

Mercy shrugged.

"Oh, I love contests of skill," Harriet said excitedly. Roy's face went pale.

"What's the matter, hayfoot, you scared?" the Whammer taunted.

"Not of you," Roy said.

"Let's go across the tracks where nobody'll get hurt," Mercy suggested.

"Nobody but the busher and his bazooka. What's in it, busher?"

"None of your business." Roy picked up the bassoon case.

The crowd moved in a body across the tracks, the kids circling around to get a good view, and the engineer and fireman watching from their cab window.

Sam cornered one of the kids who lived nearby and sent him home for a fielder's glove and his friend's catcher's mitt. While they were waiting, for protection he buttoned underneath his coat the washboard Roy had won. Max drew a batter's box alongside a piece of slate. He said he would call the throws and they would count as one of the three pitches only if they were over or if the Whammer swung and missed.

When the boy returned with the gloves, the sun was going down, and though the sky was aflame with light all the way to the snowy mountain peak, it was chilly on the ground.

Breaking the seal, Sam squeezed the baseball box and the pill shot up like a greased egg. He tossed it to Mercy, who inspected the hide and stitches, then rubbed the shine off and flipped it to Roy.

"Better throw a couple of warm-ups."

"My arm is loose," said Roy.

"It's your funeral."

Placing his bassoon case out of the way in the grass, Roy shed his coat. One of the boys came forth to hold it.

"Be careful you don't spill the pockets," Roy told him.

Sam came forward with the catcher's glove on. It was too small for his big hand but he said it would do all right.

"Sam, I wish you hadn't bet that money on me," Roy said.

"I won't take it if we win, kiddo, but just let it stand if we lose," Sam said, embarrassed.

"We came by it too hard."

"Just let it stand so."

He cautioned Roy to keep his pitches inside, for the Whammer was known to gobble them on the outside corner.

Sam returned to the plate and crouched behind the batter, his knees spread wide because of the washboard. Roy drew on his glove and palmed the ball behind it. Mercy, rubbing his hands to warm them, edged back about six feet behind Sam.

The onlookers retreated to the other side of the tracks, except Harriet, who stood without fear of fouls up close.

Her eyes shone at the sight of the two men facing one another.

Mercy called, "Batter up."

The Whammer crowded the left side of the plate, gripping the heavy bat low on the neck, his hands jammed together and legs plunked evenly apart. He hadn't bothered to take off his coat. His eye on Roy said it spied a left-handed monkey.

"Throw it, Rube, it won't get no lighter."

Though he stood about sixty feet away, he loomed up gigantic to Roy, with the wood held like a caveman's ax on his shoulder. His rocklike frame was motionless, his face impassive, unsmiling, dark.

Roy's heart skipped a beat. He turned to gaze at the mountain.

Sam whacked the leather with his fist. "Come on, kiddo, wham it down his whammy."

The Whammer out of the corner of his mouth told the drunk to keep his mouth shut.

"Burn it across his button."

"Close your trap," Mercy said.

"Cut his throat with it."

"If he tries to dust me, so help me I will smash his skull," the Whammer threatened.

Roy stretched loosely, rocked back on his left leg, twirling the right a little like a dancer, then strode forward and threw with such force his knuckles all but scraped the ground on the follow-through.

At thirty-three the Whammer still enjoyed exceptional eyesight. He saw the ball spin off Roy's fingertips and it reminded him of a white pigeon he had kept as a boy, that he would send into flight by flipping it into the air. The ball flew at him and he was conscious of its bird-form and white flapping wings, until it suddenly disappeared from view. He heard a noise like the bang of a firecracker at his feet and Sam had the ball in his mitt. Unable to believe his ears he heard Mercy intone a reluctant strike.

Sam flung off the glove and was wringing his hand.

"Hurt you, Sam?" Roy called.

"No, it's this dang glove."

Though he did not show it, the pitch had bothered the Whammer no end. Not just the speed of it but the sensation of surprise and strangeness that went with it—him batting here on the railroad tracks, the crazy carnival, the drunk catching and a clown pitching, and that queer dame Harriet, who had five minutes ago been patting him on the back for his skill in the batting cage, now eyeing him coldly for letting one pitch go by.

He noticed Max had moved farther back.

"How the hell you expect to call them out there?"

"He looks wild to me." Max moved in.

"Your knees are knockin'," Sam tittered.

"Mind your business, rednose," Max said.

"You better watch your talk, mister," Roy called to Mercy.

"Pitch it, greenhorn," warned the Whammer.

Sam crouched with his glove on. "Do it again, Roy. Give him something simular."

"Do it again," mimicked the Whammer. To the crowd, maybe to Harriet, he held up a vaunting finger showing there were other pitches to come.

Roy pumped, reared and flung.

The ball appeared to the batter to be a slow spinning planet looming toward the earth. For a long light-year he waited for this globe to whirl into the orbit of his swing so he could bust it to smithereens that would settle with dust and dead leaves into some distant cosmos. At last the unseeing eye, maybe a fortuneteller's lit crystal ball—anyway, a curious combination of circles—drifted within range of his weapon, or so he thought, because he lunged at it

23

ferociously, twisting round like a top. He landed on both knees as the world floated by over his head and hit with a *whup* into the cave of Sam's glove.

"Hey, Max," Sam said, as he chased the ball after it had bounced out of the glove, "how do they pernounce Whammer if you leave out the W?"

"Strike," Mercy called long after a cheer (was it a jeer?) had burst from the crowd.

"What's he throwing," the Whammer howled, "spitters?"

"In the pig's poop." Sam thrust the ball at him. "It's drier than your granddaddy's scalp."

"I'm warning him not to try any dirty business."

Yet the Whammer felt oddly relieved. He liked to have his back crowding the wall, when there was a single pitch to worry about and a single pitch to hit. Then the sweat began to leak out of his pores as he stared at the hard, lanky figure of the pitiless pitcher, moving, despite his years and a few waste motions, like a veteran undertaker of the diamond, and he experienced a moment of depression.

Sam must have sensed it, because he discovered an unexpected pity in his heart and even for a split second hoped the idol would not be tumbled. But only for a second, for the Whammer had regained confidence in his known talent and experience and was taunting the greenhorn to throw.

Someone in the crowd hooted and the Whammer raised aloft two fat fingers and pointed where he would murder the ball, where the gleaming rails converged on the horizon and beyond was invisible.

Roy raised his leg. He smelled the Whammer's blood and wanted it, and through him the worm's he had with him, for the way he had insulted Sam.

The third ball slithered at the batter like a meteor, the flame swallowing itself. He lifted his club to crush it into a universe of sparks but the heavy wood dragged, and though he willed to destroy the sound he heard a gong bong and realized with sadness that the ball he had expected to hit had long since been part of the past; and though Max could not cough the fatal word out of his throat, the Whammer understood he was, in the truest sense of it, out.

The crowd was silent as the violet evening fell on their shoulders.

For a night game, the Whammer harshly shouted, it was customary to turn on lights. Dropping the bat, he trotted off to the train, an old man.

The ball had caught Sam smack in the washboard and lifted him off his feet. He lay on the ground, extended on his back. Roy pushed everybody aside to get him air. Unbuttoning Sam's coat, he removed the dented washboard.

"Never meant to hurt you, Sam."

"Just knocked the wind outa me," Sam gasped. "Feel better now." He was pulled to his feet and stood steady.

The train whistle wailed, the echo banging far out against the black mountain.

Then the doctor in the broadbrimmed black hat appeared, flustered and morose, the conductor trying to pacify him, and Eddie hopping along behind.

The doctor waved the crumpled yellow paper around. "Got a telegram says somebody on this train took sick. Anybody out here?"

Roy tugged at Sam's sleeve.

"Ixnay."

"What's that?"

"Not me," said Roy.

The doctor stomped off. He climbed into his Ford, whipped it up and drove away.

The conductor popped open his watch. "Be a good hour late into the city."

"All aboard," he called.

"Aboard," Eddie echoed, carrying the bassoon case.

The buxom girl in yellow broke through the crowd and threw her arms around Roy's neck. He ducked but she hit him quick with her pucker four times upon the right eye, yet he could see with the other that Harriet Bird (certainly a snappy goddess) had her gaze fastened on him.

They sat, after dinner, in Eddie's dimmed and empty Pullman, Roy floating through drifts of clouds on his triumph as Harriet went on about the recent tourney, she put it, and the unreal forest outside swung forward like a gate shutting. The odd way she saw things interested him, yet he was aware of the tormented trees fronting the snaky lake they were passing, trees bent and clawing, plucked white by icy blasts from the black water, their bony branches twisting in many a broken direction.

Harriet's face was flushed, her eyes gleaming with new insights. Occasionally she stopped and giggled at herself for the breathless volume of words that flowed forth, to his growing astonishment, but after a pause was on her galloping way again—a girl on horseback—reviewing the inspiring sight (she said it was) of David jawboning the Goliath-Whammer, or was it Sir Percy lancing Sir Maldemer, or the first son (with a rock in his paw) ranged against the primitive papa?

Roy gulped. "My father? Well, maybe I did want to skull him sometimes. After my grandma died, the old man dumped me in one orphan home after the other, wherever he happened to be working—when he did—though he did used to take me out of there summers and teach me how to toss a ball."

No, that wasn't what she meant, Harriet said. Had he ever read Homer?

Try as he would he could only think of four bases and not a book. His head spun at her allusions. He found her lingo strange with all the college stuff and hoped she would stop it because he wanted to talk about baseball.

Then she took a breather. "My friends say I have a fantastic imagination."

He quickly remarked he wouldn't say that. "But the only thing I had on my mind when I was throwing out there was that Sam had bet this ten spot we couldn't afford to lose out on, so I had to make him whiff."

"To whiff—oh, Roy, how droll," and she laughed again.

He grinned, carried away by the memory of how he had done it, the hero, who with three pitched balls had nailed the best the American League had to offer. What didn't that say about the future? He felt himself falling into sentiment in his thoughts and tried to steady himself but couldn't before he had come forth with a pronouncement: "You have to have the right stuff to play good ball and I have it. I bet some day I'll break every record in the book for throwing and hitting."

Harriet appeared startled then gasped, hiding it like a cough behind her tense fist, and vigorously applauded, her bracelets bouncing on her wrists. "Bravo, Roy, how wonderful."

"What I mean," he insisted, "is I feel that I have got it in me—that I am due for something very big. I have to do it. I mean," he said modestly, "that's of course when I get in the game."

Her mouth opened. "You mean you're not—" She seemed, to his surprise, disappointed, almost on the verge of crying.

"No," he said, ashamed. "Sam's taking me for a tryout."

Her eyes grew vacant as she stared out the window. Then she asked, "But Walter—*he* is a successful professional player, isn't he?"

"The Whammer?" Roy nodded.

"And he has won that award three times—what was it?"

"The Most Valuable Player." He had a panicky feeling he was losing her to the Whammer.

She bit her lip. "Yet you defeated him," she murmured.

He admitted it. "He won't last much longer I don't think —the most a year or two. By then he'll be too old for the game. Myself, I've got my whole life ahead of me."

Harriet brightened, saying sympathetically. "What will you hope to accomplish, Roy?"

He had already told her but after a minute remarked, "Sometimes when I walk down the street I bet people will say there goes Roy Hobbs, the best there ever was in the game."

She gazed at him with touched and troubled eyes. "Is that all?"

He tried to penetrate her question. Twice he had answered it and still she was unsatisfied. He couldn't be sure what she expected him to say. "Is that all?" he repeated. "What more is there?"

"Don't you know?" she said kindly.

Then he had an idea. "You mean the bucks? I'll get them too."

She slowly shook her head. "Isn't there something over and above earthly things—some more glorious meaning to one's life and activities?"

"In baseball?"

"Yes."

He racked his brain—

"Maybe I've not made myself clear, but surely you can see (I was saying this to Walter just before the train stopped) that yourself alone—alone in the sense that we are all terribly alone no matter what people say—I mean by that perhaps if you understood that our values must derive from—oh, I really suppose—" She dropped her hand futilely. "Please forgive me. I sometimes confuse myself with the little I know."

Her eyes were sad. He felt a curious tenderness for her, a little as if she might be his mother (That bird.) and tried very hard to come up with the answer she wanted—something you said about LIFE.

"I think I know what you mean," he said. "You mean the fun and satisfaction you get out of playing the best way that you know how?"

She did not respond to that.

Roy worried out some other things he might have said but had no confidence to put them into words. He felt curiously deflated and a little lost, as if he had just flunked a test. The worst of it was he still didn't know what she'd been driving at.

Harriet yawned. Never before had he felt so tongue-tied in front of a girl, a looker too. Now if he had her in bed—

Almost as if she had guessed what he was thinking and her mood had changed to something more practical than asking nutty questions that didn't count, she sighed and edged closer to him, concealing the move behind a query about his bassoon case. "Do you play?"

"Not any music," he answered, glad they were talking about something different. "There's a thing in it that I made for myself."

"What, for instance?"

He hesitated. "A baseball bat."

She was herself again, laughed merrily. "Roy, you are priceless."

"I got the case because I don't want to get the stick all banged up before I got the chance to use it."

"Oh, Roy." Her laughter grew. He smiled broadly.

She was now so close he felt bold. Reaching down he lifted the hat box by the string and lightly hefted it.

"What's in it?"

She seemed breathless. "In it?" Then she mimicked, "—Something I made for myself."

"Feels like a hat."

"Maybe a head?" Harriet shook a finger at him.

"Feels more like a hat." A little embarrassed, he set the box down. "Will you come and see me play sometime?" he asked.

She nodded and then he was aware of her leg against his and that she was all but on his lap. His heart slapped against his ribs and he took it all to mean that she had dropped the last of her interest in the Whammer and was putting it on the guy who had buried him.

As they went through a tunnel, Roy placed his arm around her shoulders, and when the train lurched on a curve, casually let his hand fall upon her full breast. The nipple rose between his fingers and before he could resist the impulse he had tweaked it.

Her high-pitched scream lifted her up and twirling like a dancer down the aisle.

Stricken, he rose—had gone too far.

Crooking her arms like broken branches she whirled back to him, her head turned so far around her face hung between her shoulders.

"Look, I'm a twisted tree."

Sam had sneaked out on the squirming, apologetic Mercy, who, with his back to the Whammer—he with a newspaper raised in front of his sullen eyes—had kept up a leechlike prodding about Roy, asking where he had come from (oh, he's just a home town boy), how it was no major league scout had got at him (they did but he turned them down for me) even with the bonus cash that they are tossing around these days (yep), who's his father (like I said, just an old semipro who wanted awful bad to be in the big

30

leagues) and what, for God's sake, does he carry around in that case (that's his bat, Wonderboy). The sportswriter was greedy to know more, hinting he could do great things for the kid, but Sam, rubbing his side where it pained, at last put him off and escaped into the coach to get some shuteye before they hit Chicago, sometime past 1 A.M.

After a long time trying to settle himself comfortably, he fell snoring asleep flat on his back and was at once sucked into a long dream that he had gone thirsty mad for a drink and was threatening the slickers in the car get him a bottle or else. Then this weasel of a Mercy, pretending he was writing on a pad, pointed him out with his pencil and the conductor snapped him up by the seat of his pants and ran his free-wheeling feet lickity-split through the sawdust, giving him the merry heave-ho off the train through the air on a floating trapeze, ploop into a bog where it rained buckets. He thought he better get across the foaming river before it flooded the bridge away so he set out, all bespattered, to cross it, only this queer duck of a doctor in oilskins, an old man with a washable white mustache and a yellow lamp he thrust straight into your eyeballs, swore to him the bridge was gone. You're plumb tootin' crazy, Sam shouted in the storm, I saw it standin' with me own eyes, and he scuffled to get past the geezer, who dropped the light setting the rails afire. They wrestled in the rain until Sam slyly tripped and threw him, and helter-skeltered for the bridge, to find to his crawling horror it was truly down and here he was scratching space till he landed with a splishity-splash in the whirling waters, sobbing (whoa whoa) and the white watchman on the embankment flung him a flare but it was all too late because he heard the roar of the falls below (and restless shifting of the sea) and felt with his red hand where the knife had stabbed him . . .

Roy was dreaming of an enormous mountain—Christ,

the size of it—when he felt himself roughly shaken—Sam, he thought, because they were there—only it was Eddie holding a lit candle.

"The fuse blew and I've had no chance to fix it."

"What's the matter?"

"Trou-ble. Your friend has collapsed."

Roy hopped out of the berth, stepped into moccasins and ran, with Eddie flying after him with the snuffed wax, into a darkened car where a pool of people under a blue light hovered over Sam, unconscious.

"What happened?" Roy cried.

"Sh," said the conductor, "he's got a raging fever."

"What from?"

"Can't say. We're picking up a doctor."

Sam was lying on a bench, wrapped in blankets with a pillow tucked under his head, his gaunt face broken out in sweat. When Roy bent over him, his eyes opened.

"Hello, kiddo," he said in a cracked voice.

"What hurts you, Sam?"

"Where the washboard banged me—but it don't hurt so much now."

"Oh, Jesus,"

"Don't take it so, Roy. I'll be better."

"Save his strength, son," the conductor said. "Don't talk now."

Roy got up. Sam shut his eyes.

The train whistled and ran slow at the next town then came to a draggy halt. The trainman brought a half-dressed doctor in. He examined Sam and straightened up. "We got to get him off and to the hospital."

Roy was wild with anxiety but Sam opened his eyes and told him to bend down.

Everyone moved away and Roy bent low.

"Take my wallet outa my rear pocket."

Roy pulled out the stuffed cowhide wallet.

"Now you go to the Stevens Hotel—"

"No, oh no, Sam, not without you."

"Go on, kiddo, you got to. See Clarence Mulligan tomorrow and say I sent you—they are expecting you. Give them everything you have got on the ball—that'll make me happy."

"But, Sam—"

"You got to. Bend lower."

Roy bent lower and Sam stretched his withered neck and kissed him on the chin.

"Do like I say."

"Yes, Sam."

A tear splashed on Sam's nose.

Sam had something more in his eyes to say but though he tried, agitated, couldn't say it. Then the trainmen came in with a stretcher and they lifted the catcher and handed him down the steps, and overhead the stars were bright but he knew he was dead.

Roy trailed the anonymous crowd out of Northwest Station and clung to the shadowy part of the wall till he had the courage to call a cab.

"Do you go to the Stevens Hotel?" he asked, and the driver without a word shot off before he could rightly be seated, passed a red light and scuttled a cripple across the deserted street. They drove for miles in a shadow-infested, street-lamped jungle.

He had once seen some stereopticon pictures of Chicago and it was a boxed-up ant heap of stone and crumbling wood buildings in a many-miled spreading checkerboard of streets without much open space to speak of except the railroads, stockyards, and the shore of a windy lake. In the Loop, the offices went up high and the streets were jampacked with people, and he wondered how so many of them could live together in any one place. Suppose there was a fire or something and they all ran out of their houses to see—how could they help but trample all over themselves? And Sam had warned him against strangers, because there were so many bums, sharpers, and gangsters around, people you were dirt to, who didn't know you and didn't want to, and for a dime they would slit your throat and leave you dying in the streets.

"Why did I come here?" he muttered and felt sick for home.

The cab swung into Michigan Avenue, which gave a view of the lake and a white-lit building spiring into the sky, then before he knew it he was standing flatfooted (Christ, the size of it) in front of the hotel, an enormous four-sectioned fortress. He hadn't the nerve to go through the whirling doors but had to because this bellhop grabbed his things—he wrested the bassoon case loose—and led him across the thick-carpeted lobby to a desk where he signed a card and had to count out five of the wallet's pulpy dollars for a room he would give up as soon as he found a house to board in.

But his cubbyhole on the seventeenth floor was neat and private, so after he had stored everything in the closet he lost his nervousness. Unlatching the window brought in the lake breeze. He stared down at the lit sprawl of Chicago, standing higher than he ever had in his life except for a night or two on a mountain. Gazing down upon the city, he felt as if bolts in his knees, wrists, and neck had loosened and he had spread up in height. Here, so high in the world, with the earth laid out in small squares so far below, he knew he would go in tomorrow and wow them with his fast one, and they would know him for the splendid pitcher he was.

The telephone rang. He was at first scared to answer it. In a strange place, so far from everybody he knew, it couldn't possibly be for him.

It rang again. He picked up the phone and listened.

"Hello, Roy? This is Harriet."

He wasn't sure he had got it right. "Excuse me?"

"Harriet Bird, silly."

"Oh, Harriet." He had completely forgotten her.

"Come down to my room," she giggled, "and let me say welcome to the city."

"You mean now?"

"Right away." She gave him the room number.

"Sure." He meant to ask her how she knew he was here but she had hung up.

Then he was elated. So that's how they did it in the city. He combed his hair and got out his bassoon case. In the elevator a drunk tried to take it away from him but Roy was too strong for him.

He walked—it seemed ages because he was impatient—through a long corridor till he found her number and knocked.

"Come on in."

Opening the door, he was astonished at the enormous room. Through the white-curtained window the sight of the endless dark lake sent a shiver down his spine.

Then he saw her standing shyly in the far corner of the room, naked under the gossamer thing she wore, held up on her risen nipples and the puffed wedge of hair beneath her white belly. A great weight went off his mind.

As he shut the door she reached into the hat box which lay open next to a vase of white roses on the table and fitted the black feathered hat on her head. A thick veil fell to her breasts. In her hand she held a squat, shining pistol.

He was greatly confused and thought she was kidding

but a grating lump formed in his throat and his blood shed ice. He cried out in a gruff voice, "What's wrong here?"

She said sweetly, "Roy, will you be the best there ever was in the game?"

"That's right."

She pulled the trigger (thrum of bull fiddle). The bullet cut a silver line across the water. He sought with his bare hands to catch it, but it eluded him and, to his horror, bounced into his gut. A twisted dagger of smoke drifted up from the gun barrel. Fallen on one knee he groped for the bullet, sickened as it moved, and fell over as the forest flew upward, and she, making muted noises of triumph and despair, danced on her toes around the stricken hero.

batter up!

I shoulda been a farmer," Pop Fisher said bitterly. "I shoulda farmed since the day I was born. I like cows, sheep, and those hornless goats—I am partial to nanny goats, my daddy wore a beard—I like to feed animals and milk 'em. I like fixing things, weeding poison oak out of the pasture, and seeing to the watering of the crops. I like to be by myself on a farm. I like to stand out in the fields, tending the vegetables, the corn, the winter wheat—greenest looking stuff you ever saw. When Ma was alive she kept urging me to leave baseball and take up farming, and I always meant to but after she died I had no heart for it." Pop's voice all but broke and Red Blow shifted nervously on the bench but Pop didn't cry. He took out his handkerchief, flipped it, and blew his nose. "I have that green thumb," he said huskily, "and I shoulda farmed instead of playing wet nurse to a last place, dead-to-the-neck ball team."

They were sitting in the New York Knights' dugout,

scanning the dusty field, the listless game and half-empty stands.

"Tough," said Red. He kept his eye on the pitcher.

Removing his cap, Pop rubbed his bald head with his bandaged fingers. "It's been a blasted dry season. No rains at all. The grass is worn scabby in the outfield and the infield is cracking. My heart feels as dry as dirt for the little I have to show for all my years in the game."

He got up, stooped at the fountain and spat the warm, rusty water into the dust. "When the hell they going to fix this thing so we can have a decent drink of water? Did you speak to that bastard partner I have, like I said to?"

"Says he's working on it."

"Working on it," Pop grunted. "He's so tight that if he was any tighter he'd be too stiff to move. It was one of the darkest days of my life when that snake crawled into this club. He's done me out of more dough than I can count."

"Kid's weakening again," Red said. "He passed two."

Pop watched Fowler for a minute but let him stay. "If those boy scouts could bring in a coupla runs once in a while I'd change pitchers, but they couldn't bring their own grandmother in from across the street. What a butchering we took from the Pirates in the first game and here we are six runs behind in this. It's Memorial Day, all right, but not for the soldiers."

"Should've had some runs. Bump had four for four in the first and two hits before he got himself chucked out of this."

Pop's face burned. "Don't mention that ape man to me —getting hisself bounced out of the game the only time we had runners on the bases when he come up."

"I'd've thrown him out too if I was the ump and he slid dry ice down my pants."

"I'd like to stuff him with ice. I never saw such a disgusting screwball for practical jokes."

Pop scratched violently under his loosely bandaged fingers. "And to top it off I have to go catch athlete's foot on my hands. Now ain't that one for the books? Everybody I have ever heard of have got it on their feet but I have to go and get it on both of my hands and be itchy and bandaged in this goshdarn hot weather. No wonder I am always asking myself is life worth the living of it."

"Tough," Red said. "He's passed Feeber, bases loaded."

Pop fumed. "My best pitcher and he blows up every time I put him against a first place team. Yank him."

The coach, a lean and freckled man, got nimbly up on the dugout steps and signaled to the bullpen in right field. He sauntered out to the mound just as somebody in street clothes came up the stairs of the tunnel leading from the clubhouse and asked the player at the end of the bench, "Who's Fisher?" The player jerked his thumb toward the opposite side of the dugout, and the man, dragging a large, beat-up valise and a bassoon case, treaded his way to Pop.

When Pop saw him coming he exclaimed, "Oh, my eight-foot uncle, what have we got here, the Salvation Army band?"

The man set his things on the floor and sat down on a concrete step, facing Pop. He beheld an old geezer of sixty-five with watery blue eyes, a thin red neck and a bitter mouth, who looked like a lost banana in the overgrown baseball suit he wore, especially his skinny legs in loose blue-and-white stockings.

And Pop saw a tall, husky, dark-bearded fellow with old eyes but not bad features. His face was strong-boned, if a trifle meaty, and his mouth seemed pleasant though its expression was grim. For his bulk he looked lithe, and he appeared calmer than he felt, for although he was sitting here on this step he was still in motion. He was traveling (on the train that never stopped). His self, his mind, raced on and he felt he hadn't stopped going wherever he was going because he hadn't yet arrived. Where hadn't he arrived? Here. But now it was time to calm down, ease up on the old scooter, sit still and be quiet, though the inside of him was still streaming through towns and cities, across forests and fields, over long years.

"The only music I make," he answered Pop, patting the bassoon case, "is with my bat." Searching through the pockets of his frayed and baggy suit, worn to threads at the knees and elbows, he located a folded letter that he reached over to the manager. "I'm your new left fielder, Roy Hobbs."

"My what!" Pop exploded.

"It says in the letter."

Red, who had returned from the mound, took the letter, unfolded it, and handed it to Pop. He read it in a single swoop then shook his head in disbelief.

"Scotty Carson sent you?"

"That's right."

"He must be daffy."

Roy wet his dry lips.

Pop shot him a shrewd look. "You're thirty-five if you're a day."

"Thirty-four, but I'm good for ten years."

"Thirty-four—Holy Jupiter, mister, you belong in an old man's home, not baseball."

The players along the bench were looking at him. Roy licked his lips.

"Where'd he pick you up?" Pop asked.

"I was with the Oomoo Oilers."

"In what league?"

"They're semipros."

"Ever been in organized baseball?"

"I only recently got back in the game."

"What do you mean got back?"

"Used to play in high school."

Pop snorted. "Well, it's a helluva mess." He slapped the letter with the back of his fingers. "Scotty signed him and the Judge okayed it. Neither of them consulted me. They can't do that," he said to Red. "That thief in the tower might have sixty per cent of the stock but I have it in writing that I am to manage this team and approve all player deals *as long as I live.*"

"I got a contract," said Roy.

"Lemme see it."

Roy pulled a blue-backed paper out of his inside coat pocket.

Pop scanned it. "Where in blazes did he get the figure of three thousand dollars?"

"It was for a five thousand minimum but the Judge said I already missed one-third of the season."

Pop burst into scornful laughter. "Sure, but that entitles you to about thirty-three hundred. Just like that godawful deadbeat. He'd skin his dead father if he could get into the grave."

He returned the contract to Roy. "It's illegal."

"Scotty's your chief scout?" Roy asked.

"That's right."

"He signed me to a contract with an open figure and the Judge filled it in. I asked about that and Scotty said he had the authority to sign me."

"He has," Red said to Pop. "You said so yourself if he found anybody decent."

"That's right, that's what I said, but who needs a fielder old enough to be my son? I got a left fielder," he said to Roy, "a darn good one when he feels like it and ain't playing practical jokes on everybody."

Roy stood up. "If you don't want me, Merry Christmas."

"Wait a second," said Red. He fingered Pop up close to the fountain and spoke to him privately.

Pop calmed down. "I'm sorry, son," he apologized to Roy when he returned to the bench, "but you came across me at a bad time. Also thirty-four years for a rookie is starting with one foot in the grave. But like Red says, if our best scout sent you, you musta showed him something. Go on in the clubhouse and have Dizzy fit you up with a monkey suit. Then report back here and I will locate you a place on this bench with the rest of my All-Stars." He threw the players a withering look and they quickly turned away.

"Listen, mister," Roy said, "I know my way out of this jungle if you can't use me. I don't want any second pickings."

"Do as he told you," Red said.

Roy rose, got his valise and bassoon case together, and headed into the tunnel. His heart was thumping like a noisy barrel.

"I shoulda bought a farm," Pop muttered.

The pitcher in the shower had left the door wide open so the locker room was clouded with steam when Roy came in. Unable to find anybody he yelled into the shower room where was the prop man, and the one in the shower yelled back in the equipment room and close the door it was drafty. When the steam had thinned out and Roy could see his way around he located the manager's office, so labeled in black letters on the door, but not the equipment room. In the diagonally opposite corner were the trainer's quarters, and here the door was ajar and gave forth an oil of wintergreen smell that crawled up his nose. He could see the trainer, in a gray sweat-shirt with KNIGHTS stenciled across his chest, working on a man mountain on the rubbing table. Catching sight of Roy, the trainer called out in an Irish brogue who was he looking for?

"Prop man," Roy said.

"That's Dizzy—down the hall." The trainer made with his eyes to the left so Roy opened the door there and went down the hall. He located a sign, "Equipment," and through the window under it saw the prop man in a baseball jersey sitting on a uniform trunk with his back to the wall. He was reading the sports page of the *Mirror*.

Roy rapped on the ledge and Dizzy, a former utility pitcher, hastily put the paper down. "Caught me at an interesting moment," he grinned. "I was reading about this catcher that got beaned in Boston yesterday. Broke the side of his skull."

"The name's Roy Hobbs, new hand here. Fisher told me to get outfitted."

"New man—fielder, eh?"

Roy nodded.

"Yeah, we been one man short on the roster for two weeks. One of our guys went and got himself hit on the head with a fly ball and both of his legs are now paralyzed."

Roy winked.

"Honest to God. And just before that our regular third baseman stepped on a bat and rolled down the dugout steps. Snapped his spine in two places." Dizzy grimaced. "We sure been enjoying an unlucky season."

He came forth with a tape measure and took Roy's measurements, then he went back and collected a pile of stuff from the shelves.

"Try this for size." He handed him a blue cap with a white K stitched on the front of it.

Roy tried it. "Too small."

"You sure got some size noggin there."

"Seven and a half." Roy looked at him.

"Just a social remark. No offense meant or intended." he gave Roy a size that fitted.

"How's it look?" Roy asked.

"A dream but why the tears?"

"I have a cold." He turned away.

Dizzy asked him to sign for the stuff—Judge Banner insisted. He helped Roy carry it to his locker.

"Keep anything you like inside of here but for goodness' sakes no booze. Pop throws fits if any of the players drink."

Roy stood the bassoon case in upright. "Got a lock for the door?"

"Nobody locks their doors here. Before the game you deposit your valuables in that trunk there and I will lock them up."

"Okay, skip it."

Dizzy excused himself to get back to his paper and Roy began to undress.

The locker room was tomblike quiet. The pitcher who had been in the showers—his footsteps were still wet on the floor—had dressed rapidly and vanished. As he put his things away, Roy found himself looking around every so often to make sure he was here. He was, all right, yet in all his imagining of how it would be when he finally hit the majors, he had not expected to feel so down in the dumps. It was different than he had thought it would be. So different he almost felt like walking out, jumping back on a train, and going wherever people went when they were running out on something. Maybe for a long rest in one of those towns he had lived in as a kid. Like the place where he had that shaggy mutt that used to scamper through the woods, drawing him after it to the deepest, stillest part, till the silence was so pure you could crack it if you threw a rock. Roy remained lost in the silence till the dog's yapping woke him, though as he came out of it, it was not barking he heard but the sound of voices through the trainer's half-open door.

He listened closely because he had the weird impression that he knew all the voices in there, and as he sorted them he recognized first the trainer's brogue and then a big voice that he did not so much recall, as remember having heard throughout his life—a strong, rawboned voice, familiar from his boyhood and some of the jobs he had worked at later, and the different places he had bummed around in, slop joints, third-rate hotels, prize fight gyms and such; the big voice of a heavy, bull-necked, strong-muscled guy, the kind of gorilla he had more than once fought half to death for no reason he could think of. Oh, the Whammer, he thought, and quickly ducked but straightened up when he remembered the Whammer was almost fifty and long since retired out of the game. But what made him most uneasy was a third voice, higher than the other two, a greedy, penetrating, ass-kissing voice he had definitely heard before. He strained his ears to hear it again but the big voice was talking about this gag he had pulled on Pop Fisher, in particular, spraying white pepper in Pop's handkerchief, which made him sneeze and constantly blow his beak. That commenced an epidemic of base stealing, to Pop's fury, because the signal to steal that day was for him to raise his handkerchief to his schnozzle.

At the end of the story there was a guffaw and a yelp of laughter, then the trainer remarked something and this other voice, one that stood on stilts, commented that Bump certainly got a kick out of his jokes, and Bump, he must have been, said Pop wouldn't agree to his release, so if he was going to be stuck in this swamp he would at least have a little fun.

He laughed loudly and said, "Here's one for your colyum, kid. We were in Cincy in April and had a free day on our hands because this exhibition game was called off, so in the Plaza lobby that morning we get to bulling about players and records, and you know Pop and this line of his about how lousy the modern player is compared to those mustached freaks he played with in the time of King Tut. He was saying that the average fielder nowadays could maybe hit the kangaroo ball we got—he was looking at me—but you couldn't count on him to catch a high fly. 'How high?' I ask him, innocent, and he points up and says, 'Any decent height. They either lose them in the sun or misjudge them in the wind.' So I say, 'Could you catch the real high ones, Pop?' And he pipes up, 'As high as they went up I could catch them.' He thinks a minute and says, 'I bet I could catch a ball that is dropped from the top of the Empire State Building.' 'No,' I says, like I was surprised, and 'Yes,' he says. So I say, 'We have nothing on for today, and although there isn't any Empire State Building in Cincinnati, yet I do have this friend of mine at the airport who owns a Piper Cub. I will give him a National League baseball and he will drop it at the height of the building if you will catch it.' 'Done,' he says, as perky as a turkey, so I call up this guy I know and arrange it and off we go across the bridge to the Kentucky side of the river, where there is plenty of room to move around in. Well, sir, soon this yellow plane comes over and circles a couple of times till he has the right height, and then he lets go with something that I didn't tell Pop, but which the boys are onto, is a grapefruit so that if it hits him it will not crack his skull open and kill him. Down the thing comes like a cannonball and Pop, in his black two-piece bathing suit, in case he has to go a little in the water, and wearing a mitt the size of a basket, circles under it like a dizzy duck, holding the sun out of his eyes as he gets a line on where it is coming down. Faster it falls, getting bigger by the second, then Pop, who is now set for the catch, suddenly lets out a howl, 'My Christ, the moon is falling on me,' and the next second, bong—the grapefruit busts him on the conk and we have all we can do to keep him from drowning in the juice."

Now there was a loud cackle of laughter in the trainer's room. The voice Roy didn't like—the frightening thought dawned on him that the voice *knew* what he was hiding—it changed the subject and wanted to know from Bump if there was any truth to the rumor about him and Pop's niece.

"Naw," Bump said, and cagily asked, "What rumor?"

"That you and Memo are getting hitched."

Bump laughed. "She must've started that one herself."

"Then you deny it?"

The door was shoved open and Bump waltzed out in his shorts, as husky, broadbacked, and big-shouldered as Roy had thought, followed by the trainer and a slightly pop-eyed gent dressed in an expensive striped suit, whose appearance gave Roy a shooting pain in the pit of the stomach —Max Mercy.

Ashamed to be recognized, to have his past revealed like an egg spattered on the floor, Roy turned away, tucking his jersey into his pants.

But Bump paraded over with his hairy arm outstretched.

"Hiya, Buster, you the latest victim they have trapped?"

Roy felt an irritable urge to pitch his fist at the loud-mouth, but he nodded and shook hands.

"Welcome to the lousiest team in the world, barring none," Bump said. "And this is ol' Doc Casey, the trainer, who has got nobody but cripples on his hands except me. And the hawkshaw with the eyes is Max Mercy, the famous sports colyumist. Most newspaper guys are your pals and know when to keep their traps shut, but to Max a private life is a personal insult. Before you are here a week he will tell the public how much of your salary you send to your grandma and how good is your sex life."

Max, whose mustache and sideboards were graying, laughed hollowly. He said to Roy, "Didn't catch the name."

"Roy Hobbs," he said stiffly, but no one seemed to think it mattered very much.

The game was over and the players hoofed through the tunnel into the locker room. They tore out of their uniforms and piled into the showers. Some stayed in only long enough to wet their skins. Wiping themselves dry, they tumbled into street clothes. Their speed, however, did them no good, for Red, after courteously asking Mercy to leave, posted himself and Earl Wilson, the third base coach, at the door and they let nobody else out. The players waited nervously, except Bump, who slapped backs and advised everybody to cheer up. A few of the boys were working the strategy of staying in the showers so long they hoped Pop would grow sick and tired and leave. But Pop, a self-sustaining torch in the shut managerial office, outwaited them, and when he got the quiet knock from Red that the lobsters were in the pot, yanked open the door and strode sulphurously forth. The team shriveled.

Pop stepped up on a chair where for once, a bald, bristling figure, he towered over them. Waving his bandaged hands he began to berate them but immediately stopped, choked by his rage into silence.

"If he coughs now," Bump boomed, "he will bust into dust."

Pop glared at him, his head glowing like a red sun. He savagely burst out that not a single blasted one of them here was a true ballplayer. They were sick monkeys, broken-down mules, pigeon-chested toads, slimy horned worms, but not real, honest-to-god baseball players.

"How's about flatfooted fish?" Bump wisecracked. "Get it, boys, fish—Fisher," and he fell into a deep gargle of laughter at his wit, but the semi-frozen players in the room did not react.

"How's he get away with it?" Roy asked the ghost standing next to him. The pale player whispered out of the corner of his mouth that Bump was presently the leading hitter in the league.

Pop ignored Bump and continued to give the team the rough side of his tongue. "What beats me is that I have spent thousands of dollars for the best players I could lay my hands on. I hired two of the finest coaches in the game. I sweat myself sick trying to direct you, and all you can deliver is those goddamn goose eggs." His voice rose. "Do you dimwits realize that we have been skunked for the last forty-five innings in a row?"

"Not Bumpsy," the big voice said, "I am terrific."

"You now hold the record of the most consecutive games lost in the whole league history, the most strikeouts, the most errors—"

"Not Bumpsy—"

"—the most foolishness and colossal stupidities. In plain words, you all stink. I am tempted to take pity on those poor dopes who spend a buck and a half to watch you play and trade the whole lousy lot of you away."

Bump dropped down on his knees and raised his clasped hands. "Me first, Lawdy, me first."

"—and start from scratch to build up a team that will know how to play together and has guts and will fight the other guy to death before they drop seventeen games in the cellar."

The players in the locker room were worn out but Bump was singing, "Many brave hearts are asleep in the deep."

"Beware," he croaked low in his throat, "bewaaare—"

Pop shook a furious finger at him that looked as if it would fly off and strike him in the face. "As for you, Bump Baily, high and mighty though you are, some day you'll pay for your sassifras. Remember that lightning cuts down the tallest trees too."

Bump didn't like warnings of retribution. His face turned surly.

"Lightning, maybe, but no burnt out old fuse."

Pop tottered. "Practice at eight in the morning," he said brokenly. But for Red he would have tumbled off the chair. In his office behind the slammed and smoking door they could hear him sobbing, "Sometimes I could cut my own throat."

It took the Knights a while to grow bones and crawl out after Bump. But when everybody had gone, including the coaches and Dizzy, Roy remained behind. His face was flaming hot, his clothes soaked in sweat and shame, as if the old man's accusations had been leveled at his head.

When Pop came out in his street clothes, a yellowed Panama and a loud sport jacket, he was startled to see Roy sitting there in the gloom and asked what he was waiting for.

"No place to go," Roy said.

"Whyn't you get a room?"

"Ain't got what it takes."

Pop looked at him. "Scotty paid you your bonus cash, didn't he?"

"Two hundred, but I had debts."

"You shoulda drawn an advance on your first two weeks' pay from the office when you came in today. It's too late now, they quit at five, so I will write you out my personal check for twenty-five dollars and you can pay me back when you get the money."

Pop balanced his checkbook on his knee. "You married?"

"No."

"Whyn't you ask around among the married players to see who has got a spare room? That way you'd have a more regular life. Either that, or in a respectable boarding house. Some of the boys who have their homes out of town prefer to stay at a moderate-priced hotel, which I myself have done since my wife passed away, but a boarding house is more homelike and cheaper. Anyway," Pop advised, "tonight you better come along with me to the hotel and tomorrow you can find a place to suit your needs."

Roy remarked he wasn't particularly crazy about hotels.

They left the ball park, got into a cab and drove downtown. The sky over the Hudson was orange. Once Pop broke out of his reverie to point out Grant's Tomb.

At the Midtown Hotel, Pop spoke to the desk clerk and he assigned Roy a room on the ninth floor, facing toward the Empire State Building. Pop went up with him and pumped the mattress.

"Not bad," he said.

After the bellhop had left he said he hoped Roy wasn't the shenanigan type.

"What kind?" Roy asked.

"There are all sorts of nuts in this game and I remember one of my players—seems to me it was close to twenty years ago—who used to walk out on the fifteenth floor ledge

52

and scare fits out of people in the other rooms. One day when he was walking out there he fell and broke his leg and only the darndest luck kept him from rolling right overboard. It was beginning to rain and he pulled himself around from window to window, begging for help, and everybody went into stitches at his acting but kept their windows closed. He finally rolled off and hit bottom."

Roy had unpacked his valise and was washing up.

"Lemme tell you one practical piece of advice, son," Pop went on. "You're starting way late—I was finished after fifteen years as an active player one year after the age you're coming in, but if you want to get along the best way, behave and give the game all you have got, and when you can't do that, quit. We don't need any more gold-brickers or fourflushers or practical jokers around. One Bump Baily is too much for any team."

He left the room, looking wretched.

The phone jangled and after a minute Roy got around to lifting it.

"What's the matter?" Red Blow barked. "Don't you answer your telephone?"

"I like it to ring a little, gives 'em a chance to change their mind."

"Who?"

"Anybody."

Red paused. "Pop asked me to show you around. When are you eating?"

"I am hungry now."

"Meet me in the lobby, half past six."

As Roy hung up there was a loud dum-diddy-um-dum on the door and Bump Baily in a red-flowered Hollywood shirt breezed in.

"Hiya, buster. Saw you pull in with the old geezer and tracked you down. I would like for you to do me a favor."

"Roy is the name."

"Roy is fine. Listen, I got my room on the fourth floor, which is a damn sight classier than this mouse trap. I would like you to borrow it and I will borrow this for tonight."

"What's the pitch?"

"I am having a lady friend visit me and there are too many nosy people on my floor."

Roy considered and said okay. He unconsciously wet his lips.

Bump slapped him between the shoulders. "Stick around, buster, you will get yours."

Roy knew he would never like the guy.

Bump told him his room number and they exchanged keys, then Roy put a few things into his valise and went downstairs.

Coming along the fourth floor hall he saw a door half open and figured this was it. As he pulled the knob he froze, for there with her back to him stood a slim, red-headed girl in black panties and brassiere. She was combing her hair before a mirror on the wall as the light streamed in around her through the billowy curtains. When she saw him in the mirror she let out a scream. He stepped back as if he had been kicked in the face. Then the door slammed and he had a splitting headache.

Bump's room was next door so Roy went in and lay down on the bed, amid four purple walls traced through with leaves flying among white baskets of fruit, some loaded high and some spilled over. He lay there till the pain in his brain eased.

At 6:30 he went down and met Red, in a droopy linen suit, and they had steaks in a nearby chophouse. Roy had two and plenty of mashed potatoes. Afterwards they walked up Fifth Avenue. He felt better after the meal.

"Want to see the Village?" Red said.

"What's in it?"

Red picked his teeth. "Beats me. Whatever they got I can't find it. How about a picture?"

Roy was agreeable so they dropped into a movie. It was a picture about a city guy who came to the country, where he had a satisfying love affair with a girl he met. Roy enjoyed it. As they walked back to the hotel the night was soft and summery. He thought about the black-brassiered girl in the next room.

Red talked about the Knights. "They are not a bad bunch of players, but they aren't playing together and it's mostly Bump's fault. He is for Bump and not for the team. Fowler, Schultz, Hinkle, and Hill are all good pitchers and could maybe be fifteen or twenty game winners if they got some support in the clutches, which they don't, and whatever Bump gives them in hitting he takes away with his lousy fielding."

"How's that?"

"He's just so damn lazy. Pop has thrown many a fine and suspension at him, but after that he will go into a slump on purpose and we don't win a one. If I was Pop I'da had his ass long ago, but Pop thinks a hitter like him could be a bell cow and lead the rest ahead, so he keeps hoping he will reform. If we could get the team rolling we'd be out of the cellar in no time."

They were approaching the hotel and Roy counted with his eyes up to the fourth floor and watched the curtains in the windows.

"I read Scotty's report on you," Red said. "He says you are a terrific hitter. How come you didn't start playing when you were younger?"

"I did but I flopped." Roy was evasive.

Red cringed. "Don't say that word around here."

"What word?"

"Flopped—at least not anywhere near Pop. He starts to cry when he hears it."

"What for?"

"Didn't you ever hear about Fisher's Flop?"

"Seems to me I did but I am not sure."

Red told him the story. "About forty years ago Pop was the third sacker for the old Sox when they got into their first World Series after twenty years. They sure wanted to take the flag that year but so did the Athletics, who they were playing, and it was a rough contest all the way into the seventh game. That one was played at Philly and from the first inning the score stood at 3-3, until the Athletics drove the tie-breaker across in the last of the eighth. In the ninth the Sox's power was due up but they started out bad. The leadoffer hit a blooper to short, the second struck out, and the third was Pop. It was up to him. He let one go for a strike, then he slammed a low, inside pitch for a tremendous knock.

"The ball sailed out to deep center," Red said, "where the center fielder came in too fast and it rolled through him to the fence and looked good for an inside-the-park homer, or at least a triple. Meanwhile, Pop, who is of course a young guy at this time, was ripping around the bags, and the crowd was howling for him to score and tie up the game, when in some crazy way as he was heading for home, his legs got tangled under him and he fell flat on his stomach, the living bejesus knocked out of him. By the time he was up again the ball was in the catcher's glove and he ran up the baseline after Pop. In the rundown that followed, the third baseman tagged him on the behind and the game was over."

Red spat into the street. Roy tried to say something but couldn't.

"That night Fisher's Flop, or as they mostly call it,

'Fisher's Famous Flop,' was in every newspaper in the country and was talked about by everybody. Naturally Pop felt like hell. I understand that Ma Fisher had the phone out and hid him up in the attic. He stayed there two weeks, till the roof caught fire and he had to come out or burn. After that they went to Florida for a vacation but it didn't help much. His picture was known to all and wherever he went they yelled after him, 'Flippity-flop, flippity-flop.' It was at this time that Pop lost his hair. After a while people no longer recognized him, except on the ball field, yet though the kidding died down, Pop was a marked man."

Roy mopped his face. "Hot," he said.

"But he had his guts in him," Red said, "and stayed in the game for ten years more and made a fine record. Then he retired from baseball for a couple of years, which was a good thing but he didn't know it. Soon one of Ma's rich relatives died and left them a pile of dough that Pop used to buy himself a half share of the Knights. He was made field manager and the flop was forgotten by now except for a few wise-egg sportswriters that, when they are too drunk to do an honest day's work, would raise up the old story and call it Fisher's Fizzle, or Farce, or Fandango—you wouldn't guess there are so many funny words beginning with an f—which some of them do to this day when the Knights look foolish. The result is that Pop has the feeling he has been jinxed since the time of his flop, and he has spent twenty-five years and practically all of his pile trying to break the jinx, which he thinks he can do by making the Knights into the world champs that the old Sox never did become. Eight times he has finished in second place, five in third, and the rest in fourth or fifth, but last season when the Judge bought into the club and then took advantage of Pop's financial necessity to get hold of ten per cent of his shares and make himself the majority stockholder, was our worst season. We ended up in the sewer and this year it looks like a repeat."

"How come?"

"The Judge is trying to push Pop out of his job although he has a contract to manage for life—that's what the Judge had to promise to get that ten per cent of stock. Anyway, he's been trying everything he can think of to make things tough for Pop. He has by his sly ways forced all sorts of trades on us which make money all right but hurt the team. It burns me up," Red said, "because I would give my right arm if I could get Pop the pennant. I am sure that if he took one and the Series after that, he would feel satisfied, quit baseball, and live in peace. He is one helluva white guy and deserves better than he got. That's why I am asking you to give him the best you have in you."

"Let him play me," Roy said, "and he will get the best."

In the lobby Red said he had enjoyed Roy's company and they should eat together more. Before he left he warned Roy to be careful with his earnings. They weren't much, he knew, but if in the future Roy had a chance to invest in something good, he advised him to do so. "There is a short life in baseball and we have to think of the future. Anything can happen to you in this game. Today you are on top and tomorrow you will be on your way out to Dubuque. Try to protect your old age. It don't pay to waste what you earn."

To his surprise, Roy answered, "To hell with my old age. I will be in this game a long time."

Red rubbed his chin. "How are you so sure?"

"It wasn't for nothing it took me fifteen years to get here. I came for more than the ride and I will leave my mark around here."

Red waited to hear more but Roy shut up.

Red shrugged, "Well, each to their choice."

Roy said good night and went upstairs. Entering Bump's room, he picked up a gilt hairpin from the carpet and put

58

it into his wallet because some claimed it brought luck. For a while he stood at the window and watched the lit Empire State Building. It was a great big city, all right. He undressed, thinking of Pop's flop that changed his whole life, and got into bed.

In the dark the bed was in motion, going round in wide, sweeping circles. He didn't like the feeling so he lay deathly still and let everything go by—the trees; mountains, states. Then he felt he was headed into a place where he did not want to go and tried urgently to think of ways to stop the bed. But he couldn't and it went on, a roaring locomotive now, screaming into the night, so that he was tensed and sweating and groaned aloud why did it have to be me? what did I do to deserve it? seeing himself again walking down the long, lonely corridor, carrying the bassoon case, the knock, the crazy Harriet (less and more than human) with the shiny pistol, and him, cut down in the very flower of his youth, lying in a red pool of his own blood.

No, he cried, oh no, and lashed at his pillow, as he had a thousand times before.

Finally, as the sight of him through the long long years of suffering faded away, he quieted down. The noise of the train eased off as it came to a stop, and Roy found himself set down in a field somewhere in the country, where he had a long and satisfying love affair with this girl he had seen in the picture tonight.

He thought of her till he had fallen all but deep asleep, when a door seemed to open in the mind and this naked redheaded lovely slid out of a momentary flash of light, and the room was dark again. He thought he was still dreaming of the picture but the funny part of it was when she got into bed with him he almost cried out in pain as her icy hands and feet, in immediate embrace, slashed his hot body, but there among the apples, grapes, and melons, he found what he wanted and had it.

at the clubhouse

the next morning the unshaven Knights were glum and redeyed. They moved around listlessly and cursed each step. Angry fist fights broke out among them. They were sore at themselves and the world, yet when Roy came in and headed for his locker they looked up and watched with interest. He opened the door and found his new uniform knotted up dripping wet on a hook. His sanitary socks and woolen stockings were slashed to shreds and all the other things were smeared black with shoe polish. He located his jock, with two red apples in it, swinging from a cord attached to the light globe, and both his shoes were nailed to the ceiling. The boys let out a bellow of laughter. Bump just about doubled up howling, but Roy yanked the wet pants off the hook and caught him with it smack in the face. The players let out another yowl.

Bump comically dried himself with a bath towel, digging deep into his ears, wiping under the arms, and shimmying as he rubbed it across his fat behind.

"Fast guesswork, buster, and to show you there's no hard feelings, how's about a Camel?"

Roy wanted nothing from the bastard but took the cigarette because everyone was looking on. When he lit it, someone in the rear yelled. "Fire!" and ducked as it burst in Roy's face. Bump had disappeared. The players fell into each other's arms. Tears streamed down their cheeks. Some of them could not unbend and limped around from laughing so.

Roy flipped the ragged butt away and began to mop up his wet locker.

Allie Stubbs, the second baseman, danced around the room in imitation of a naked nature dancer. He pretended to discover a trombone at the foot of a tree and marched around blowing oompah, oompah, oompah.

Roy then realized the bassoon case was missing. It startled him that he hadn't thought of it before.

"Who's got it, boys?"—but no one answered. Allie now made out like he was flinging handfuls of rose petals into the trainer's office.

Going in there, Roy saw that Bump had broken open the bassoon case and was about to attack Wonderboy with a hacksaw.

"Lay off of that, you goon."

Bump turned and stepped back with the bat raised. Roy grabbed it and with a quick twist tore it out of his sweaty hands, turning him around as he did and booting him hard with his knee. Bump grunted and swung but Roy ducked. The team crowded into the trainer's office, roaring with delight.

But Doc Casey pushed his way through them and stepped between Roy and Bump. "That'll do, boys. We want no trouble here. Go on outside or Pop will have your hides."

Bump was sweaty and sore. "You're a lousy sport, alfalfa."

"I don't like the scummy tricks you play on people you have asked for a favor," Roy said.

"I hear you had a swell time, wonderboy."

Again they grappled for each other, but Doc, shouting for help, kept them apart until the players pinned Roy's arms and held on to Bump.

"Lemme at him," Bump roared, "and I will skin the skunk."

Held back by the team, they glared at one another over the trainer's head.

"What's going on in there?" Pop's shrill blast came from inside the locker room. Earl Wilson poked his grayhaired, sunburned head in and quickly called, "All out, men, on the double." The players scurried past Pop and through the tunnel. They felt better.

Dizzy hustled up a makeshift rig for Roy. He dressed and polished his bat, a little sorry he had lost his temper, because he had wanted to speak quietly to the guy and find out whether he was expecting the redhead in his room last night.

Thinking about her made him uneasy. He reported to Pop in the dugout.

"What was that trouble in there between Bump and you?" Pop asked.

Roy didn't say and Pop got annoyed. "I won't stand for any ructions between players so cut it out or you will find yourself chopping wood back in the sticks. Now report to Red."

Roy went over to where Red was catching Chet Schultz, today's pitcher, and Red said to wait his turn at the batting cage.

The field was overrun with droopy players. Half a dozen were bunched near the gate of the cage, waiting to be pitched to by Al Fowler, whom Pop had ordered to throw batting practice for not bearing down in the clutches yesterday. Some of the men were at the sidelines, throwing catch. A few were shagging flies in the field, a group was playing pepper. On the line between home and first Earl Wilson was hacking out grounders to Allie Stubbs, Cal Baker at short, Hank Benz, the third baseman, and Emil Lajong, who played first. At the edge of the outfield, Hinkle and Hill, two of the regular starters, and McGee, the reliefer, were doing a weak walk-run-walk routine. No one seemed to be thoroughly awake, but when Roy went into the batting cage they came to life and observed him.

Fowler, a southpaw, was in a nasty mood. He didn't like having his ears burned by Pop, called a showboat in front of the other men, and then shoved into batting practice the day after he had pitched. Fowler was twenty-three but looked thirty. He was built rangy, with very light hair and eyelashes, and small blue eyes. As a pitcher he had the stuff and knew it, but all season long he had been erratic and did a great amount of griping. He was palsy with Bump, who as a rule had no friends.

When Roy came up with Wonderboy, he hugged the plate too close to suit Fowler, who was in there anyway only to help the batters find their timing. In annoyance Fowler pitched the ball at Roy's head. Roy hit the dirt.

Pop shrieked, "Cut that out, you blasted fool." Fowler mumbled something about the ball slipping. Yet he wanted to make Roy look silly and burned the next one in. Roy swung and the ball sailed over the right field fence. Red-faced, Fowler tried a hard, sharp-breaking curve. Roy caught it at the end of his bat and pulled it into the left field stands.

"Try this one, grandpa." Fowler flung a stiff-wrist knuckler that hung in the air without spin before it took a sudden dip, but Roy scooped it up with the stick and lifted it twenty rows up into the center field stands. Then he quit. Fowler was scowling at his feet. Everybody else stared at Roy.

Pop called out, "Lemme see that bat, son."

Both he and Red examined it, hefting it and rubbing along the grain with their fingers.

"Where'd you get it?" Pop asked.

Roy cleared his throat. He said he had made it himself.

"Did you brand this name Wonderboy on it?"

"That's right."

"What's it mean?"

"I made it long ago," Roy said, "when I was a kid. I wanted it to be a very good bat and that's why I gave it that name."

"A bat's cheap to buy," Red said.

"I know it but this tree near the river where I lived was split by lightning. I liked the wood inside of it so I cut me out a bat. Hadn't used it much until I played semipro ball, but I always kept it oiled with sweet oil and boned it so it wouldn't chip."

"Sure is white. Did you bleach the wood?"

"No, that's the true color."

"How long ago d'you make it?" Pop asked.

"A long time—I don't remember."

"Whyn't you get into the game then?"

Roy couldn't answer for a minute. "I sorta got side-tracked."

But Pop was all smiles. "Red'll measure and weigh it. if there's no filler and it meets specifications you'll be allowed to use it."

"There's nothing in it but wood."

Red clapped him on the back. "I feel it in my bones that you will have luck with it." He said to Pop, "Maybe we can start Roy in the line-up soon?"

Pop said they would see how it worked out.

But he sent Roy out to left field and Earl hit fungos to him all over the lot. Roy ran them down well. He took one shot over his shoulder and two caroming off the wall below the stands. His throwing was quick, strong, and bull's eye.

When Bump got around to his turn in the cage, though he did not as a rule exert himself in practice, he now whammed five of Fowler's fast pitches into the stands. Then he trotted out to his regular spot in the sun field and Earl hit him some long flies, all of which he ran for and caught with gusto, even those that went close to the wall, which was unusual for him because he didn't like to go too near it.

Practice picked up. The men worked faster and harder than they had in a long time. Pop suddenly felt so good, tears came to his eyes and he had to blow his nose.

In the clubhouse about an hour and a half before game time, the boys were sitting around in their underwear after showers. They were bulling, working crossword puzzles, shaving and writing letters. Two were playing checkers, surrounded by a circle of others, and the rest were drinking soda, looking at the *Sporting News,* or just resting their eyes. Though they tried to hide it they were all nervous, always glancing up whenever someone came into the room. Roy couldn't make sense of it.

Red took him around to meet some of the boys and Roy spoke a few words to Dave Olson, the squat catcher, also to the shy Mexican center fielder, Juan Flores, and to Gabby Laslow, who patrolled right field. They sidestepped Bump, sitting in front of his locker with a bath towel around his rump, as he worked a red thread across the yellowed foot of a sanitary sock.

"Changes that thread from sock to sock every day," Red said in a low voice. "Claims it keeps him hitting."

As the players began to get into clean uniforms, Pop,

wearing halfmoon specs, stepped out of his office. He read aloud the batting order, then flipping through his dog-eared, yellow-paged notebook he read the names of the players opposing them and reminded them how the pitchers were to pitch and the fielders field them. This information was scribbled all over the book and Pop had to thumb around a lot before he had covered everybody. Roy then expected him to lay on with a blistering mustard plaster for all, but he only glanced anxiously at the door and urged them all to be on their toes and for gosh sakes get some runs.

Just as Pop finished his pep talk the door squeaked open and a short and tubby man in a green suit peeked in. Seeing they were ready, he straightened up and entered briskly, carrying a briefcase in his hand. He beamed at the players and without a word from anybody they moved chairs and benches and arranged themselves in rows before him. Roy joined the rest, expecting to hear some kind of talk. Only Pop and the coaches sat behind the man, and Dizzy lounged, half open-mouthed, at the door leading to the hall.

"What's the act?" Roy asked Olson.

"It's Doc Knobb." The catcher looked sleepy.

"What's he do?"

"Pacifies us."

The players were attentive, sitting as if they were going to have their pictures snapped. The nervousness Roy had sensed among them was all but gone. They looked like men whose worries had been lifted, and even Bump gave forth a soft grunt of contentment.

The doctor removed his coat and rolled up his shirt-sleeves. "Got to hurry today," he told Pop, "got a polo team to cheer up in Brooklyn."

He smiled at the men and then spoke so softly, at first they couldn't hear him. When he raised his voice it exuded calm.

"Now, men," he purred, "all of you relax and let me have your complete attention. Don't think of a thing but me." He laughed, brushed a spot off his pants, and continued. "You know what my purpose is. You're familiar with that. It's to help you get rid of the fears and personal inferiorities that tie you into knots and keep you from being aces in this game. Who are the Pirates? Not supermen, only mortals. What have they got that you haven't got? I can't think of a thing, absolutely not one. It's the attitude that's licking you—your own, not the Pirates'. What do you mean to yourselves? Are you a flock of bats flying around in a coffin, or the sun shining calmly on a blue lake? Are you sardines being swallowed up in the sea, or the whale that does the swallowing? That's why I'm here, to help you answer that question in the affirmative, to help you by mesmerism and autosuggestion, meaning you do the suggesting, not I. I only assist by making you receptive to your own basic thoughts. If you think you are winners, you will be. If you don't, you won't. That's psychology. That's the way the world works. Give me your whole attention and look straight into my eyes. What do you see there? You see sleep. That's right, sleep. So relax, sleep, relax . . ."

His voice was soft, lulling, peaceful. He had raised his pudgy arms and with stubby fingers was making ripples on a vast calm sea. Already Olson was gently snoring. Flores, with the tip of his tongue protruding, Bump, and some of the other players were fast asleep. Pop looked on, absorbed.

Staring at the light gleaming on Pop's bald bean, Roy felt himself going off . . . way way down, drifting through the tides into golden water as he searched for this lady fish, or mermaid, or whatever you called her. His eyes grew big in the seeking, first fish eyes, then bulbous frog eyes. Sailing lower into the pale green sea, he sought everywhere for the reddish glint of her scales, until the water became dense and dark green and then everything gradually got so black he lost all sight of where he was. When he tried to rise up into the light he couldn't find it. He darted in all directions, and though there were times he saw flashes of her green tail, it was dark everywhere. He threshed up a storm of luminous bubbles but they gave out little light and he did not know where in all the glass to go.

Roy ripped open his lids and sprang up. He shoved his way out from between the benches.

The doctor was startled but made no attempt to stop him. Pop called out, "Hey, where do you think you're going?"

"Out."

"Sit down, dammit, you're on the team."

"I might be on the team but no medicine man is going to hypnotize me."

"You signed a contract to obey orders," Pop snapped shrilly.

"Yes, but not to let anybody monkey around in my mind."

As he headed into the tunnel he heard Pop swear by his eight-foot uncle that nobody by the name of Roy Hobbs would ever play ball for him as long as he lived.

He had waited before . . . and he waited now, on a spike-scuffed bench in the dugout, hidden from sky, wind and weather, from all but the dust that blew up from Knights Field and lodged dry in the throat, as the grass grew browner. And from time ticking off balls and strikes, batters up and out, halves and full innings, games won and (mostly) lost, days and nights, and the endless train miles from Philly, with in-between stops, along the arc to St. Louis, and circling back by way of Chi, Boston, Brooklyn . . . still waiting.

68

"C'mon, Roy," Red had urged, "apologize to Pop, then the next time Knobb comes around, join the boys and everything will be okay."

"Nix on that," said Roy, "I don't need a shyster quack to shoot me full of confidence juice. I want to go through on my own steam."

"He only wants everybody to relax and be able to do their best."

Roy shook his head. "I been a long time getting here and now that I am, I want to do it by myself, not with that kind of bunk."

"Do what?" Red asked.

"What I have to do."

Red shrugged and gave him up as too stubborn. Roy sat around, and though it said on his chest he was one of the team, he sat among them alone; at the train window, gazing at the moving trees, in front of his locker, absorbed in an untied shoe lace, in the dugout, squinting at the great glare of the game. He traveled in their company and dressed where they did but he joined them in nothing, except maybe batting practice, entering the cage with the lumber on his shoulder glistening like a leg bone in the sun and taking his chops at the pill. Almost always he hammered the swift, often murderous throws (the practice pitchers dumped their bag of tricks on him) deep into the stands, as the players watched and muttered at the swift flight of the balls, then forgot him when the game started. But there were days when the waiting got him. He could feel the strength draining from his bones, weakening him so he could hardly lift Wonderboy. He was unwilling to move then, for fear he would fall over on his puss and have to crawl away on all fours. Nobody noticed he did not bat when he felt this way except Pop; and Bump, seeing how white his face was, squirted contemptuous tobacco juice in the dust. Then when Roy's strength ebbed back, he would once again go into the batters' cage and do all sorts of marvelous things that made them watch in wonder.

He watched *them* and bad as he felt he had to laugh. They were a nutty bunch to begin with but when they were losing they were impossible. It was like some kind of sickness. They threw to the wrong bases, bumped heads together in the outfield, passed each other on the baselines, sometimes batted out of order, throwing both Pop and the ump into fits, and cussed everybody else for their mistakes. It was not uncommon to see them pile three men on a bag, or behold a catcher on the opposing team, in a single skip and jump, lay the tag on two of them as they came thundering together into home plate. Or watch Gabby Laslow, in a tight spot, freeze onto the ball, or Allie Stubbs get socked with it in the jaw, thrown by Olson on a steal as Allie admired a lady in the stands. Doc Knobb's hypnotism cut down their jitters but it didn't much help their coordination, yet when they were left unhypnotized for a few days, they were afflicted with more than the usual number of hexes and whammies and practiced all sorts of magic to undo them. To a man they crossed their fingers over spilled salt, or coffee or tea, or at the sight of a hearse. Emil Lajong did a backward flip whenever he located a cross-eyed fan in the stands. Olson hated a woman who wore the same drab brown-feathered hat every time she showed up. He spat through two fingers whenever he spotted her in the crowd. Bump went through his ritual with the colored threads in his socks and shorts. Pop sometimes stroked a rabbit's foot. Red Blow never changed his clothes during a "winning streak," and Flores secretly touched his genitals whenever a bird flew over his head.

They were not much different from the fans in the patched and peeling stands. On weekdays the stadium usually looked like a haunted house but over the weekend crowds developed. The place often resembled a zoo full of oddballs, including gamblers, bums, drunks, and some ugly crackpots. Many of them came just to get a laugh out of the bonehead plays. Some, when the boys were losing, cursed and jeered, showering them—whenever they came close enough—with rotten cabbages, tomatoes, blackened bananas and occasionally an eggplant. Yet let the umpire call a close play against the Knights and he became a target for pop bottles, beer cans, old shoes or anything that happened to be lying around loose. Surprisingly, however, a few players were chosen for affection and even admiration by their fans. Sadie Sutter, a girl of sixty-plus, who wore large flowered hats, bobby sox, and short skirts, showed her undying love for Dave Olson every time he came up to the plate by banging with all her might on a Chinese gong she dragged into the stadium every day. A Hungarian cook, a hearty man with a hard yellow straw hat jammed tight on his skull, hopped up on his seat and crowed like a rooster whenever Emil Lajong originated a double play. And there was a girl named Gloria from Mississippi, a washed-out flower of the vestibules, who between innings when her eyes were not on the game, lined up a customer or two for a quickie later. She gave her heart to Gabby, yelling, "Get a move on, mo-lasses," to set him in motion after a fly ball. Besides these, there had appeared early in the present season, a pompous Otto P. Zipp, whose peevish loudspeaker could be heard all over the park, his self-chosen mission to rout the critics of Bump Baily, most of whom razzed the big boy for short legging on the other fielders. The dwarf honked a loud horn at the end of a two-foot walking stick, and it sounded as if a flock of geese had been let loose at the offenders, driving them—his purple curses ringing in their ears—to seek shelter in some hidden hole in the stands or altogether out of the ballpark. Zipp was present at every home game, sitting at the rail in short left field, and Bump made it his much publicized business, as he trotted out to his position at the start of the game, to greet him with a loud kiss on the forehead, leaving Otto in a state of creamy bliss.

Roy got to know them all as he waited, all one if you looked long enough through the haze of cigarette smoke, except one . . . Memo Paris, Pop's redheaded niece, sad, spurned lady, who sat without wifehood in the wives' box behind third base. He could, if she would let him, find her with his eyes shut, with his hands alone as he had in the dark. Always in the act of love she lived in his mind, the only way he knew her, because she would not otherwise suffer his approach. *He* was to blame, she had wept one bitter midnight, so she hated his putrid guts. Since the team's return to the city (the phone banged in his ear and she ripped up his letters when they were delivered) whenever he got up from his seat in the hotel lobby as she stepped out of the elevator, to say how sorry he was for beginning at the wrong end, she tugged at her summer furpiece and breezed past him in greeneyed scorn, withering in the process Bump at the cigar stand, who had laughed aloud at Roy's rout. ("Honeybunch," he had explained, "it was out of the pity of my heart that I took that shmo into my room, because they didn't have one for him and I was intending to pass the night at the apartment of my he cousin from Mobile. How'd I know you'd go in there when you said you weren't speaking to me?" He swore it hadn't been a gag—had he ever pulled one on her?—but Memo punished him in silence, punishing herself, and he knew it because she still came every day to see him play.) She walked out of the lobby, with her silver bracelets tinkling, swaying a little on her high heels, as if she had not too long ago learned to walk on them, and went with her beautiful body away, for which Roy everlastingly fried Bump Baily in the deep fat of his abomination.

It was for her he waited.

On the morning of the twenty-first of June Pop told Roy that as of tomorrow he was being shipped to a Class B team in the Great Lakes Association. Roy said he was quitting baseball anyway, but that same day, in answer to an angry question of Pop's as to why the team continued to flop, Doc Knobb said that the manager's hysterical behavior was undoing all the good he had done, and he offered to hypnotize Pop along with the others without hiking his fee. Pop shrilly told the psychologist he was too old for such bamboozlement, and Knobb retorted that his attitude was not only ridiculous but stupid. Pop got redfaced and told him to go to perdition with his hocus pocus and as of right then the doctor was canned.

That afternoon the Knights began a series with the second-place Phils. Instead of falling into a swoon when they learned there was to be no further hypnosis, the team played its best ball in weeks. Against superior pitching, in the sixth they bunched three singles for a run, and though Schultz had already given up five hits to the Phils, they were scattered and came to nothing. The Phils couldn't score till the top of the eighth, when with two out Schultz weakened, walking one man and handing the next a good enough throw to hit for a sharp single, so that there were now men on first and third. Up came Rogers, the Phils' slugger, and hit a fast curve for what looked like no more than a long fly ball, a routine catch, to left center. Now it happened that Bump was nearer to the ball than Flores, who was shifted to the right, but he was feeling horny in the sun and casting about in his mind for who to invite to his bed tonight, when he looked up and noticed this ball coming. He still had time to get

73

under it but then saw Flores going for it like a galloping horse, and the anguished look on the Mexican's face, his black eyes popping, neck like a thick rope, and mouth haunted, fascinated Bump so, he decided to let him have it if he wanted it that bad. At the last minute he tried to take it away from the Mex, risking a head-on collision, but the wind whipped the ball closer to the wall than he had bargained for, so Bump fell back to cover Flores in case he misplayed it.

The ball fell between them, good for a double, and scoring two of the Phils. Pop tore at what was left of his gray hair but couldn't grip it with his oily, bandaged fingers so he pulled at his ears till they were lit like red lamps. Luckily the next Phil smothered the fire by rolling to first, which kept the score at 2-1. When Bump returned to the dugout Pop cursed him from the cradle to the grave and for once Bump had no sassy answers. When it came his time to go out on deck, Pop snarled for him to stay where he was. Flores found a ripe one and landed on first but Pop stuck to his guns and looked down the line past Bump. His eye lit on Roy at the far end of the bench, and he called his name to go out there and hit. Bump turned purple. He grabbed a bat and headed for Roy but half the team jumped on him. Roy just sat there without moving and it looked to everyone like he wouldn't get up. The umpire roared in for a batter to come out, and after a while, as the players fidgeted and Pop fumed, Roy sighed and picked up Wonderboy. He slowly walked up the steps.

"Knock the cover off of it," Pop yelled.

"Attention, please," the P.A. man announced. "Roy Hobbs, number forty-five, batting for Baily."

A groan rose from the stands and turned into a roar of protest.

Otto Zipp jumped up and down on his seat, shaking his furious little fist at home plate.

"Throw him to the dogs," he shouted, and filled the air with his piercing curses.

Glancing at the wives' box, Roy saw that Memo had her head turned away. He set his jaw and advanced to the plate. His impulse was to knock the dirt out of his cleats but he refrained because he did not want to harm his bat in any way. Waiting for the pitcher to get set, Roy wiped his palms on his pants and twitched his cap. He lifted Wonderboy and waited rocklike for the throw.

He couldn't tell the color of the pitch that came at him. All he could think of was that he was sick to death of waiting, and tongue-out thirsty to begin. The ball was now a dew drop staring him in the eye so he stepped back and swung from the toes.

Wonderboy flashed in the sun. It caught the sphere where it was biggest. A noise like a twenty-one gun salute cracked the sky. There was a straining, ripping sound and a few drops of rain spattered to the ground. The ball screamed toward the pitcher and seemed suddenly to dive down at his feet. He grabbed it to throw to first and realized to his horror that he held only the cover. The rest of it, unraveling cotton thread as it rode, was headed into the outfield.

Roy was rounding first when the ball plummeted like a dead bird into center field. Attempting to retrieve and throw, the Philly fielder got tangled in thread. The second baseman rushed up, bit the cord and heaved the ball to the catcher but Roy had passed third and made home, standing. The umpire called him safe and immediately a rhubarb boiled. The Phils' manager and his players charged out of the dugout and were joined by the nine men on the field. At the same time, Pop, shouting in defense of the ump, rushed forth with all the Knights but Bump. The umpire, caught between both teams, had a troublesome time of it and was shoved this way and that. He tossed out two men on each side but by then came to the decision that the hit was a ground rules double. Flores had scored and the game was tied up. Roy was ordered back to second, and Pop announced he was finishing the game under protest. Somebody then shouted it was raining cats and dogs. The stands emptied like a yawn and the players piled into the dugouts. By the time Roy got in from second he was wading in water ankle deep. Pop sent him into the clubhouse for a change of uniform but he could have saved himself the trouble because it rained steadily for three days. The game was recorded as a 2-2 tie, to be replayed later in the season.

In the locker room Pop asked Roy to explain why he thought the cover had come off the ball.

"That's what you said to do, wasn't it?"

"That's right," said Pop scratching his bean.

The next day he told Roy he was withdrawing his release and would hereafter use him as a pinch hitter and substitute fielder.

The rain had washed out the Phils' series but the Knights were starting another with the seventh-place Redbirds. In batting practice, Roy, who was exciting some curiosity for his freak hit of yesterday, looked tremendous but so did Bump. For the first time in a long while Roy went out to left field to limber up. Bump was out there too and Earl swatted fungos to both.

As they were changing into clean uniforms before the start of the game, Bump warned Roy in front of everybody, "Stay out of my way, busher, or you will get your head bashed."

Roy squirted spit on the floor.

When Pop later handed the batting order to Stuffy Briggs, the plate umpire, it had Bump's name scribbled on it as usual in the fourth slot, but Pop had already warned him that if he didn't hustle his behind when a ball was hit out to his field, he would rest it a long time on the bench.

Bump made no reply but it was obvious that he took Pop's words to heart, because he was a bang-up fielder that day. He accepted eight chances, twice chasing into center field to take them from Flores. He caught them to his left and right, dove for and came up with a breathtaking shoestringer, and running as if on fire, speared a fantastic catch over his shoulder. Still not satisfied, he pounded like a bull after his ninth try, again in Flores' territory, a smoking ball that sailed up high, headed for the wall. As Bump ran for it he could feel fear leaking through his stomach, and his legs unwillingly slowed down, but then he had this vision of himself as the league's best outfielder, acknowledged so by fans and players alike, even Pop, whom he'd be nothing less than forever respectful to, and in love with and married to Memo. Thinking this way he ran harder, though Zipp's geese honked madly at his back, and with a magnificent twisting jump, he trapped the ball in his iron fingers. Yet the wall continued to advance, and though the redheaded lady of his choice was on her feet shrieking, Bump bumped it with a skull-breaking bang, and the wall embraced his broken body.

Though Bump was on the critical list in the hospital, many newspapers continued to speculate about that ball whose cover Roy had knocked off. It was explained as everything from an optical illusion (neither the ball nor the cover was ever found, the remnant caught by the catcher disappeared, and it was thought some fan had snatched the cover) to a feat of prodigious strength. Baseball records and newspaper files were combed but no one could find any evidence that it had happened before, although some of the older scribes swore it had. Then it leaked out that Pop had ordered Roy to skin the ball and Roy had obliged, but no one took that very seriously. One of the sportswriters suggested that a hard downward chop could shear off the outer covering. He had tried it in his cellar and had split the horsehide. Another pointed out that such a blow would have produced an infield grounder, therefore maybe a tremendous upward slash? The first man proved that would have uncorked a sure pop fly whereas the ball, as everyone knew, had sailed straight out over the pitcher's head. So it had probably resulted from a very very forceful sock. But many a hitter had plastered the ball forcefully before, still another argued, and his idea was that it was defective to begin with, a fact the company that manufactured the ball vigorously denied. Max Mercy had his own theory. He wrote in his column, "My Eye in the Knot Hole" (the year he'd done the Broadway stint for his paper his eye was in the key hole), that Roy's bat was a suspicious one and hinted it might be filled with something a helluva lot stronger than wood. Red Blow publicly denied this. He said the bat had been examined by league authorities and was found to be less than forty-two inches long, less than two and three-quarters inches thick at its fattest part, and in weight less than two pounds, which made it a legal weapon. Mercy then demanded that the wood be X-rayed but Roy turned thumbs down on that proposition and kept Wonderboy hidden away when the sports columnist was nosing around in the clubhouse.

On the day after the accident Pop soberly gave Roy the nod to play in Bump's place. As Roy trotted out to left, Otto Zipp was in his usual seat but looking worn and aged. His face, tilted to the warming rays of the sun, was like a pancake with a cherry nose, and tears were streaming through slits where the eyes would be. He seemed to be waiting for his pre-game kiss on the brow but Roy passed without looking at him.

The long rain had turned the grass green and Roy romped in it like a happy calf in its pasture. The Redbirds,

78

probing his armor, belted the ball to him whenever they could, which was often, because Hill was not too happy on the mound, but Roy took everything they aimed at him. He seemed to know the soft, hard, and bumpy places in the field and just how high a ball would bounce on them. From the flags on the stadium roof he noted the way the wind would blow the ball, and he was quick at fishing it out of the tricky undercurrents on the ground. Not sun, shadow, nor smoke-haze bothered him, and when a ball was knocked against the wall he estimated the angle of rebound and speared it as if its course had been plotted on a chart. He was good at gauging slices and knew when to charge the pill to save time on the throw. Once he put his head down and ran ahead of a shot going into the concrete. Though the crowd rose with a thunderous warning, he caught it with his back to the wall and did a little jig to show he was alive. Everyone laughed in relief, and they liked his long-legged loping and that he resembled an acrobat the way he tumbled and came up with the ball in his glove. For his performance that day there was much whistling and applause, except where he would have liked to hear it, an empty seat in the wives' box.

His batting was no less successful. He stood at the plate lean and loose, right-handed with an open stance, knees relaxed and shoulders squared. The bat he held in a curious position, lifted slightly above his head as if prepared to beat a rattlesnake to death, but it didn't harm his smooth stride into the pitch, nor the easy way he met the ball and slashed it out with a flick of the wrists. The pitchers tried something different every time he came up, sliders, sinkers, knucklers, but he swung and connected, spraying them to all fields. He was, Red Blow said to Pop, a natural, though somewhat less than perfect because he sometimes hit at bad ones, which caused Pop to frown.

"I mistrust a bad ball hitter."

"There are all kinds of hitters," Red answered. "Some are bucket foots, and some go for bad throws but none of them bother me as long as they naturally connect with anything that gets in their way."

Pop spat up over the dugout steps. "They sometimes make some harmful mistakes."

"Who don't?" Red asked.

Pop then muttered something about this bad ball hitter he knew who had reached for a lemon and cracked his spine.

But the only thing Roy cracked that day was the record for the number of triples hit in a major league debut and also the one for chances accepted in the outfield. Everybody agreed that in him the Knights had uncovered something special. One reporter wrote, "He can catch everything in creation," and Roy just about proved it. It happened that a woman who lived on the sixth floor of an apartment house overlooking the stadium was cleaning out her bird cage, near the end of the game, which the Knights took handily, when her canary flew out of the window and darted down across the field. Roy, who was waiting for the last out, saw something coming at him in the low rays of the sun, and leaping high, bagged it in his glove.

He got rid of the bloody mess in the clubhouse can.

when Bump died Memo went wild with grief. Bump, Bump, she wailed, pounding on the wall. Pop, who hovered over her at first, found her in bed clutching strands of red hair. Her cheeks were scratched where the tears rolled down. He was frightened and urged her to have the doctor but her piercing screams drove him away. She wept for days. Clad in black pajamas she lay across the white bed like a broken candle still lit. In her mind she planted kisses all over the corpse and when she kissed his mouthless mouth, blew back the breath of life, her womb stirring at the image of his restoration. Yet she saw down a dark corridor that he was laid out dead, gripping in his fingers the glowing ball he had caught, and that there were too many locked doors to go through to return. She stopped trying to think of him alive and thought of him dead. Then she really hit the wall.

She could not stop weeping, as if the faucet were broken. Or she were a fountain they had forgotten to turn off. There was no end to her tears. They flowed on as if she had never wept before. Wherever she turned she cried, the world was wet. Her thoughts dripped on flowers, dark, stained ones in night fields. She moved among them, tasting their many darknesses, could not tell them from the rocks on the ground. His shade was there. She saw it drifting before her and recognized it by the broken places. Bump, oh Bump, but her voice was drowned in water. She heard a gurgle and the bubbles breaking and felt the tears go searing down a hurt face (hers) and though she wanted always to be with him she was (here) weeping.

After unnumbered days she dragged herself out of bed, disturbed by all the space, her bare feet with lacquered nails, her shaky presence among changeless things. She sought in the hollow closet souvenirs of him, an autographed baseball "to my Honey from her Bump" (tears), a cigarette lighter shaped like a bat, click-open-light. She blew it out and searching further found an old kewpie doll he had won for her and a pressed, yellowed gardenia, but couldn't with her wept-out nose detect the faintest odor; also a pair of purple shorts she herself had laundered and placed in the drawer among her soft (and useless) underthings. Going through her scrapbook, only rarely could she find menus (Sardi's, Toots Shor, and once the Diamond Horseshoe) or movie ticket stubs (Palace, Paramount, Capitol) and other such things of them both that one could paste in, but most were pictures she had clipped from the sports pages, showing Bump at bat, on the basepaths, and crossing the plate. She idly turned the pages, sighed deeply and put the book away, then picked up the old picture album, and here was her sadeyed mother, and the torn up, patched together one was of Daddy grinning, who with a grin had (forever) exited dancing with his dancing partner, and here she was herself, a little girl weeping, as if nothing ever changed . . . The heartbreak was always present—he had not been truly hers when he died (she tried not to think whose, in many cities, he had been) so that she now mourned someone who even before his death had made her a mourner. That was the thorn in her grief.

When the July stifle drove her out of her room she appeared in the hotel lobby in black, her hair turned a lighter, golden shade as though some of the fire had burned out of it, and Roy was moved by her appearance. He had imagined how she would look when he saw her again but both the black and red, though predictable, surprised him. They told him with thunderclap quickness what he wanted to be sure of, that she, despite green eyes brimming for Bump, was the one for him, the ever desirable only. Occasionally he reflected what if the red were black and ditto the other way? Here, for example, was this black-haired dame in red and what about it? He could take her or leave her, though there was a time in his life when a red dress would excite his fancy, but with Memo, flaming above and dark below, there was no choice—he was chosen so why not admit it though it brought pain? He had tried lately to forget her but had a long memory for what he wanted so there was only this to do, wait till she came in out of the rain.

Sometimes it was tough to, even for one used to waiting. Once a hungry desire sent him down to knock at her door but she shut it in his face although he was standing there with his hat in his embarrassed hands. He thought of asking Pop to put in a good word for him—how long was life anyhow?—but something told him to wait. And from other cities, when the team was on the road, he sent her cards, candies, little presents, which were all stuffed in his mailbox when he returned. It took the heart out of him. Yet each morning when she came out of the elevator he would look up at her as she walked by on her high heels, although she never seemed to see him. Then one day she shed black and put on white but still looked as if she were wearing black, so he waited. Only, now, when he looked at her she sometimes glanced at him. He watched her dislike of him fade to something neutral which he slowly became confident he could beat.

"One thing I hafta tell you not to do, son," Pop said to Roy in the hotel lobby one rainy morning not long after Bump's funeral, "and that is to blame yourself about what happened to Bump. He had a tough break but it wasn't your fault."

"What do you mean my fault?"

Pop looked up. "All I mean to say was he did it himself."

"Never thought anything but."

"Some have said maybe it wouldn't happen if you didn't join the team, and maybe so, but I believe such things are outside of yours and my control and I wouldn't want you to worry that you had caused it in any way."

"I won't because I didn't. Bump didn't have to go to the wall for that shot, did he? We were ahead in runs and the bases were clear. He could've taken it when it came off the wall without losing a thing, couldn't he?"

Pop scratched his baldy. "I guess so."

"Who are the people who said I did it?"

"Well, nobody exactly. My niece said you coulda wanted it to happen but that don't mean a thing. She was hysterical then."

Roy felt uneasy. Had he arranged Bump's run into the wall? No. Had he wished the guy would drop dead? Only once, after the night with Memo. But he had never consciously hoped he would crack up against the wall. That was none of his doing and he told Pop to tell it to Memo. But Pop was embarrassed now and said to drop the whole thing, it was a lot of foolishness.

Though Roy denied wishing Bump's fate on him or having been in any way involved in it, he continued to be unwillingly concerned with him even after his death. He was conscious that he was filling Bump's shoes, not only because he batted in the clean-up slot and fielded in the sun field (often watched his shadow fly across the very spot Bump had dived into) and became, in no time to speak of, one of the leading hitters in the league and at present certainly the most sensational, but also because the crowds made no attempt to separate his identity from Bump's. To his annoyance, when he made a hot catch, the kind Bump in all his glory would have left alone, he could hear through the curtain of applause, "Nice work, Bumpsy, 'at's grabbin' th' old apple," or "Leave it to Bump, he will be where they drop." It was goddamn stupid. The same fans who a month ago were hissing Bump for short legging on the other fielders now praised his name so high Roy felt like painting up a sandwich sign to wear out on the field, that said, ROY HOBBS PLAYING.

Even Otto Zipp made no effort to distinguish him from his predecessor and used the honker to applaud his doings, though there were some who said the dwarf sounded half-hearted in his honking. And Roy also shared the limelight with Bump on the sports page, where the writers were constantly comparing them for everything under the sun. One of them went so far as to keep a tally of their batting averages—Roy's total after his first, second, and third weeks of play, as compared with Bump's at the beginning of the season. One paper even printed pictures showing the living and dead facing each other with bats held high, as white arrows pointed at various places in their anatomies to show how much alike their measurements and stances were.

All this irritated Roy no end until he happened to notice Memo walk into the lobby one night with a paper turned to the sports page. From having read the same paper he knew she had seen a column about Bump and him as batsmen,

85

so he decided there might be some percentage to all these comparisons. He came to feel more kindly to the memory of Bump and thought he was not such a bad egg after all, even if he did go in for too many screwball gags. Thinking back on him, he could sort of understand why Memo had been interested in him, and he felt that, though he was superior to Bump as an athlete, they were both money players, both showmen in the game. He figured it was through these resemblances that Memo would gradually get used to him and then come over all the way, although once she did, it would have to be for Hobbsie himself and not for some ghost by another name.

So he blazed away for her with his golden bat. It was not really golden, it was white, but in the sun it sometimes flashed gold and some of the opposing pitchers complained it shone in their eyes. Stuffy Briggs told Roy to put it away and use some other club but he stood on his rights and wouldn't. There was a hot rhubarb about that until Roy promised to rub some of the shine off Wonderboy. This he did with a hambone, and though the pitchers shut up, the bat still shone a dull gold. It brought him some wondrous averages in hits, runs, RBI's and total bases, and for the period of his few weeks in the game he led the league in homers and triples. (He was quoted in an interview as saying his singles were "mistakes." And he never bunted. "There is no percentage in bunts." Pop shook his head over that, but Red chuckled and said it was true for a wonderful hitter like Roy.) He also destroyed many short-term records, calling down on his performance tons of newspaper comment. However, his accomplishments were not entirely satisfying to him. He was gnawed by a nagging impatience—so much more to do, so much of the world to win for himself. He felt he had nothing of value yet to show for what he was accomplishing, and in his dreams he still sped over endless miles of monotonous rail toward something he desperately wanted. Memo, he sighed.

Pop couldn't believe his amazed eyes. "Beginner's luck," he muttered. Many a rookie had he seen come out blasting them in the breeze only to blow out in it with his tail between his legs. "The boy's having hisself a shower of luck. Usually they end up with a loud bust, so let's wait and see," he cautioned. Yet Roy continued on as before, by his own efforts winning many a ball game. The team too were doubtful he could go on like this, and doubtful of their doubt. They often discussed him when he wasn't around, compared him to Bump, and argued whether he was for the team or for himself. Olson said he was for the team. Cal Baker insisted no. When asked for a reason he could give none except to say, "Those big guys are always for themselves. They are not for the little guy. If he was for us why don't he come around more? Why does he hang out so much by himself?" "Yeah," answered Olson, "but we're outa the cellar now and who done that—the wind? That's what counts, not if he sits around chewin' his ass with us." Most of them agreed with Olson. Even if Roy wasn't actively interested in them he was a slick ballplayer and his example was having a good effect on them. In the course of three weeks they had achieved a coordination of fielding, hitting and pitching (Fowler and Schultz were whipping the opposition, and Hinkle and Hill, with an assist here and there from McGee, were at least breaking even) such as they had not for seasons known. Like a rusty locomotive pulling out of the roundhouse for the first time in years, they ground down the tracks, puffing, wheezing, belching smoke and shooting sparks. And before long they had dislodged the Reds, who had been living on the floor above them since the season started. When, near the end of July, they caught up with the Cubs and, twelve games behind the league-leading Pirates, took possession of sixth place, Pop rubbed his unbelieving eyes. The players thought now that the team is on its way up he will change his crabby ways and give us a smile once in a while, but Pop surprised them by growing sad, then actually melancholy at the thought that but for his keeping Roy out of the line-up for three weeks they might now be in first division.

A new day dawned on Knights Field. Looking down upon the crowds from his office in the curious tower he inhabited that rose on a slight tilt above the main entrance of the ball park, Judge Goodwill Banner was at first made uneasy by what he saw, for every rise in attendance would make it more difficult for him to get Pop to give up the managerial reins, a feat he hoped to accomplish by next season. However, the sound of the merry, clicking turnstiles was more than he could resist, so, although reluctantly, he put on extra help to sweep the stands and ramps and dust off seats that hadn't been sat in for years but were now almost always occupied.

The original Knights "fans," those who had come to see them suffer, were snowed under by this new breed here to cheer the boys on. Vegetables were abolished, even at the umps, and the crowd assisted the boys by working on the nerves of the visiting team with whammy words, catcalls, wisecracks, the kind of sustained jockeying that exhausted the rival pitchers and sometimes drove them out of the game. Now the old faithful were spouting steam—the Hungarian cook outcrowed a flock of healthy roosters, Gloria, the vestibule lady, acquired a better type customer, and Sadie Sutter gave up Dave Olson and now beat her hectic gong for the man of the hour. "Oh, you Roy," she screeched in her yolky cackle, "embracez moy," and the stands went wild with laughter. Victory was sweet, except for Otto Zipp, who no longer attended the games. Someone who met him waddling out of a subway station in Carnarsie asked how come, but the dwarf only waved a pudgy palm in disgust. Nobody could guess what he meant by that and his honker lay dusty and silent on a shelf in the attic.

Even the weather was better, more temperate after the insulting early heat, with just enough rain to keep the grass a bright green and yet not pile up future double headers. Pop soon got into the spirit of winning, lowered the boom on his dismal thoughts, and showed he had a lighter side. He unwound the oily rags on his fingers and flushed them down the bowl. His hands healed and so did his heart, for even during the tensest struggle he looked a picture of contentment. And he was patient now, extraordinarily so, giving people the impression he had never been otherwise. Let a man bobble a hot one, opening the gate for a worrisome run, and he no longer jumped down his throat but wagged his head in silent sympathy. And sometimes he patted the offender on the surprised back. Formerly his strident yell was everywhere, on the field, in the dugout, clubhouse, players' duffel bags, also in their dreams, but now you never heard it because he no longer raised his voice, not even to Dizzy's cat when it wet on his shoes. Nobody teased him or played jokes on him any more and every tactic he ordered on the field was acted on, usually successfully. He was in the driver's seat. His muscles eased, the apoplexy went out of his system, and for his star fielder a lovelight shone in his eyes.

As Roy's fame grew, Bump was gradually forgotten. The fans no longer confused talent with genius. When they cheered, they cheered for Roy Hobbs alone. People wondered about him, wanted news of his life and career. Reporters kept after him for information and Max Mercy, who for some reason felt he ought to know a lot more about Roy than he did, worked a sharp pickax over his shadow but gathered no usable nugget. All that was known was that Roy had first played ball on an orphan asylum team, that his father was a restless itinerant worker and his mother rumored to have been a burlesque actress. Stingy with facts, Roy wouldn't confirm a thing. Mercy sent a questionnaire to one thousand country papers in the West but there were no towns or cities that claimed the hero as their own.

It came about that Roy discovered Memo at one of the home games, though not, as formerly, sitting in the wives' box. Happening to meet her later in the hotel elevator, where they were pressed close together because of the crowd, he got off at her floor. Taking her arm he said, "Memo, I don't know what more I can do to show you how sorry I am about that time and tell you how I feel in my heart for you now."

But Memo stared at him through a veil of tears and said, "I'm strictly a dead man's girl."

He figured she had to be made to forget. If she would go out with him he would give her a good time at the night clubs and musical shows. But to do that and buy her some decent presents a guy needed cash, and on the meager three thousand he got he had beans—barely enough to pay his hotel bill. He considered selling his name for endorsements and approached a sporting goods concern but they paid him only fifty dollars. Elsewhere he got a suit and a pair of shoes but no cash. An agent he consulted advised him that the companies were suspicious he might be a flash in the pan. "Lay low now," he advised. "By the end of the season, if you keep on like you're going, they'll be ready to talk turkey, then we'll put the heat on."

The newspaper boys supplied him with the cue for what to do next. They pointed out how he filled up Knights Field; and on the road, as soon as the Knights blew into town the game was a sellout and the customers weren't exactly coming to see a strip-tease. One of the columnists (not Mercy) wrote an open letter to the Judge, saying it was a crying shame that a man as good as Roy should get a rock-bottom salary when he was playing better ball than some of the so-called stars who drew up to a hundred grand. Roy was being gypped, the columnist wrote, and he called on the Judge to burn up his old contract and write a decent one instead. Why, even Bump had earned thirty-five thousand. That decided Roy. He figured for himself a flat forty-five thousand for the rest of the season, plus a guarantee of a percentage of the gate. He thought that if he got this sort of arrangement and really piled in the dough, it would do him no harm with Memo.

So one day after a long double header, both ends of which the Knights finally took, Roy climbed the slippery stairs up the tower to the Judge's office. The Judge's male secretary said he was busy but Roy sat down to wait so they soon let him in. The huge office was half dark, though lit on the double-windowed street side (the Judge counted the customers going in and from the opposite window he counted them in the stands) by the greenish evening sky. The Judge, a massive rumpled figure in a large chair before an empty mahogany desk, was wearing a black fedora with a round pot crown and smoking, under grizzled eyebrows, a fat, black King Oscar I. This always looked to be the same size in the rare newspaper photographs of the Judge, and many people maintained it was the same picture of him all the time, because it was a known fact that the Judge never left the tower and no photographer ever got in. Roy noted a shellacked half of stuffed shark, mounted on pine board on the faded green wall, and a framed motto piece that read:

"Be it ever so humble, there is no place like home"
"Nihil nisi bonum"
"All is not gold that glitters"
"The dog is turned to his vomit again"

The floor of the office was, of course, slanted—because of the way the tower, an addition to the stadium structure, had settled—and to level it the Judge had a rug made a quarter of an inch thick on one side and a good inch on the other, but the few visitors to the place noticed they were not standing strictly on keel so they quickly sat down, which was what Roy did too. He had heard that the door on the opposite side of the room led up to the Judge's apartment. Pop said that though the Judge was a sluggish man with a buck it was a lavish place, and the bathroom had a television set and a sunken bathtub inlaid with mother of pearl. It was also rumored that he kept in there two enormous medicine cabinets loaded with laxatives and cathartics.

The Judge looked Roy over, struck a match under the top of his desk and drew a flame into his dead King Oscar. He blew out a smelly cloud of yellow smoke that hid his face a full minute.

"Nice of you to come," he rumbled. "To what good cause may I attribute this pleasant surprise?"

"I guess you know, Judge," said Roy, trying to make himself comfortable.

The Judge rumbled in his belly.

"I'm reminded of a case that came before me once. 'What do you plead?' I asked the defendant. 'I leave it to you, Judge, take your choice,' he responded. I did and sent him to the penitentiary for twenty years."

The Judge coughed and cackled over that. Roy regarded him closely. Everybody had warned him he was a slick trader, especially Pop who had poured out a hot earful about his partner. "He will peel the skin off of your behind without you knowing it if you don't watch out." That was what had happened to him, he said, and he went on to tell Roy that not long after the Judge had bought into the club—after working up Charlie Gulch, Pop's old-time partner, against him and getting him to sell out—he had taken advantage of some financial troubles Pop was having with his two brothers who owned a paint factory, and also because of his own sickness that kept him in a hospital under expensive medical care all winter long, and the Judge put the squeeze on him to get ten per cent of his stock for a pittance, which had then looked like a life saver because Pop was overdrawn at the bank and they wouldn't lend him another cent on his share of the Knights. Later, when he realized how much of a say in things he had lost to the Judge he kicked himself all over the lot, for the Judge, as Red Blow had told Roy, drummed up all sorts of player deals to turn a buck, and though Pop fought him on these, he showed on paper that they were losing money at the gate and this was the only way to cover their losses and keep the team going, so Pop had to give in on most of them although he had fought the Judge to a standstill when he wanted to sell Bump and would do the same if he tried it with Roy. It beat Pop where Goodie Banner, as he called him, had got the money to operate with in the first place. He had known him years ago as an impoverished shyster but once he got on the bench his fortunes improved. Yet his salary was only twelve thousand a year for the three years he had served so he must have had backing to buy into the club and later—the dratted nerve of the worm—to offer to buy Pop out altogether. He said he wouldn't exactly call the Judge a thief but he wouldn't exactly call him honest either. For instance, the Judge had once casually asked Pop if he wanted to go in for any sideline activities over what they had already contracted for, meaning concessions and the like. Pop said no, he was only interested in the game end of it, so the Judge drew up an agreement offering Pop five per cent of all receipts from enterprises initiated by himself, and he began to rent the place to miniature auto races, meetings, conventions, and dog races, making all sorts of money for himself, while things necessary to the team were being neglected. "When triple talk is invented," Pop said bitterly, "he will own the copyright."

It was dark in the office but the Judge made no attempt to switch on the lights. He sat there motionless, a lumpy figure aglow around the edges against the darkening sky.

Roy thought he better get down to brass tacks. "Well, Judge," he said, shifting in his chair, "I thought you might be expecting me to drop in and see you. You know what I am doing to the ball both here and on the road. The papers have been writing that you might be considering a new contract for me."

The Judge blew at the ash of his cigar.

Roy grew restless. "I figure forty-five thousand is a fair price for my work. That's only ten grand more than Bump was getting—and you can subtract off the three thousand in my contract now." This last was an afterthought and he had decided to leave out the percentage of the gate till next year.

The Judge rumbled, Roy couldn't tell if it was in his throat or belly.

"I was thinking of Olaf Jespersen." The Judge's eyes took on a faraway, slightly glazed look. "He was a farmer I knew in my youth—terrible life. Yet as farmers often do, he managed to live comfortably because he owned a plot of ground with a house on it and had come into possession of an extraordinary cow, Sieglinde. She was a splendid animal with soft and silky front and well-shaped hooves. Her milk yield was some nine gallons per diem, altogether exceptional. In a word she was a superior creature and had the nicest ways with children—her own of course; but

Olaf was deeply disturbed by an ugly skin discoloration that ran across her rump. For a long while he had been eyeing Gussie, an albino cow of his neighbor down the road. One day he approached the man and asked if Gussie was for sale. The neighbor said yes, frankly admitting she gave very little milk although she consumed more than her share of fodder. Olaf said he was willing to trade Sieglinde for her and the neighbor readily agreed. Olaf went back for the cow but on the way to the neighbor's she stepped into a rut in the road and keeled over as if struck dead. Olaf suffered a heart attack. Thus they were found but Sieglinde recovered and became, before very long, her splendid nine-gallon self, whereas Olaf was incapacitated for the remainder of his days. I often drove past his place and saw him sitting on the moldy front porch, a doddering cripple starving to death with his tubercular albino cow."

Roy worked the fable around in his mind and got the point. It was not an impressive argument: be satisfied with what you have, and he said so to the Judge.

" 'The love of money is the root of all evil,' " intoned the Judge.

"I do not love it, Judge. I have not been near enough to it to build up any affection to speak of."

"Think, on the one hand, of the almost indigent Abraham Lincoln, and on the other of Judas Iscariot. What I am saying is that emphasis upon money will pervert your values. One cannot begin to imagine how one's life may alter for the worse under the impetus of wealth-seeking."

Roy saw how the land lay. "I will drop it to thirty-five thousand, the same as Bump, but not a cent less."

The Judge struck a match, throwing shadows on the wall. It was now night. He sucked a flame into his cigar. It went in like a slug, out like a moth—in and out, then forever in and the match was out. The cigar glowed, the Judge blew out a black fog of smoke, then they were once more in the dark.

Lights on, you stingy bastard, Roy thought.

"Pardon the absence of light," the Judge said, almost making him jump. "As a youngster I was frightened of the dark—used to wake up sobbing in it, as if it were water and I were drowning—but you will observe that I have disciplined myself so thoroughly against that fear, that I much prefer a dark to a lit room, and water is my favorite beverage. Will you have some?"

"No."

"There is in the darkness a unity, if you will, that cannot be achieved in any other environment, a blending of self with what the self perceives, an exquisite mystical experience. I intend some day to write a disquisition 'On the Harmony of Darkness; Can Evil Exist in Harmony?' It may profit you to ponder the question."

"All I know about the dark is that you can't see in it."

"A pure canard. You know you can."

"Not good enough."

"You see me, don't you?"

"Maybe I do and maybe I don't."

"What do you mean?"

"I see somebody but I am not sure if it is you or a guy who sneaked in and took your chair."

The cigar glowed just enough to light up the Judge's rubbery lips. It was him all right.

"Twenty-five thousand," Roy said in a low voice. "Ten less than Bump."

The cigar lit for a long pull then went out. Its smell was giving Roy a headache. The Judge was silent so long Roy wasn't sure he would ever hear from him again. He wasn't even sure he was there anymore but then he thought yes he is, I can smell him. He is here in the dark and if I come back tomorrow he will still be here and also the year after that.

"'He that maketh haste to be rich shall not be innocent,'" spoke the Judge.

"Judge," said Roy, "I am thirty-four, going on thirty-five. That's not haste, that's downright slow."

"I hear that you bet money on horse races?"

"In moderation, not more than a deuce on the daily double."

"Avoid gambling like a plague. It will cause your downfall. And stay away from loose ladies. 'Put a knife to thy throat if thou be a man given to appetite.'"

Roy could hear him open a drawer and take something out. Handing it to him, he lit a match over it and Roy read: "The Curse of Venereal Disease."

He tossed the pamphlet on the desk.

"Yes or no?" he said.

"Yes or no what?" The Judge's voice was edged with anger.

"Fifteen thousand."

The Judge rose. "I shall have to ask you to fulfill the obligations of your contract."

Roy got up. "I wouldn't exactly say you were building up my good will for next year."

"I have learned to let the future take care of itself."

The Judge took some other papers out of the drawer. "I presume these are your signatures?" He scratched up another match.

"That's right."

"The first acknowledging the receipt of two uniforms and sundry articles?"

"Right."

"And the second indicating the receipt of a third uniform?"

"That's what it says."

"You were entitled to only two. I understand that some of the other clubs issue four, but that is an extravagance. Here, therefore, is a bill to the amount of fifty-one dollars for property destroyed. Will you remit or shall I deduct the sum from your next check?"

"I didn't destroy them, Bump did."

"They were your responsibility."

Roy picked up the receipts and bill and tore them to pieces. He did the same with the VD pamphlet, then blew the whole business over the Judge's head. The scraps of paper fluttered down like snow on his round hat.

"The interview is ended," snapped the Judge. He scratched up a match and with it led Roy to the stairs. He stood on the landing, his oily shadow dripping down the steps as Roy descended.

"Mr. Hobbs."

Roy stopped.

"Resist all evil—"

The match sputtered and went out. Roy went the rest of the way down in the pitch black.

"How'd you make out, kid?"

It was Max Mercy lurking under a foggy street lamp at the corner. He had tailed Roy from the dressing room and had spent a frustrated hour thinking I know the guy but who is he? It was on the tip of his tongue but he couldn't spit it out. He saw the face as he thought he had seen it before somewhere, but what team, where, in what league, and doing what that caused him to be remembered? The mystery was like an itch. The more he scratched the more he drew his own blood. At times the situation infuriated him. Once he dreamed he had the big s.o.b. by the throat and was forcing him to talk. Then he told the world Mercy knew.

The sight of the columnist did not calm Roy as he came

out of the tower. Why does he haunt me? He thought he knew what Max sensed and he knew that he didn't want him to know. I don't want his dirty eyes peeking into my past. What luck for me that I had Sam's wallet in my pocket that night, and they wrote down his name. This creep will never find that out, or anything else about me unless I tell him, and the only time I'll do that is when I am dead.

"Listen, El Smearo," he said, "why don't you stay home in bed?"

Max laughed hollowly.

"Who has ever seen the like of it?" he said, trying to put some warmth into his voice. "Here's the public following everything a man does with their tongue hanging out and all he gives out with is little balls of nothing. What are you hiding? If it was something serious you woulda been caught long ago—your picture has been in the papers every day for weeks."

"I ain't hiding a thing."

"Who says you are? But what's all the mystery about? Where were you born? Why'd you stay out of the game so long? What was your life like before this? My paper will guarantee you five grand in cash for five three-thousand word articles on your past life. I'll help you write them. What do you say?"

"I say no. My life is my own business."

"Think of your public."

"All they're entitled to is to pay a buck and watch me play."

"Answer me this—is it true you once tried out with another major league team?"

"I got nothing to say."

"Then you don't deny it?"

"I got nothing to say."

"Were you once an acrobat or something in a circus?"

"Same answer as before."

Max scratched in his mustache. "Hobbs, the man nobody knows. Say, kid, you're not doing it on purpose, are you?"

"What do you mean?"

"To raise speculation and get publicity?"

"Nuts I am."

"I don't catch. You're a public figure. You got to give the fans something once in a while to keep up their good will to you."

Roy thought a second. "Okay, tell them my cheapskate of a boss has turned me down flat on a raise and I am still his slave for a lousy three thousand bucks."

Max wrote a hasty note in his black book.

"Listen, Roy, let's you and I have a little chin-chin. You'll like me better once you get to know me. Have you had your supper yet?"

"No."

"Then have a steak with me at the Pot of Fire. Know the place?"

"I have never been there."

"It's a night club with a nice girlie show. All the hotshot celebrities like yourself hang out there. They have a good kitchen and a first class bar."

"Okay with me." He was in a mood for something for nothing.

In the cab Max said, "You know, I sometimes get the funny feeling that I have met you some place before. Is that right?"

Roy thrust his head forward. "Where?"

Max contemplated his eyes and solid chin.

"It musta been somebody else."

At the entrance to the Pot of Fire a beggar accosted them.

"Jesus," Max said, "can't I ever get rid of you?"

"All I ask is a buck."

"Go to hell."

The beggar was hurt. "You'll get yours," he said.

"You'll get yours," said Max. "I'll call a cop."

"You'll get yours," the beggar said. "You too," he said to Roy and spat on the sidewalk.

"Friend of yours?" Roy asked as they went down the stairs into the nightspot.

Max's face was inflamed. "I can't get rid of that scurvy bastard. Picks this place to hang around and they can't flush him outa here."

Inside the club the audience was in an uproar. The show was on and some screaming, half-naked girls were being chased by masked devils with tin pitchforks. Then the lights went out and the devils ran around poking at the customers. Roy was jabbed in the rear end. He grabbed at the devil but missed, then he heard a giggle and realized it was a girl. He grabbed for her again but the devil jabbed him and ran. When the lights went on all the girls and devils were gone. The customers guffawed and applauded.

"Come on," Max said.

The captain had recognized him and was beckoning them to a ringside table. Roy sat down. Max looked around and bounced up.

"See a party I know. Be right back."

The band struck up a number and the chorus wriggled out amid weaving spotlights for the finale. They were wearing red spangled briefs and brassieres and looked so pretty that Roy felt lonely.

Max was back.

"We're changing tables. Gus Sands wants us with him."

"Who's he?"

Max looked to see if Roy was kidding.

"You don't know Gus Sands?"

"Never heard of him."

"What d'ye read, the Podunk Pipsqueak? They call him

the Supreme Bookie, he nets at least ten million a year. Awfully nice guy and he will give you the silk shirt off his back. Also somebody you know is with him."

"Who's that?"

"Memo Paris."

Roy got up. What's she doing here? He followed Max across the floor to Gus Sands's table. Memo was sitting there alone in a black strapless gown and wearing her hair up. The sight of her, so beautiful, hit him hard. He had been picturing her alone in her room nights. She said hello evasively. At first he thought she was still sore at him, but then he heard voices coming from the floor at the other side of the table and understood that was where she was looking.

A surprising semi-bald dome rose up above the table and Roy found himself staring into a pair of strange eyes, a mournful blue one and the other glowing weirdly golden. His scalp prickled as the bookie, a long stretch of bone, rose to his full height. The angle at which the spotlight had caught his glass eye, lighting it like a Christmas tree, changed, and the eye became just a ball of ice.

"S'matter, Gus?" Mercy said.

"Memo lost two bits." His voice was sugar soft. "Find it yet?" he asked the waiter, still down on all fours.

"Not yet, sir." He got up. "No, sir."

"Forget it." Sands flicked a deft fiver into the man's loose fist.

He shook hands with Roy. "Glad to meet you, slugger. Whyn't you sit down?"

"Tough luck, babyface," he said, giving Memo a smile. Roy sat down facing her but she barely glanced at him. Though dressed up, she was not entirely herself. The blue eye shadow she had on could not hide the dark circles around her eyes and she looked tired. Her chair was close to Gus's. Once he chucked her under the chin and she giggled. It sickened Roy because it didn't make sense.

The busboy cleaned up the remains of two lobsters. Gus slipped him a fiver.

"Nice kid," he said softly. Reaching for the menu, he handed it to Roy.

Roy read it and although he was hungry couldn't concentrate on food. What did this glass-eye bookie, a good fifty years if not more, mean to a lively girl like Memo, a girl who was, after all, just out of mourning for a young fellow like Bump? Over the top of the menu he noticed Gus's soft-boned hands and the thick, yellow-nailed fingers. He had pouches under both the good and fake eyes, and though he smiled a lot, his expression was melancholy. Roy disliked him right off. There was something wormy about him. He belonged in the dark with the Judge. Let them both haunt themselves there.

"Order, guys," Gus said.

Roy did just to have something to do.

The captain came over and asked was everything all right.

"Check and double check." Gus pressed two folded fives into his palm. Roy didn't like the way he threw out the bucks. He thought of the raise he didn't get and felt bad about it.

"Lemme buy you a drink, slugger," Gus said, pointing to his own Scotch.

"No, thanks."

"Clean living, eh?"

"The eyes," Roy said, pointing to his. "Got to keep 'em clear."

Gus smiled. "Nice goin', slugger."

"He needs a drink," Max said. "The Judge gave him nix on a raise."

Roy could have bopped him for telling it in front of Memo.

Gus was interested.

"Y'mean he didn't pull out his pouch and shake you out some rusty two-dollar gold pieces?"

Everybody laughed but Roy.

"I see you met him," Max said.

Gus winked the glass eye. "We had some dealings."

"How'd you make out?"

"No evidence. We were acquitted." He chuckled softly.

Max made a note in his book.

"Don't write that, Max," said Gus.

Max quickly tore out the page. "Whatever you say, Gus."

Gus beamed. He turned to Roy. "How'd it go today, slugger?"

"Fine," Roy said.

"He got five for five in the first, and four hits in the nightcap," Max explained.

"Say, what d'ye know?" Gus whistled softly. "That'll cost me a pretty penny." He focused his good eye on Roy. "I was betting against you today, slugger."

"You mean the Knights?"

"No, just you."

"Didn't know you bet on any special player."

"On anybody or anything. We bet on strikes, balls, hits, runs, innings, and full games. If a good team plays a lousy team we will bet on the spread of runs. We cover anything anyone wants to bet on. Once in a Series game I bet a hundred grand on three pitched balls."

"How'd you make out on that?"

"Guess."

"I guess you didn't."

"Right, I didn't." Gus chuckled. "But it don't matter. The next week I ruined the guy in a different deal. Sometimes we win, sometimes we don't but the percentage is for us. Today we lost on you, some other time we will clean up double."

"How'll you do that?"

"When you are not hitting so good."

"How'll you know when to bet on that?"

Gus pointed to his glass eye. "The Magic Eye," he said. "It sees everything and tells me."

The steaks came and Roy cut into his.

"Wanna see how it works, slugger? Let's you and I bet on something."

"I got nothing I want to bet on," Roy said, his mouth full of meat and potatoes.

"Bet on any old thing and I will come up with the opposite even though your luck is running high now."

"It's a helluva lot more than luck."

"I will bet anyway."

Memo looked interested. Roy decided to take a chance.

"How about that I will get four hits in tomorrow's game?"

Gus paused. "Don't bet on baseball now," he said. "Bet on something we can settle here."

"Well, you pick it and I'll bet against you."

"Done," said Gus. "Tell you what, see the bar over by the entrance?"

Roy nodded.

"We will bet on the next order. You see Harry there, don't you? He's just resting now. In a minute somebody's gonna order drinks and Harry will make them. We'll wait till a waiter goes over and gives him an order—any one of them in the joint any time you say, so nobody thinks it's rigged. Then I will name you one of the drinks that will go on the waiter's tray, before Harry makes them. If there is only one drink there I will have to name it exactly—for a grand."

Roy hesitated. "Make it a hundred."

Max tittered.

"A 'C' it is," Gus said. "Say when."

"Now."

Gus shut his eyes and rubbed his brow with his left hand. "One of the drinks on the tray will be a Pink Lady."

The way they were seated everybody but Mercy could see the bar, so he turned his chair around to watch.

"Your steak might get cold, Max."

"This I got to see."

Memo looked on, amused.

They waited a minute, then a waiter went over to the bar and said something to the bartender. Harry nodded and turned around for a bottle, but they couldn't see what he was mixing because a customer was standing in front of him. When he left, Roy saw a tall pink drink standing on the counter. He felt sick but then he thought maybe it's a sloe gin fizz. Harry poured a Scotch and soda for the same tray and the waiter came for it.

As he passed by, Gus called him over to the table.

"What is that red drink that you have got there?"

"This one?" said the waiter. "A Pink Lady, Mr. Sands."

Gus slipped him a fiver.

Everybody laughed.

"Nothing to it," said Gus.

"It never fails." Max had turned his chair and was eating. "Nice work, Gus."

Gus beamed. Memo patted his hand. Roy felt annoyed.

"That's a hundred," he said.

"It was a freak win," Gus said, "so we will write it off."

"No, I owe it to you but give me a chance to win it back."

He thought Memo was mocking him and it made him stubborn.

"Anything you say," Gus shrugged.

"You can say it," said Roy. "I'll cover you for two hundred."

Gus concentrated a minute. Everybody watched him, Roy tensely. It wasn't the money he was afraid of. He wanted to win in front of Memo.

"Let's play on some kind of a number," Gus said.

"What kind?"

"Of the amount of bills you are carrying on you."

A slow flush crept up Roy's cheeks.

"I will bet I can guess by one buck either way how much you have got on you now," Gus said.

"You're on." Roy's voice was husky.

Gus covered his good eye and pretended he was a mind reader trying to fathom the number. His glass eye stared unblinking.

"Ten bucks," he announced.

Roy's throat went dry. He drew his wallet out of his pants pocket. Max took it from him and loudly counted up a five and four single dollar bills. "Nine." He slapped the table and guffawed.

"Wonderful," Memo murmured.

"Three hundred I owe to you."

"Don't mention it."

"It was a bet. Will you take my IOU?"

"Wanna try again?"

"Sure."

"You'll lose your panties," Max warned.

"On what?" Gus asked.

Roy thought. "What about another number?"

"Righto. What kind?"

"I'll pick out a number from one to ten. You tell me what it is."

Gus considered. "For the three hundred?"

"Yes."

Okay."

"Do you want me to write the number?"

"Keep it in your head."

"Go ahead."

"Got the number?"

"I have it."

Again Gus eclipsed his good eye and took a slow breath. He made it seem like a kind of magic he was doing. Memo was fascinated.

"Deuce," Gus quickly announced.

Roy felt as if he had been struck on the conk. He considered lying but knew they could tell if he did.

"That's right, how'd you do it?" He felt foolish.

Gus winked.

Max was all but coming apart with laughter. Memo looked away.

Gus swallowed his Scotch. "Two is a magic number," he crooned at Memo. "Two makes the world go around." She smiled slightly, watching Roy.

He tried to eat but felt numbed.

Max just couldn't stop cackling. Roy felt like busting him one in the snoot.

Gus put his long arm around Memo's bare shoulders. "I have lots of luck, don't I, babyface?"

She nodded and sipped her drink.

The lights went on. The m.c. bobbed up from a table he had been sitting at and went into his routine.

"Six hundred I owe to you," Roy said, throwing Max into another whoop of laughter.

"Forget it, slugger. Maybe some day you might be able to do me a favor."

They were all suddenly silent.

"What kind of favor?" Roy asked.

"When I am down and out you can buy me a cup o' coffee."

They laughed, except Roy.

"I'll pay you now." He left the table and disappeared.

In a few minutes he returned with a white tablecloth over his arm.

Roy flapped out the cloth and one of the spotlights happened to catch it in the air. It turned red, then gold.

"What's going on?" Max said.

Roy whisked the cloth over Gus's head.

"The first installment."

He grabbed the bookie's nose and yanked. A stream of silver dollars clattered into his plate.

Gus stared at the money. Memo looked at Roy in intense surprise.

People at the nearby tables turned to see what was going on. Those in the rear craned and got up. The m.c. gave up his jokes and waved both spots to Roy.

"For Pete's sake, sit down," Max hissed.

Roy rippled the green cloth in front of Max's face and dragged out of his astonished mouth a dead herring.

Everybody in the place applauded.

From Memo's bosom, he plucked a duck egg.

Gus got red in the face. Roy grabbed his beak again and twisted—it shed more cartwheels.

"Second installment."

"What the hell is this?" Gus sputtered.

The color wheels spun. Roy turned purple, red, and yellow. From the glum Mercy's pocket he extracted a long salami. Gus's ears ran a third installment of silver. A whirl of the cloth and a white bunny hopped out of Memo's purse. From Max's size sixteen shirt collar, he teased out a pig's tail.

As the customers howled, Max pulled out his black book and furiously scribbled in it. Gus's blue, depressed eye hunted around for a way out but his glass one gleamed like a lamp in a graveyard. And Memo laughed and laughed till the tears streamed down her cheeks.

maybe I might break my back while I am at it," Roy spoke into the microphone at home plate before a hushed sellout crowd jampacked into Knights Field, "but I will do my best—the best I am able—to be the greatest there ever was in the game.

"I thank you." He finished with a gulp that echoed like an electric hiccup through the loudspeakers and sat down, not quite happy with himself despite the celebration, because when called on to speak he had meant to begin with a joke, then thank them for their favor and say what a good team the Knights were and how he enjoyed working for Pop Fisher, but it had come out this other way. On the other hand, so what the hell if they knew what was on his mind?

It was "Roy Hobbs Day," that had been in the making since two weeks ago, when Max Mercy printed in his column: "Roy Hobbs, El Swatto, has been ixnayed on a pay raise. Trying to kill the bird that lays the golden baseball,

Judge?" A grass roots movement developed among the loyal fans to put the Judge to shame (if possible) and they had quickly arranged a Day for Roy, which was held after the Knights had bounced into third place, following a night game win over the Phils, who now led them by only four games, themselves two behind the first-place Pirates.

The whole thing was kept a surprise, and after batting practice was over on this particular Saturday afternoon in early August, the right field gate had swung open and a whole caravan of cars, led by a limousine full of officials and American Legionnaires, and followed by a gorgeous, underslung white Mercedes-Benz and a lumbering warehouse van loaded with stuff, drove in and slowly circled the field to the music of a band playing "Yankee Doodle," while the crowd cheered shrilly. Someone then tapped Roy and said it was all for him.

"Who, me?" he said, rising . . .

When he had made his speech and retired to the dugout, after a quick, unbelieving glance at the mountain of gifts they were unpacking for him, the fans sat back in frozen silence, some quickly crossing their fingers, some spitting over their left shoulders, onto the steps so they wouldn't get anyone wet, almost all hoping he had not jinxed himself forever by saying what he had said. "The best there ever was in the game" might tempt the wrath of some mighty powerful ghosts. But they quickly recovered from the shock of his audacity and clapped up a thick thunder of applause.

It was everyman's party and they were determined to enjoy it. No one knew exactly who had supplied the big dough, but the loyal everyday fans had contributed all sorts of small change and single bucks to buy enough merchandise to furnish a fair-sized general store. When everything was unloaded from the van, Roy posed in front of it, fiddling with a gadget or two for the benefit of the photographers, though he later tipped off Dizzy to sell whatever he could to whoever had the cash. Mercy himself counted two television sets, a baby tractor, five hundred feet of pink plastic garden hose, a nanny goat, lifetime pass to the Paramount, one dozen hand-painted neckties offering different views of the Grand Canyon, six aluminum traveling cases, and a credit for seventy-five taxi rides in Philadelphia. Also three hundred pounds of a New Jersey brand Swiss cheese, a set of andirons and tongs, forty gallons of pistachio ice cream, six crates of lemons, a frozen side of hog, hunting knife, bearskin rug, snowshoes, four burner electric range, deed to a lot in Florida, twelve pairs of monogrammed blue shorts, movie camera and projector, a Chris-Craft motor boat—and, because everybody thought the Judge (unashamedly looking on from his window in the tower) was too cheap to live—a certified check for thirty-six hundred dollars. Although the committee had tried to keep out all oddball contributions, a few slipped in, including a smelly package of Limburger cheese, one human skull, bundle of comic books, can of rat exterminator, and a package of dull razor blades, this last with a card attached in the crabbed handwriting of Otto Zipp: "Here, cut your throat," but Roy did not take it to heart.

When he was told, to his amazement, that the Mercedes-Benz was his too, he could only say, "This is the happiest day of my life." Getting in, he drove around the park to the frenzied waving and whistling of the fans and whirring of movie cameras. The gleaming white job was light to the touch of hand and foot and he felt he could float off in it over the stadium wall. But he stopped before Memo's box and asked if she would go with him for a jaunt after the game, to which she, lowering her eyes, replied she was agreeable.

Memo said she longed to see the ocean so they drove over the bridge and down into Long Island toward Jones Beach, stopping when she was hungry, for charcoal-broiled steaks at a roadside tavern. Afterwards it was night, lit up by a full moon swimming in lemon juice, but at intervals eclipsed by rain clouds that gathered in dark blots and shuttered the yellow light off the fields and tree tops.

She spoke little, once remarking it looked like rain.

He didn't answer. Though he had started off riding high (he had paid back the patrons of his Day by walloping a homer that drove in the winning run) he now felt somewhat heavy hearted. For the past two weeks he had been seeing Memo most every day but had made little headway. There were times when he thought yes, I am on my way up in her affections, but no sooner did he think that when something she did or said, or didn't do or didn't say, made him think no, I am not. It was a confusing proposition to want a girl you'd already had and couldn't get because you had; a situation common in his life, of having first and then wanting what he had had, as if he hadn't had it but just heard about it, and it had, in the hearing, aroused his appetite. He even wished he had not had her that night, and wondered—say he hadn't—whether he would be in the least interested in her today.

In another sense it wasn't a bad evening. He was with her, at least, and they were traveling together, relaxed, to the ocean. He didn't exactly know where it was and though he liked the water, tonight he did not much care if they never came to it. He felt contentment in moving. It rested him by cutting down the inside motion—that which got him nowhere, which was where he was and she was not, or where his ambitions were and he was chasing after. Sometimes he wished he had no ambitions—often wondered where they had come from in his life, because he remembered how satisfied he had been as a youngster, and that with the little he had had—a dog, a stick, an aloneness he loved (which did not bleed him like his later loneliness), and he wished he could have lived longer in his boyhood. This was an old thought with him.

Hoping for a better fate in the future he stepped on the gas and was at once seized by an uneasy fear they were being followed. Since the mirror showed nobody behind them, he wondered at his suspicions and then recalled a black sedan that had been on their tail, he thought, all the way down from the city, only they had lost it a while back in turning off the highway. Yet he continued to watch in the mirror, though it showed only the lifeless moonlit road.

Memo said Jones Beach was too far and told him to stop the next time they came to a brook or pond where she could take off her shoes and go wading in the water. When he spied a small stream running along the edge of a wooded section between two towns, he slowed down. They parked across the shoulder of the asphalt and got out but as they crossed this wooden bridge to the grassy side of the stream, they were confronted by a sign: DANGER. POLLUTED WATER. NO SWIMMING. Roy was all for getting into the car to find another place, but Memo said no, they could watch the water from the bridge. She lit a cigarette, all in light, her hair and green summer dress, and her naked legs and even the slave bracelet around her left ankle gleaming in the light of the moon. Smoking, she watched the water flowing under the bridge, its movement reflected on her face.

After a while, seeing how silent she was, Roy said, "I bet I got enough today to furnish a house."

Memo said, "Bump was coming up for a Day just before he died."

He felt anger rise in his heart and asked coldly, "Well, Memo, what did he have that I haven't got?" He stood to his full height, strong and handsome.

Without looking at him she spoke Bump's name thoughtfully, then shook her head to snap out of it, as if it didn't pay to be thoughtful about Bump. "Oh," she answered, "he was carefree and full of life. He did the craziest things and always kept everybody in stitches. Even when he played ball, there was something carefree and playful about it. Maybe he went all the way after a fly ball or maybe he didn't, but once he made up his mind to catch it, it was exciting how he ran and exciting how he caught it. He made you think you had been wishing for a thing to happen for a long time and then he made it happen. And the same with his hitting. When you catch one, Roy, or go up to hit, everybody knows beforehand that it will land up in your glove, or be a hit. You work at it so— sometimes you even look desperate—but to him it was a playful game and so was his life. Nobody could ever tell what would happen next with Bump, and that was the wonderful thing of it."

Roy thought this is how she sees him now that he is dead. She forgets how hopping sore she was at him after that time in bed with me.

But Bump was dead, he thought, dead and buried in his new box, an inescapable six feet under, so he subtly changed the subject to Gus.

"Gus?" Memo said. At first her face was expressionless. "Oh, he's just like a daddy to me."

He asked her in what way but she laughed and said, "That was a funny business you did with him in the Pot of Fire. How did you do all those tricks?"

"Easy. They had a magic act all laid out to go on. I

walked into the guy's dressing room and when they saw who I was they let me use his stuff just for the laughs."

"Who showed you how to use it?"

"Nobody. I have done some different things in my time, Memo."

"Such as what other ones?"

"You name it, I did it."

"What you did to Max was a scream."

A black cloud rolled like a slow wave across the moon.

"It's so strange," she murmured, looking at the moving water.

"What is?"

For a time she didn't speak, then she sighed and said she meant her life. "It's been strange ever since I can remember except for a year or two—mostly the part with Bump. That was the good part only it didn't last very long, not much of the good part ever did. When I was little my daddy walked out on us and I don't ever remember being happy again till the time I got to go to Hollywood when I was nineteen."

He waited.

"I won a beauty contest where they picked a winner from each state and she was sent to Hollywood to be a starlet. For a few weeks I felt like the Queen of the May, then they took a screen test and though I had the looks and figure my test did not come out so good in acting and they practically told me to go home. I couldn't stand the thought of that so I stayed there for three more years, doing night club work and going to an acting school besides, hoping that I would some day be a good enough actress but it didn't take. I knew what I was supposed to do but I couldn't make myself, in my thoughts, into somebody else. You're supposed to forget who you are but I couldn't. Then I came east and had some more

116

bad times after my mother died, till I met Bump.

He thought she would cry but she didn't.

Memo watched the pebbles in the flowing water. "After Bump I realized I could never be happy any more."

"How do you know that?" Roy asked slowly.

"Oh, I know. I can tell from the way I feel. Sometimes in the morning I never want to wake up."

He felt a dreary emptiness at her words.

"What about yourself?" she asked, wanting to change the subject.

"What about me?" he said gloomily.

"Max says you are sort of a mystery."

"Max is a jerk. My past life is nobody's business."

"What was it like?"

"Like yours, for years I took it on the chin." He sounded as if he had caught a cold, took out his handkerchief and blew his nose.

"What happened?"

He wanted to tell her everything, match her story and go her a couple better but couldn't bring himself to. It wasn't, he thought, that he was afraid to tell her what had happened to him that first time (though the thought of doing that raised a hot blush on his pan, for he had never told anybody about it yet), but about the miserable years after that, when everything, everything he tried somehow went to pot as if that was its destiny in the first place, a thing he couldn't understand.

"What happened?" she asked again.

"The hell with it," he said.

"I told you about myself."

He watched the water.

"I have knocked around a lot and been hard hurt in plenty of ways," he said huskily. "There were times I thought I would never get anywhere and it made me eat my guts, but all that is gone now. I know I have the stuff and will get there."

"Get where?"

"Where I am going. Where I will be the champ and have what goes with it."

She drew back but he had caught her arm and tugged her to him.

"Don't."

"You got to live, Memo."

He trapped her lips, tasting of lemon drops, kissing hard. Happening to open his eyes, he saw her staring at him in the middle of the kiss. Shutting them, he dived deep down again. Then she caught his passion, opened her mouth for his tongue and went limp around the knees.

They swayed together and he turned his hand and slipped it through the top of her dress into her loose brassiere, cupping her warm small breast in his palm.

Her legs stiffened. She pushed at him, sobbing, "Don't touch it."

He was slow to react.

She wailed, "Don't, please don't."

He pulled his hand out, angrily disappointed.

She was crying now, rubbing her hand across her bosom.

"Did I hurt you?"

"Yes."

"How the hell did I do that? I was nice with it."

"It's sick," she wept.

He felt like he had had an icy shave and haircut. "Who says so?"

"It hurts. I know."

She could be lying, only her eyes were crisscrossed with fear and her arms goosefleshed.

"Did you go to a doctor?"

"I don't like them."

118

"You ought to go."

Memo ran off the bridge. He followed her to the car. She sat at the wheel and started the motor. Figuring she would calm down quicker this way he let her.

She backed the car onto the road and drove off. The moon sank into an enormous cloud-sea. Memo sped along the asphalt and turned at a fork down a hard dirt road.

"Put on the lights."

"I like it dark." Her white arms were stiff on the wheel.

He knew she didn't but figured she was still nervous.

Dripping dark cloud spray, the moon bobbed up and flooded the road ahead with bright light. Memo pressed her foot on the gas.

A thundering wind beat across his skull. Let her, he thought. Whatever she has got on her mind, let her get it off, expecially if it is still Bump.

He thought about what she had said on the bridge about never being happy again and wondered what it meant. In a way he was tired of her—she was too complicated—but in a different way he desired her more than ever. He could not decide what to say or do next. Maybe wait, but he didn't want to any more. Yet what else was there to do?

The white moonlight shot through a stretch of woods ahead. He found himself wishing he could go back somewhere, go home, wherever that was. As he was thinking this, he looked up and saw in the moonlight a boy coming out of the woods, followed by his dog. Squinting through the windshield, he was unable to tell if the kid was an illusion thrown forth by the trees or someone really alive. After fifteen seconds he was still there. Roy yelled to Memo to slow down in case he wanted to cross the road. Instead, the car shot forward so fast the woods blurred, the trees racing along like shadows in weak light, then skipping into black and white, finally all black and the moon was gone.

"Lights!"

She sat there stiffly so he reached over and switched them on.

As the road flared up, Memo screamed and tugged at the wheel. He felt a thud and his heart sickened. It was a full minute before he realized they hadn't stopped.

"For Christ sake, stop—we hit somebody."

"No." Her face was bloodless.

He reached for the brake.

"Don't, it was just something on the road."

"I heard somebody groan."

"That was yourself."

He couldn't remember that he had.

"I want to go back and see."

"If you do, the cops will get us."

"What cops?"

"They have been after us since we started. I've been doing ninety."

He looked back and saw a black car with dimmed headlights speeding after them.

"Turn at the next bend," he ordered her, "and I will take over."

They were nearer to the Sound than he had suspected, and when a white pea-souper crawled in off the water Roy headed into it. Though the Mercedes showed no lights the whiteness of it was enough to keep it in the sedan's eye, so he welcomed the fog and within it easily ditched those who chased them.

On the way back he attempted to find the road along the woods to see if they had hit somebody. Memo had little patience with him. She was sure, despite Roy's insistence of an outside groan, that they had hit a rock or log in the road. If they went back the cops might be laying for them and they'd be arrested, which would cause no end of trouble.

He said he was going back anyway.

Roy had the feeling that the sedan was still at his shoulder—he could see it wasn't—as he tried to locate the bridge and then the road along the woods. He wasn't convinced they had not hit somebody and if he could do anything for the kid, even this late, he wanted to. So he turned the lights on bright, illuminating the swirling fog, and as they went by the fog-shrouded woods—he couldn't be sure it was the right woods—he searched the road intently for signs of a body or its blood but found nothing. Memo dozed off but was awakened when Roy, paying no heed to what lay ahead, ran off a low embankment, crashing the car into a tree. Though shaken up, neither of them was much hurt. Roy had a black eye and Memo bruised her sick breast. The car was a wreck.

Helping Memo out of a cab that same morning before dawn, Roy glanced into the hotel lobby just as Pop Fisher bounced up out of a couch and came charging at them like a runaway trolley. Memo said to run, so they raced down the street and ducked into the hotel by the side entrance, but they were barely to the stairs when Pop, who had doubled back on his tracks, came at them smoking with anger.

Memo sobbed she had taken all she could tonight and ran up the stairs. Roy had hoped to have another chance at a kiss but when Pop flew at him like a batty, loose-feathered fowl, killing the stillness of the place with his shrill crowing, he figured it best to keep him away from Memo.

He turned to Pop, who then got a closeup of Roy's rainbow eye and all but blew apart. He called him everything from a dadblamed sonovagun to a blankety blank Judas traitor for breaking training, hurting his eye, and blowing in at almost 5 A.M. on the day of an important twin bill with the Phils.

"You damn near drove me wild," he shouted. "I just about had heart failure when Red told me you weren't in your room at midnight."

He then and there fined Roy two hundred and fifty dollars, but reduced it to an even hundred when Roy sarcastically mentioned how much the Knights were paying him.

"And nothing is wrong with my eye," he said. "It don't hurt but a little and I can see out of it as clear as day, but if you want me to get some sleep before the game don't stand there jawing my head off."

Pop was quickly pacified. "I admit you are entitled to a good time on your Day but you have no idea of all that I have suffered in those hours I was waiting up for you. All kinds of terrible things ran through my mind. I don't hafta tell you it don't take much to kill off a man nowadays."

Roy laughed. "Nothing is going to kill me before my time. I am the type that will die a natural death."

Seeing the affectionate smile this raised up on Pop's puss, he felt sorry for the old man and said, "Even with one eye I will wow them for you today."

"I know you will, son," Pop almost purred. "You're the one I'm depending on to get us up there. We're hot now and I figure, barring any serious accidents, that we will catch up with the Pirates in less than two weeks. Then once we are first we should stay there till we take the flag. My God, when I think of that my legs get dizzy. I guess you know what that would mean to me after all of these years. Sometimes I feel I have been waiting for it my whole life. So take care of yourself. When all is said and done, you ain't a kid any more. At your age the body will often act up, so be wise and avoid any trouble."

"I am young in my mind and healthy in my body," Roy said. "You don't have to worry about me."

"Only be careful," Pop said.

Roy said good night but couldn't move because Pop had gripped his elbow. Leading him to the corner, he whispered to Roy not to have too much to do with Memo. Roy stiffened.

"Don't get me wrong, son, she's not a bad girl—"

Roy glared.

Pop gulped. "I am the one who is really bad. It was me who introduced her to Bump." He looked sick. "I hoped she would straighten him out and sorta hold him in the team—but—well, you know how these things are. Bump was not the marrying kind and she sorta—well, you know what I mean."

"So what?" said Roy.

"Nothing," he answered brokenly. "Only I was wrong for encouraging them to get together with maybe in the back of my mind the idea of how they would do so—without getting married, that is—and I have suffered from it since."

Roy said nothing and Pop wouldn't look him in the eye. "What I started to say," he went on, "is that although she is not really a bad person, yet she is unlucky and always has been and I think that there is some kind of whammy in her that carries her luck to other people. That's why I would like you to watch out and not get too tied up with her."

"You're a lousy uncle."

"I am considering you."

"I will consider myself."

"Don't mistake me, son. She was my sister's girl and I do love her, but she is always dissatisfied and will snarl you up in her trouble in a way that will weaken your strength if you don't watch out."

"You might as well know that I love her."

Pop listened gloomily. "Does she feel the same to you?"

"Not yet but I think she will."

"Well, you are on your own." He looked so forlorn that Roy said, "Don't worry yourself about her. I will change her luck too."

"You might at that." Pop took out his billfold and extracted a pink paper that he handed to Roy.

Roy inspected it through his good eye. It was a check for two thousand dollars, made out to him. "What's it for?"

"The balance of your salary for the time you missed before you got here. I figure that you are entitled to at least the minimum pay for the year."

"Did the Judge send it?"

"That worm? He wouldn't send you his bad breath. It's my personal check." Pop was blushing.

Roy handed it back. "I am making out okay. If the Judge wants to raise my pay, all right, but I don't want your personal money."

"My boy, if you knew what you mean to me—"

"Don't say it." Roy's throat was thick with sentiment. "Wait till I get you the pennant."

He turned to go and bumped into Max Mercy at his elbow. Max's sleepy popeyes goggled when he saw Roy's shiner. He sped back into the lobby.

"That slob is up to no good," Roy said.

"He was sleeping on the couch next to where I was waiting for you to come home. He heard Red tell me you hadn't showed up. Kept a camera with him back there."

"He better not take a picture of my eye," Roy said.

He beat it up the back stairs with Max on his tail. Though the columnist carried a camera and a pocketful of flashbulbs he ran faster than Roy had expected, so to ditch him he shot through the second-floor door and sped down the corridor. Seeing over his shoulder that Max was still after him he ducked through a pair of open glass doors into an enormous black ballroom, strewn with chairs, potted palms, and music stands from a dance last night. The lingering odor of perfume mixed with cigarette smoke reminded him of the smell of Memo's hair and haunted him even now. He thought of hiding behind something but that would make him a ridiculous sitting duck for a chance shot of Max's, so since his good eye had become accustomed to the dark he nimbly picked his way among the obstacles, hoping the four-eyed monstrosity behind him would break his camera or maybe a leg. But Max seemed to smell his way around in the dark and hung tight. Reaching the glass doors at the other end of the ballroom, Roy sidestepped out just as a bulb lit in a wavering flash that would leave Max with a snapshot of nothing but a deserted ballroom. The columnist stuck like glue to Roy's shadow, spiraling after him up the stairs and through the long empty ninth-floor corridor (broad and soft-carpeted so that their footsteps were silent) which stretched ahead, it seemed to Roy, like an endless highway.

He felt he had been running for ages, then this blurred black forest slid past him, and as he slowed down, each black tree followed a white, and then all the trees were lit in somber light till the moon burst forth through the leaves and the woods glowed. Out of it appeared this boy and his dog, and Roy in his heart whispered him a confidential message: watch out when you cross the road, kid, but he had spoken too late, for the boy lay brokenboned and bleeding in a puddle of light, with no one to care for him or whisper a benediction upon his lost youth. A groan rose in Roy's throat (he holding a flashlight over the remains) for not having forced Memo to stop and go back to undo some of the harm. A sudden dark glare flashed over his head, eerily catapulting his shadow forward, and erasing in its incandescence the boy in the road. Roy felt a burning pain in his gut, yet simultaneously remembered there had been no sign of blood on the bumper or fender, and Memo said she had screamed because she saw in the mirror that they were being chased by cops. The black sedan that trailed them had not stopped either, which it would have done if there were cops in it and somebody was dying in the road. So Memo must've been right—either it was a rock, or maybe the kid's hound, probably not even that, for it did not appear there ever was any kid in those woods, except in his mind.

Ahead was his door. Max was panting after him. As Roy shoved the key into the lock, poking his eye close to do the job quick, Max from fifteen feet away aimed the camera and snapped the shutter. The flashbulb burst in the reflector. The door slammed. Max swore blue bloody murder as Roy, inside, howled with laughing.

he had a whopping good time at the ball game. Doc Casey had squeezed the swelling of his eye down and painted out the black with a flesh-tone color, and Roy led the attack against the Phils that sank them twice that afternoon, sweeping the series for the Knights and raising them into second place, only three games behind the Pirates. Pop was hilarious. The fans went wild. The newspapers called the Knights "the wonder team of the age" and said they were headed for the pennant.

On his way to Memo's after the game, Roy met her, wearing her summer furpiece, coming along the fourth-floor hall.

"I thought I would drop around and see how you are, Memo."

She continued her slightly swaying walk to the elevator.

"I am all right," she said.

He paused. "See the doctor yet?"

Memo blushed and said quickly, "He says it's neuritis —nothing serious."

She pressed the elevator button.

"Nothing serious?"

"That's what he said." She was looking up the elevator shaft and he sensed she had not been to the doctor. He guessed her breast was not sick. He guessed she had said that to get him to slow down. Though he did not care for her technique, he controlled his anger and asked her to go to the movies.

"Sorry. Gus is picking me up."

Back in his room he felt restless. He thought he'd be better off without her but the thought only made him bitter. Red Blow called him to go to the pictures but Roy said he had a headache. Later he went out by himself. That night he dreamed of her all night long. The sick breast had turned green yet he was anxious to have a feel of it.

The next day, against the Braves, Roy got exactly no hits. The Knights won, but against the Dodgers in Brooklyn on Tuesday he went hitless once more and they lost. Since he had never before gone without a hit more than six times in a row there was talk now of a slump. That made him uneasy but he tried not to think of it, concerning himself with Memo and continuing his search through the papers for news of a hit-and-run accident on Long Island. Finding no mention of one he blamed the whole thing on his imagination and thought he'd better forget it. And he told himself not to worry about the slump—it happened to the very best—but after a third day without even a bingle he couldn't help but worry.

As his hitlessness persisted everyone was astonished. It didn't seem possible this could happen to a miracle man like Roy. Enemy pitchers were the last to believe the news. They pitched him warily, fearing an eruption of his wrath, but before long they saw the worry in his eyes and would no longer yield those free and easy walks of yore. They straightened out their curves and whizzed them over the gut of the plate, counting on him either to top a slow roller to the infield or strike himself out. True, he was the same majestic-looking figure up there, well back in the box, legs spread wide, and with Wonderboy gleaming in the sun, raised over his shoulder (he had lowered it from his head). He swung with such power you could see a circle of dust lift off the ground as the bat passed over it, yet all it amounted to was breeze. It made many a pitcher feel like a pretty tough hombre to see Roy drag himself away from the plate and with lowered head enter the dugout.

"What's the matter with me?" he thought with irritation. He didn't feel himself (wondered if he could possibly be sick). He felt blunt and dull—all thumbs, muscles, and joints, Charley horse all over. He missed the sensation of the sock—the moment the stomach galloped just before the wood hit the ball, and the satisfying sting that sped through his arms and shoulders as he belted one. Though there was plenty of fielding to do—the Knights' pitchers were getting to be loose with the hits—he missed the special exercise of running the bases, whirling round them with the speed of a race horse as nine frantic men tried to cut him down. Most of all he missed the gloating that blew up his lungs when he crossed the plate and they ran up another tally opposite his name in the record book. A whole apparatus of physical and mental pleasures was on the kibosh and without them he felt like the Hobbs he thought he had left behind dead and buried.

"What am I doing that's wrong?" he asked himself. No one on the bench or in the clubhouse had offered any advice or information on the subject or even so much as mentioned slump. Not even Pop, also worried, but hoping it would fade as suddenly as it had appeared. Roy realized that he was overanxious and pressing—either hitting impatiently in front of the ball or swinging too late—so that Wonderboy only got little bites of it or went hungry. Thinking he was maybe overstriding and getting his feet too far apart so that he could not pivot freely, he shifted his stride but that didn't help. He tried a new stance and attempted, by counting to himself, to alter his timing. It did no good. To save his eyesight he cut out all reading and going to the pictures. At bat his expression was so dark and foreboding it gave the opposing pitchers the shakes, but still they had his number.

He spent hours fretting whether to ask for help or wait it out. Some day the slump was bound to go, but when? Not that he was ashamed to ask for help but once you had come this far you felt you had learned the game and could afford to give out with the advice instead of being forced to ask for it. He was, as they say, established and it was like breaking up the establishment to go around panhandling an earful. Like making a new beginning and he was sick up to here of new beginnings. But as he continued to whiff he felt a little panicky. In the end he sought out Red Blow, drew him out to center field and asked in an embarrassed voice, "Red, what is the matter with me that I am not hitting them?" He gazed over the right field wall as he asked the question.

Red squirted tobacco juice into the grass.

"Well," he said, rubbing his freckled nose, "what's worrying your mind?"

Roy was slow to reply. "I am worrying that I am missing so many and can't get back in the groove."

"I mean besides that. You haven't knocked up a dame maybe?"

"No."

"Any financial worries about money?"

"Not right now."

"Are you doing something you don't like to do?"

"Such as what?"

"Once we had a guy here whose wife made him empty the garbage pail in the barrel every night and believe it or not it began to depress him. After that he fanned the breeze a whole month until one night he told her to take the damn garbage out herself, and the next day he hit again."

"No, nothing like that."

Red smiled. "Thought I'd get a laugh out of you, Roy. A good belly laugh has more than once broke up a slump."

"I would be glad to laugh but I don't feel much like it. I hate to say it but I feel more like crying."

Red was sympathetic. "I have seen lots of slumps in my time, Roy, and if I could tell you why they come I could make a fortune, buy a saloon and retire. All I know about them is you have to relax to beat 'em. I know how you feel now and I realize that every game we lose hurts us, but if you can take it easy and get rid of the nervousness that is for some reason in your system, you will soon snap into your form. From there on in you will hit like a house on fire."

"I might be dead by then," Roy said gloomily.

Red removed his cap and with the hand that held it scratched his head.

"All I can say is that you have got to figure this out for yourself, Roy."

Pop's advice was more practical. Roy visited the manager in his office after the next (fruitless) game. Pop was sitting at his roll top desk, compiling player averages in a looseleaf notebook. On the desk were a pair of sneakers, a picture of Ma Fisher, and an old clipping from the *Sporting News* saying how sensational the Knights were going. Pop closed the average book but not before Roy had seen

131

a large red zero for the day's work opposite his name. The Knights had dropped back to third place, only a game higher than the Cardinals, and Pop's athlete's foot on his hands was acting up.

"What do I have to do to get out of this?" Roy asked moodily.

Pop looked at him over his half-moon specs.

"Nobody can tell you exactly, son, but I'd say right off stop climbing up after those bad balls."

Roy shook his head. "I don't think that's it. I can tell when they're bad but the reason I reach for them sometimes is that the pitchers don't throw me any good ones, which hasn't been so lately. Lately, they're almost all good but not for me."

"Danged if I know just what to tell you," Pop said, scratching at his reddened fingers. He too felt a little frightened. But he recommended bunting and trying to beat them out. He said Roy had a fast pair of legs and getting on base, in which ever way, might act to restore his confidence.

But Roy, who was not much of a bunter—never had his heart in letting the ball hit the bat and roll, when he could just as well lash out and send the same pitch over the fence—could not master the art of it overnight. He looked foolish trying to bunt, and soon gave it up.

Pop then recommended hitting at fast straight ones thrown by different pitchers for thirty minutes every morning, and to do this till he had got his timing back, because it was timing that was lost in a slump. Roy practiced diligently and got so he could connect, yet he couldn't seem to touch the same pitches during the game.

Then Pop advised him to drop all batting practice and to bat cold. That didn't help either.

"How is your eye that got hurt?" Pop asked.

"Doc tested it, he says I see perfect."

Pop looked grimly at Wonderboy. "Don't you think you ought to try another stick for a change? Sometimes that will end up a slump."

Roy wouldn't hear of it. "Wonderboy made all of my records with me and I am staying with him. Whatever is wrong is wrong with me and not my bat."

Pop looked miserable but didn't argue.

Only rarely he saw Memo. She was not around much, never at the games, though she had begun to come quite often a while back. Roy had the morbid feeling she couldn't stand him while he was in this slump. He knew that other people's worries bothered her and that she liked to be where everybody was merry. Maybe she thought the slump proved he was not as good a player as Bump. Whatever it was, she found excuses not to see him and he got only an occasional glimpse of her here and there in the building. One morning when he ran into her in the hotel grill room, Memo reddened and said she was sorry to read he was having a tough time.

Roy just nodded but she went on to say that Bump used to ease his nerves when he wasn't hitting by consulting a fortuneteller named Lola who lived in Jersey City.

"What for?" Roy asked.

"She used to tell him things that gave him a lift, like the time she said he was going to be left money by some-one, and he felt so good it raised him clean out of his slump."

"Did he get the dough that she said?"

"Yes. Around Christmas his father died and left him a garage and a new Pontiac. Bump cleared nine thousand cash when he sold the property."

Roy thought it over afterwards. He had little faith that any fortuneteller could help him out of his trouble but the failure of each remedy he tried sank him deeper into the dumps and he was now clutching for any straw. Borrowing a car, he hunted up Lola in Jersey City, locating her in a two-story shack near the river. She was a fat woman of fifty, and wore black felt slippers broken at the seams, and a kitchen towel wrapped around her head.

"Step right inside the parlor," she said, holding aside the beaded curtain leading into a dark and smelly room, "and I will be with you in a jiffy, just as soon as I get rid of this loud mouth on the back porch."

Feeling ill at ease and foolish, Roy waited for her.

Lola finally came in with a Spanish shawl twisted around her. She lit up the crystal ball, passed her gnarled hands over it and peered nearsightedly into the glass. After watching for a minute she told Roy he would soon meet and fall in love with a darkhaired lady.

"Anything else?" he said impatiently.

Lola looked. A blank expression came over her face and she slowly shook her head. "Funny," she said, "there ain't a thing more."

"Nothing about me getting out of a slump in baseball?"

"Nothing. The future has closed down on me."

Roy stood up. "The trouble with what you said is that I am already in love with a swell-looking redhead."

Because of the shortness of the sitting Lola charged him a buck instead of the usual two.

After his visit to her, though Roy was as a rule not superstitious, he tried one or two things he had heard about to see how they would work. He put his socks on inside out, ran a red thread through his underpants, spat between two fingers when he met a black cat, and daily searched the stands for some crosseyed whammy who might be hexing him. He also ate less meat, though he was always hungry, and he arranged for a physical check-up. The doctor told him he was in good shape except for some high blood pressure that was caused by worrying and would diminish as soon as he relaxed. He practiced different grips on Wonderboy before his bureau mirror and sewed miraculous medals and evil-eye amulets of fish, goats, clenched fists, open scissors, and hunchbacks all over the inside of his clothes.

Little of this escaped the other Knights. While the going was good they had abandoned this sort of thing, but now that they were on the skids they felt the need of some extra assistance. So Dave Olson renewed his feud with the lady in the brown-feathered hat, Emil Lajong spun his protective backflips, and Flores revived the business with the birds. Clothes were put on from down up, gloves were arranged to point south when the players left the field to go to bat, and everybody, including Dizzy, owned at least one rabbit's foot. Despite these precautions the boys were once more afflicted by bonehead plays—failing to step on base on a simple force, walking off the field with two out as the winning run scored from first, attempting to stretch singles into triples, and fearing to leave first when the ball was good for at least two. And they were not ashamed to blame it all on Roy.

It didn't take the fans very long to grow disgusted with their antics. Some of them agreed it was Roy's fault, for jinxing himself and the team on his Day by promising the impossible out of his big mouth. Others, including a group of sportswriters, claimed the big boy had all the while been living on borrowed time, a large bag of wind burst by the law of averages. Sadie, dabbing at her eyes with the edge of her petticoat, kept her gong in storage, and Gloria disgustedly swore off men. And Otto Zipp had reappeared like a bad dream with his loud voice and pesky tooter venomously hooting Roy into oblivion. A few of the fans were ashamed that Otto was picking on somebody obviously down, but the majority approved his sentiments. The old-timers began once again to heave vegetables and oddments around, and following the dwarf's lead they heckled the players, especially Roy, calling him everything from a coward to a son of a bitch. Since Roy had always had rabbit ears, every taunt and barb hit its mark. He changed color and muttered at his tormentors. Once in a spasm of weakness he went slowly after a fly ball (lately he had to push himself to catch shots he had palmed with ease before), compelling Flores to rush into his territory to take it. The meatheads rose to a man and hissed. Roy shook his fist at their stupid faces. They booed. He thumbed his nose. "You'll get yours," they howled in chorus.

He had, a vile powerlessness seized him.

Seeing all this, Pop was darkly furious. He all but ripped the recently restored bandages off his pusing fingers. His temper flared wild and red, his voice tore, he ladled out fines like soup to breadline beggars, and he was vicious to Roy.

"It's that goshdamn bat," he roared one forenoon in the clubhouse. "When will you get rid of that danged Wonderboy and try some other stick?"

"Never," said Roy.

"Then rest your ass on the bench."

So Roy sat out the game on the far corner of the bench, from where he could watch Memo, lovelier than ever in a box up front, in the company of two undertakers, the smiling, one-eye Gus, and Mercy, catlike contented, whose lead that night would read: "Hobbs is benched. The All-American Out has sunk the Knights into second division."

He woke in the locker room, stretched out on a bench. He remembered lying down to dry out before dressing but he was still wet with sweat, and a lit match over his wristwatch told him it was past midnight. He sat up stiffly, groaned and rubbed his hard palms over his bearded face. The thinking started up and stunned him. He sat there paralyzed though his innards were in flight—the double-winged lungs, followed by the boat-shaped heart, trailing a long string of guts. He longed for a friend, a father, a home to return to—saw himself packing his duds in a suitcase, buying a ticket, and running for a train. Beyond the first station he'd fling Wonderboy out the window. (Years later, an old man returning to the city for a visit, he would scan the flats to see if it was there, glowing in the mud.) The train sped through the night across the country. In it he felt safe. He tittered.

The mousy laughter irritated him. "Am I outa my mind?" He fell to brooding and mumbled, "What am I doing that's wrong?" Now he shouted the question and it boomed back at him off the walls. Lighting matches, he hurriedly dressed. Before leaving, he remembered to wrap Wonderboy in flannel. In the street he breathed easier momentarily, till he suspected someone was following him. Stopping suddenly, he wheeled about. A woman, walking alone in the glare of the street lamp, noticed him. She went faster, her heels clicking down the street. He hugged the stadium wall, occasionally casting stealthy glances behind. In the tower burned a dark light, the Judge counting his shekels. He cursed him and dragged his carcass on.

A cabbie with a broken nose and cauliflower ear stared but did not recognize him. The hotel lobby was deserted. An old elevator man mumbled to himself. The ninth-floor hall was long and empty. Silent. He felt a driblet of fear . . . like a glug of water backing up the momentarily opened drain and polluting the bath with a dead spider, three lice, a rat turd, and things he couldn't stand to name or look at. For the first time in years he felt afraid to enter his room. The telephone rang. It rang and rang. He waited for it to stop. Finally it did. He warned himself he was acting like a crazy fool. Twisting the key in the lock, he pushed open the door. In the far corner of the room, something moved. His blood changed to falling snow.

Bracing himself to fight without strength he snapped on the light. A white shadow flew into the bathroom. Rushing in, he kicked the door open. An ancient hoary face stared at him. "Bump!" He groaned and shuddered. An age passed . . . His own face gazed back at him from the bathroom mirror, his past, his youth, the fleeting years. He all but blacked out in relief. His head, a jagged rock on aching shoulders, throbbed from its rocky interior. An oppressive sadness weighed like a live pain on his heart. Gasping for air, he stood at the open window and looked down at the dreary city till his legs and arms were drugged with heaviness. He shut the hall door and flopped into bed. In the dark he was lost in an overwhelming weakness . . . I am finished, he muttered. The pages of the record book fell apart and fluttered away in the wind. He slept and woke, finished. All night long he waited for the bloody silver bullet.

On the road Pop was in a foul mood. He cracked down on team privileges: no more traveling wives, no signing of food checks—Red dispensed the cash for meals every morning before breakfast—curfew at eleven and bed check every night. But Roy had discovered that the old boy had invited Memo to come along with them anyway. He went on the theory that Roy had taken to heart his advice to stay away from her and it was making a wreck out of him. Memo had declined the invitation and Pop guiltily kicked himself for asking her.

Roy was thinking about her the morning they came into Chicago and were on their way to the hotel in a cab—Pop, Red, and him. For a time he had succeeded in keeping her out of his thoughts but now, because of the renewed disappointment, she was back in again. He wondered whether Pop was right and she had maybe jinxed him into a slump. If so, would he do better out here, so far away from her?

The taxi turned up Michigan Avenue, where they had a clear view of the lake. Roy was silent. Red happened to glance out the back window. He stared at something and then said, "Have either of you guys noticed the black Cadillac that is following us around? I've seen that damn auto most everywhere we go."

Roy turned to see. His heart jumped. It looked like the car that had chased them halfway across Long Island.

"Drat 'em," Pop said. "I fired those guys a week ago. Guess they didn't get my postcard."

Red asked who they were.

"A private eye and his partner," Pop explained. "I hired them about a month back to watch the Great Man here and keep him outa trouble but it's a waste of good money now." He gazed back and fumed. "Those goshdarn saps."

Roy didn't say anything but he threw Pop a hard look and the manager was embarrassed.

As the cab pulled up before the hotel, a wild-eyed man in shirtsleeves, hairy-looking and frantic, rushed up to them.

"Any of you guys Roy Hobbs?"

"That's him," Pop said grimly, heading into the hotel with Red. He pointed back to where Roy was getting out of the cab.

"No autographs." Roy ducked past the man.

"Jesus God, Roy," he cried in a broken voice. He caught Roy's arm and held on to it. "Don't pass me by, for the love of God."

"What d'you want?" Roy stared, suspicious.

"Roy, you don't know me," the man sobbed. "My name's Mike Barney and I drive a truck for Cudahy's. I don't want a thing for myself, only a favor for my boy Pete. He was hurt in an accident, playin' in the street. They operated him for a broken skull a coupla days ago and he ain't doin' so good. The doctor says he ain't fightin' much."

Mike Barney's mouth twisted and he wept.

"What has that got to do with me?" Roy asked, white-faced.

The truck driver wiped his eyes on his sleeve. "Pete's a fan of yours, Roy. He got a scrapbook that thick fulla pictures of you. Yesterday they lemme go in and see him and I said to Pete you told me you'd sock a homer for him in the game tonight. After that he sorta smiled and looked better. They gonna let him listen a little tonight, and I know if you will hit one it will save him."

"Why did you say that for?" Roy said bitterly. "The way I am now I couldn't hit the side of a barn."

Holding to Roy's sleeve, Mike Barney fell to his knees. "Please, you gotta do it."

"Get up," Roy said. He pitied the guy and wanted to help him yet was afraid what would happen if he couldn't. He didn't want that responsibility.

Mike Barney stayed on his knees, sobbing. A crowd had collected and was watching them.

"I will do the best I can if I get the chance." Roy wrenched his sleeve free and hurried into the lobby.

"A father's blessing on you," the truck driver called after him in a cracked voice.

Dressing in the visitors' clubhouse for the game that night, Roy thought about the kid in the hospital. He had been thinking of him on and off and was anxious to do something for him. He could see himself walking up to the plate and clobbering a long one into the stands and then he imagined the boy, healed and whole, thanking him for saving his life. The picture was unusually vivid, and as he polished Wonderboy, his fingers itched to carry it into the batter's box and let go at a fat one.

But Pop had other plans. "You are still on the bench, Roy, unless you put that Wonderboy away and use a different stick."

Roy shook his head and Pop gave the line-up card to the ump without his name on it. When Mike Barney, sitting a few rows behind a box above third base, heard the announcement of the Knights' line-up without Roy in it, his face broke out in a sickish sweat.

The game began, Roy taking his non-playing position on the far corner of the bench and holding Wonderboy between his knees. It was a clear, warm night and the stands were just about full. The floods on the roof lit up the stadium brighter than day. Above the globe of light lay the dark night, and high in the sky the stars glittered. Though unhappy not to be playing, Roy, for no reason he could think of, felt better in his body than he had in a week. He had a hunch things could go well for him tonight, which was why he especially regretted not being in the game. Furthermore, Mike Barney was directly in his line of vision and sometimes stared at him. Roy's gaze went past him, farther down the stands, to where a young blackhaired woman, wearing a red dress, was sitting at an aisle seat in short left. He could clearly see the white flower she wore pinned on her bosom and that she seemed to spend more time craning to get a look into the Knights' dugout—at him, he could swear—than in watching the game. She interested him, in that red dress, and he would have liked a close gander at her but he couldn't get out there without arousing attention.

Pop was pitching Fowler, who had kept going pretty well during the two dismal weeks of Roy's slump, only he was very crabby at everybody—especially Roy—for not getting him any runs, and causing him to lose two well-pitched games. As a result Pop had to keep after him in the late innings, because when Fowler felt disgusted he wouldn't bear down on the opposing batters.

Up through the fifth he had kept the Cubs bottled up but he eased off the next inning and they reached him for two runs with only one out. Pop gave him a fierce glaring at and Fowler then tightened and finished off the side with a pop fly and strikeout. In the Knights' half of the seventh, Cal Baker came through with a stinging triple, scoring Stubbs, and was himself driven in by Flores' single. That tied the score but it became untied when, in their part of the inning, the Cubs placed two doubles back to back, to produce another run.

As the game went on Roy grew tense. He considered telling Pop about the kid and asking for a chance to hit. But Pop was a stubborn cuss and Roy knew he'd continue to insist on him laying Wonderboy aside. This he was afraid to do. Much as he wanted to help the boy—and it really troubled him now—he felt he didn't stand a Chinaman's chance at a hit without his own club. And if he once abandoned Wonderboy there was no telling what would happen to him. Probably it would finish his career for keeps, because never since he had made the bat had he swung at a ball with any other.

In the eighth on a double and sacrifice, Pop worked a runner around to third. The squeeze failed so he looked around anxiously for a pinch hitter. Catching Roy's eye, he said, as Roy had thought he would, "Take a decent stick and go on up there."

Roy didn't move. He was sweating heavily and it cost him a great effort to stay put. He could see the truck driver suffering in his seat, wiping his face, cracking his knuckles, and sighing. Roy averted his glance.

There was a commotion in the lower left field stands. This lady in the red dress, whoever she was, had risen, and standing in a sea of gaping faces, seemed to be searching for someone. Then she looked toward the Knights' dugout and sort of half bowed her head. A murmur went up from the crowd. Some of them explained it that she had got mixed up about the seventh inning stretch and others answered how could she when the scoreboard showed the seventh inning was over? As she stood there, so cleanly etched in light, as if trying to communicate something she couldn't express, some of the fans were embarrassed. And the stranger sitting next to her felt a strong sexual urge which he concealed behind an impatient cigarette. Roy scarcely noticed her because he was lost in worry, seriously considering whether he ought to give up on Wonderboy.

Pop of course had no idea what was going on in Roy's head, so he gave the nod to Ed Simmons, a substitute infielder. Ed picked a bat out of the rack and as he approached the plate the standing lady slowly sat down. Everyone seemed to forget her then. Ed flied out. Pop looked scornfully at Roy and shot a stream of snuff into the dust.

Fowler had a little more trouble in the Cubs half of the eighth but a double play saved him, and the score was still 3-2. The ninth opened. Pop appeared worn out. Roy had his eyes shut. It was Fowler's turn to bat. The second guessers were certain Pop would yank him for a pinch hitter but Fowler was a pretty fair hitter for a pitcher, and if the Knights could tie the score, his pitching tonight was too good to waste. He swung at the first ball, connecting for a line drive single, to Pop's satisfaction. Allie Stubbs tried to lay one away but his hard-hit fly ball to center was caught. To everybody's surprise Fowler went down the white line on the next pitch and dove safe into second under a cloud of dust. A long single could tie the score, but Cal Baker, to his disgust, struck out and flung his bat away. Pop again searched the bench for a pinch hitter. He fastened his gaze on Roy but Roy was unapproachable. Pop turned bitterly away.

Mike Barney, a picture of despair, was doing exercises of grief. He stretched forth his long hairy arms, his knobby hands clasped, pleading. Roy felt as though they were reaching right into the dugout to throttle him.

He couldn't stand it any longer. "I give up." Placing Wonderboy on the bench he rose and stood abjectly in front of Pop.

Pop looked up at him sadly. "You win," he said. "Go on in."

Roy gulped. "With my own bat?"

Pop nodded and gazed away.

Roy got Wonderboy and walked out into the light. A roar of recognition drowned the announcement of his name but not the loud beating of his heart. Though he'd been at bat only three days ago, it felt like years—an ageless time. He almost wept at how long it had been.

Lon Toomey, the hulking Cub hurler, who had twice in the last two weeks handed Roy his lumps, smiled behind his glove. He shot a quick glance at Fowler on second, fingered the ball, reared and threw. Roy, at the plate, watched it streak by.

"Stuh-rike."

He toed in, his fears returning. What if the slump did not give way? How much longer could it go on without destroying him?

Toomey lifted his right leg high and threw. Roy swung from his heels at a bad ball and the umpire sneezed in the breeze.

"Strike two!"

Wonderboy resembled a sagging baloney. Pop cursed

the bat and some of the Knights' rooters among the fans booed. Mike Barney's harrowed puss looked yellow.

Roy felt sick with remorse that he hadn't laid aside Wonderboy in the beginning and gone into the game with four licks at bat instead of only three miserable strikes, two of which he already used up. How could he explain to Barney that he had traded his kid's life away out of loyalty to a hunk of wood?

The lady in the stands hesitantly rose for the second time. A photographer who had stationed himself nearby snapped a clear shot of her. She was an attractive woman, around thirty, maybe more, and built solid but not too big. Her bosom was neat, and her dark hair, parted on the side, hung loose and soft. A reporter approached her and asked her name but she wouldn't give it to him, nor would she, blushing, say why she was standing now. The fans behind her hooted, "Down in front," but though her eyes showed she was troubled she remained standing.

Noticing Toomey watching her, Roy stole a quick look. He caught the red dress and a white rose, turned away, then came quickly back for another take, drawn by the feeling that her smile was for him. Now why would she do that for? She seemed to be wanting to say something, and then it flashed on him the reason she was standing was to show her confidence in him. He felt surprised that anybody would want to do that for him. At the same time he became aware that the night had spread out in all directions and was filled with an unbelievable fragrance.

A pitch streaked toward him. Toomey had pulled a fast one. With a sob Roy fell back and swung.

Part of the crowd broke for the exits. Mike Barney wept freely now, and the lady who had stood up for Roy absently pulled on her white gloves and left.

The ball shot through Toomey's astounded legs and began to climb. The second baseman, laying back on the grass

145

on a hunch, stabbed high for it but it leaped over his straining fingers, sailed through the light and up into the dark, like a white star seeking an old constellation.

Toomey, shrunk to a pygmy, stared into the vast sky.

Roy circled the bases like a Mississippi steamboat, lights lit, flags fluttering, whistle banging, coming round the bend. The Knights poured out of their dugout to pound his back, and hundreds of their rooters hopped about in the field. He stood on the home base, lifting his cap to the lady's empty seat.

And though Fowler goose-egged the Cubs in the last of the ninth and got credit for the win, everybody knew it was Roy alone who had saved the boy's life.

it seemed perfectly natural to Iris to be waiting for him, with her shoes off to ease her feet, here on the park grass. He had been in her mind so often in the past month she could not conceive of him as a stranger, though he certainly was. She remembered having fallen asleep thinking of him last night. She had been gazing at the stars through her window, unaware just when they dissolved into summer rain, although she remembered opening a brown eye in time to see the two-pronged lightning plunge through a cloud and spread its running fire in all directions. And though she was sometimes afraid she would be hurt by it (this was her particular fear) she did not get up to shut the window but watched the writhing flame roll across the sky, until it disappeared over the horizon. The night was drenched and fragrant. Without the others knowing, she had slipped on a dress and gone across the road to walk in a field of daisies whose white stars lit up her bare feet as she thought of tomorrow in much the way she had at sixteen.

Tonight was a high, free evening, still green and gold above the white fortress of buildings on Michigan Avenue, yet fading over the lake, from violet to the first blue of night. A breeze with a breath of autumn in it, despite that afternoon's heat in the city, blew at intervals through the trees. From time to time she caught herself glancing, sometimes frowning, at her wristwatch although it was her own fault she had come so early. Her arms showed gooseflesh and she wondered if she had been rash to wear a thin dress at night but that was silly because the night was warm. It did not take her long to comprehend that the gooseflesh was not for now but another time, long ago, a time she was, however, no longer afraid to remember.

Half her life ago, just out of childhood it seemed, but that couldn't be because she was too strangely ready for the irrevocable change that followed, she had one night alone in the movies met a man twice her age, with whom she had gone walking in the park. Sensing at once what he so unyieldingly desired, she felt instead of fright, amazement at her willingness to respond, considering she was not, like some she later met, starved of affection. But a mother's love was one thing, and his, when he embraced her under the thick-leaved tree that covered them, was something else again. She had all she could do to tear herself away from him, and rushed through the branches, scratching her face and arms in the bargain. But he would not let her go, leading her always into dark places, hidden from all but the light of the stars, and taught her with his kisses that she could race without running. All but bursting with motion she cried don't look, and when he restlessly turned away, undressed the bottom half of her. She offered herself in a white dress and bare feet and was considerably surprised when he pounced like a tiger.

A horn hooted.

It was Roy driving a hired car. He looked around for a

parking place but she had slipped on her shoes and waved she was coming.

He had come across her picture in one of the morning papers the day after he had knocked out the homer for the kid. Slicing it out carefully with his knife, he folded it without creasing the face and kept it in his wallet. Whenever he had a minute to himself (he was a smashing success at bat—five for five, three home runs—and was lionized by all) he took the picture out and studied it, trying to figure out why she had done that for him; nobody else ever had. Usually when he was down he was down alone, without flowers or mourners. He suspected she might be batty or a grownup bobby soxer gone nuts over him for having his name and picture in the papers. But from the intelligent look of her it didn't seem likely. There were some players the ladies might fall for through seeing their pictures but not him—not that he was bad-looking or anything, just that he was no dream boy—nor was she the type to do it. In her wide eyes he saw something which caused him to believe she knew what life was like, though you really couldn't be sure.

He made up his mind and telephoned the photographer who had taken this shot of her, for any information he might have as to where she lived, but at his office they said he was covering a forest fire in Minnesota. During the game that afternoon Roy scanned the stands around him and in the fifth frame located her practically at his elbow in deep left. He got one of the ushers to take her a note saying could she meet him tonight? She wrote back not tonight but enclosed her phone number. After a shot of Scotch he called her. Her voice was interesting but she said frankly she wondered if their acquaintance ought to end now, because these things could be disillusioning when they dragged past their time. He said he didn't think she would disappoint him. After some coaxing she yielded, chiefly

149

because Roy insisted he wanted to thank her in person for her support of him.

He held the door open and she stepped in.

"I'm Iris Lemon," she said with a blush.

"Roy Hobbs." He felt foolish for of course she knew his name. Despite his good intentions he was disappointed right off, because she was heavier than he had thought— the picture didn't show that so much or if it did he hadn't noticed—and she had lost something, in this soft brown dress, that she'd had in the red. He didn't like them hefty, yet on second thought it couldn't be said she really was. Big, yes, but shapely too. Her face and hair were pretty and her body—she knew what to wear on her feet—was well proportioned. He admitted she was attractive although as a rule he never thought so unless they were slim like Memo.

So he asked her right out was she married.

She seemed startled, then smiled and said, "No, are you?"

"Nope."

"How is it the girls missed you?"

Though tempted to go into a long explanation about that, he let it pass with a shrug. Neither of them was looking at the other. They both stared at the road ahead. The car hadn't moved.

Iris felt she had been mistaken to come. He seemed so big and bulky next to her, and close up looked disappointingly different from what she had expected. In street clothes he gained little and lost more, a warrior's quality he showed in his uniform. Now he looked like any big-muscled mechanic or bartender on his night off. Whatever difference could it have made to her that this particular one had slumped? She was amazed at her sentimentality.

Roy was thinking about Memo. If not for her he wouldn't

150

be here trying to make himself at ease with this one. She hadn't treated him right. For a while things had looked good between them but no sooner had he gone into a slump when she began again to avoid him. Had she been nice to him instead, he'd have got out of his trouble sooner. However, he wasn't bitter, because Memo was remote, even unreal. Strange how quick he forgot what she was like, though he couldn't what she looked like. Yet with that thought even her image went up in smoke. Iris, a stranger, had done for him what the other wouldn't, in public view what's more. He felt for her a gratitude it was hard to hold in.

"When you get to know me better you will like me more." He surprised himself with that—the hoarse remark echoed within him—and she, sure she had misjudged him, felt a catch in her throat as she replied, "I like you now."

He stepped on the starter and they drove off in the lilac dusk. Where to? he had asked and she had said it made no difference, she liked to ride. He felt, once they started, as if he had been sprung from the coop, and only now, as the white moon popped into the sky, did he begin to appreciate how bad it had been with him during the time of his slump.

They drove so they could almost always see the lake. The new moon climbed higher in the blue night, shedding light like rain. They drove along the lit highway to where the lake turned up into Indiana and they could see the lumpy yellow dunes along the shore. Elsewhere the land was shadowless and flat except for a few trees here and there. Roy turned into a winding dirt road and before long they came to this deserted beach, enclosed in a broken arc of white birches. The wind here was balmy and the water lit on its surface.

He shut off the motor. In the silence—everything but the

lapping of the lake water—they too were silent. He hesitated at what next move to make and she prayed it would be the right one although she was not quite sure what she meant.

Roy asked did she want to get out. She understood he wanted her to so she said yes. But she surprised him by saying she had been here before.

"How's the water?" he asked.

"Cold. The whole lake is, but you get used to it soon."

They walked along the shore and then to a cluster of birches. Iris sat on the ground under one of the trees and slipped off her shoes. Her movements were graceful, she made her big feet seem small.

He sat nearby, his eyes on her. She sensed he wanted to talk but now felt curiously unconcerned with his problems. She had not expected the night to be this beautiful. Since it was, she asked no more than to be allowed to enjoy it.

But Roy impatiently asked her why she had stood up for him the other night.

She did not immediately reply.

After a minute he asked again.

"I don't know," Iris sighed.

That was not the answer he had expected.

"How come?"

"I've been trying to explain it to myself." She lit a cigarette.

He was now a little in awe of her, something he had not foreseen, though he pretended not to be.

"You're a Knights fan, ain't you?"

"No."

"Then how come—I don't get it."

"I'm not a baseball fan but I like to read about the different players. That's how I became interested in you—your career."

"You read about my slump?" His throat tightened at the word.

"Yes, and before that of your triumphs."

"Ever see me play—before the other night?"

She shook her head. "Once then and again yesterday."

"Why'd you come—the first time?"

She rubbed her cigarette into the dirt. "Because I hate to see a hero fail. There are so few of them."

She said it seriously and he felt she meant it.

"Without heroes we're all plain people and don't know how far we can go."

"You mean the big guys set the records and the little buggers try and bust them?"

"Yes, it's their function to be the best and for the rest of us to understand what they represent and guide ourselves accordingly."

He hadn't thought of it that way but it sounded all right.

"There are so many young boys you influence."

"That's right," said Roy.

"You've got to give them your best."

"I try to do that."

"I mean as a man too."

He nodded.

"I felt that if you knew people believed in you, you'd regain your power. That's why I stood up in the grandstand. I hadn't meant to before I came. It happened naturally. Of course I was embarrassed but I don't think you can do anything for anyone without giving up something of your own. What I gave up was my privacy among all those people. I hope you weren't ashamed of me?"

He shook his head. "Were you praying for me to smack one over the roof?"

"I hoped you might become yourself again."

"I was jinxed," Roy explained to her. "Something was

153

keeping me out of my true form. Up at the plate I was
blind as a bat and Wonderboy had the heebie jeebies. But
when you stood up and I saw you with that red dress on
and thought to myself she is with me even if nobody else is,
it broke the whammy."

Iris laughed.

Roy crawled over to her and laid his head in her lap.
She let him. Her dress was scented with lilac and clean
laundry smell. Her thighs were firm under his head. He
got a cigar out of his pocket and lit it but it stank up the
night so he flung it away.

"I sure am glad you didn't stand me up," he sighed.

"Who would?" she smiled.

"You don't know the half of it."

She softly said she was willing to.

Roy struggled with himself. The urge to tell her was
strong. On the other hand, talk about his inner self was
always like plowing up a graveyard.

She saw the sweat gleaming on his brow. "Don't if you
don't feel like it."

"Everything came out different than I thought." His
eyes were clouded.

"In what sense?"

"Different."

"I don't understand."

He coughed, tore his voice clear and blurted, "My goddamn life didn't turn out like I wanted it to."

"Whose does?" she said cruelly. He looked up. Her expression was tender.

The sweat oozed out of him. "I wanted everything." His
voice boomed out in the silence.

She waited.

"I had a lot to give to this game."

"Life?"

"Baseball. If I had started out fifteen years ago like

I tried to, I'da been the king of them all by now."

"The king of what?"

"The best in the game," he said impatiently.

She sighed deeply. "You're so good now."

"I'da been better. I'da broke most every record there was."

"Does that mean so much to you?"

"Sure," he answered. "It's like what you said before. You break the records and everybody else tries to catch up with you if they can."

"Couldn't you be satisfied with just breaking a few?"

Her pinpricking was beginning to annoy him. "Not if I could break most of them," he insisted.

"But I don't understand why you should make so much of that. Are your values so—"

He heard a train hoot and went freezing cold.

"Where's that train?" he cried, jumping to his feet.

"What train?"

He stared into the night.

"The one I just heard."

"It must have been a bird cry. There are no trains here."

He gazed at her suspiciously but then relaxed and sat down.

"That way," he continued with what he had been saying, "if you leave all those records that nobody else can beat—they'll always remember you. You sorta never die."

"Are you afraid of death?"

Roy stared at her listening face. "Now what has that got to do with it?"

She didn't answer. Finally he laid his head back on her lap, his eyes shut.

She stroked his brow slowly with her fingers.

"What happened fifteen years ago, Roy?"

Roy felt like crying, yet he told her—the first one he ever had. "I was just a kid and I got shot by this batty dame on the night before my tryout, and after that I just couldn't get started again. I lost my confidence and everything I did flopped."

He said this was the shame in his life, that his fate, somehow, had always been the same (on the train going nowhere)—defeat in sight of his goal.

"Always?"

"Always the same."

"Always with a woman?"

He laughed harshly. "I sure met some honeys in my time. They burned me good."

"Why do you pick that type?"

"It's like I say—they picked me. It's the breaks."

"You could say no, couldn't you?"

"Not to that type dame I always fell for—they weren't like you."

She smiled.

"I mean you are a different kind."

"Does that finish me?"

"No," he said seriously.

"I won't ever hurt you, Roy."

"No."

"Don't ever hurt me."

"No."

"What beats me," he said with a trembling voice, "is why did it always have to happen to me? What did I do to deserve it?"

"Being stopped before you started?"

He nodded.

"Perhaps it was because you were a good person?"

"How's that?"

"Experience makes good people better."

She was staring at the lake.

"How does it do that?"

"Through their suffering."

"I had enough of that," he said in disgust.

"We have two lives, Roy, the life we learn with and the life we live with after that. Suffering is what brings us toward happiness."

"I had it up to here." He ran a finger across his windpipe.

"Had what?"

"What I suffered—and I don't want any more."

"It teaches us to want the right things."

"All it taught me is to stay away from it. I am sick of all I have suffered."

She shrank away a little.

He shut his eyes.

Afterwards, sighing, she began to rub his brow, and then his lips.

"And is that the mystery about you, Roy?"

"What mystery?"

"I don't know. Everyone seems to think there is one."

"I told you everything."

"Then there really isn't?"

"Nope."

Her cool fingers touched his eyelids. It was unaccountably sweet to him.

"You broke my jinx," he muttered.

"I'm thirty-three," she said, looking at the moonlit water.

He whistled but said, "I am no spring chicken either, honey."

"Iris."

"Iris, honey."

"That won't come between us?"

"What?"

"My age?"

"No."

"Nothing?"

"If you are not married?"

"No."

"Divorced?"

"No."

"A widow?"

"No," said Iris.

He opened his eyes. "How come with all your sex appeal that you never got hitched?"

She gazed away.

Roy suddenly sat up and bounced to his feet. "Jesus, will you look at that water. What are we waiting for?" He tore at his tie.

Iris was saying that she had, however, brought a child into the world, a girl now grown, but Roy seemed not to hear, he was so busy getting out of his clothes. In no time to speak of he stood before her stripped to his shorts.

"Get undressed."

The thought of standing naked before him frightened her. She told herself not to be—she was no longer a child about the naked body. But she couldn't bring herself to remove her clothes in front of him so she went back to the car and undressed there. He waited impatiently, then before he expected her, she stepped out without a thing on and ran in the moonlight straight into the water, through the shallow part, and dived where it was deep.

Hopping high through the cold water, Roy plunged in after her. He dived neatly, kicked hard underwater and came up almost under her. Iris fell back out of his reach and swam away. He pursued her with less skill than she had but more strength. At first he damn near froze but as he swam his blood warmed. She would not stop and before long the white birches near the beach looked to be the size of match sticks.

Though they were only a dozen strokes apart she wouldn't let him gain, and after another fifty tiring yards he wondered how long this would go on. He called to her but she didn't answer and wouldn't stop. He was beginning to be winded and considered quitting, only he didn't want to give up. Then just about when his lungs were frying in live coals, she stopped swimming. As she trod water, the light on the surface hid all but her head from him.

He caught up with her at last and attempted to get his arms around her waist. "Give us a kiss, honey."

She was repelled and shoved him away.

He saw she meant it, realized he had made a mistake, and felt terrible.

Roy turned tail, kicking himself down into the dark water. As he sank lower it got darker and colder but he kept going down. Before long the water turned murky yet there was no bottom he could feel with his hands. Though his legs and arms were numb he continued to work his way down, filled with icy apprehensions and weird thoughts.

Iris couldn't believe it when he did not quickly rise. Before long she felt frightened. She looked everywhere but he was still under water. A sense of abandonment gripped her. She remembered standing up in the crowd that night, and said to herself that she had really stood up because he was a man whose life she wanted to share . . . a man who had suffered. She thought distractedly of a home, children, and him coming home every night to supper. But he had already left her . . .

. . . At last in the murk he touched the liquid mud at the bottom. He dimly thought he ought to feel proud to have done that but his mind was crammed with old memories flitting back and forth like ghostly sardines, and there wasn't a one of them that roused his pride or gave him any comfort.

So he forced himself, though sleepily, to somersault up

and begin the slow task of climbing through all the iron bars of the currents . . . too slow, too tasteless, and he wondered was it worth it.

Opening his bloodshot eyes he was surprised how far down the moonlight had filtered. It dripped down like oil in the black water, and then, unexpectedly, there came into his sight this pair of golden arms searching, and a golden head with a frantic face. Even her hair sought him.

He felt relieved no end.

I am a lucky bastard.

He was climbing a long, slow ladder, broad at the base and narrowing on top, and she, trailing clusters of white bubbles, was weaving her way to him. She had golden breasts and when he looked to see, the hair between her legs was golden too.

With a watery howl bubbling from his blistered lungs he shot past her inverted eyes and bobbed up on the surface, inhaling the soothing coolness of the whole sky.

She rose beside him, gasping, her hair plastered to her naked skull, and kissed him full on the lips. He tore off his shorts and held her tight. She stayed in his arms.

"Why did you do it?" she wept.

"To see if I could touch the bottom."

They swam in together, taking their time. As they dragged themselves out of the water, she said, "Go make a fire, otherwise we will have nothing to dry ourselves with."

He covered her shoulders with his shirt and went hunting for wood. Under the trees he collected an armload of branches. Near the dunes he located some heavy boxwood. Then he came back to where she was sitting and began to build a fire. He set an even row of birch sticks down flat and with his knife shaved up a thick branch till he had a pile of dry shavings. These he lit with the only match he had. When they were burning he added some dry birch pieces he had cut up. He split the boxwood against a rock and when the fire was crackling added that, hunk by hunk, to the flames. Before long he had a roaring blaze going. The fire reddened the water and the lacy birches.

It reddened her naked body. Her thighs and rump were broad but her waist was narrow and virginal. Her breasts were hard, shapely. From above her hips she looked like a girl but the lower half of her looked like a woman.

Watching her, he thought he would wait for the fire to die down, when she was warm and dry and felt not rushed.

She was sitting close to the fire with her hair pulled over her head so the inside would dry first. She was thinking why did he go down? Did he touch the bottom of the lake out of pride, because he wants to make records, or did he do it in disappointment, because I wouldn't let him kiss me?

Roy was rubbing his hands before the fire. She looked up and said in a tremulous voice, "Roy, I have a confession to you. I was never married, but I am the mother of a grown girl."

He said he had heard her the first time.

She brushed her hair back with her fingers. "I don't often talk about it, but I want to tell you I made a mistake long ago and had a hard time afterwards. Anyway, the child meant everything to me and made me happy. I gave her a good upbringing and now she is grown and on her own, and I am free to think of myself and young enough to want to."

That was the end of it because Roy asked no questions.

He watched the fire. The flames sank low. When they had just about been sucked into the ashes he crept toward her and took her in his arms. Her breasts beat like hearts against him.

"You are really the first," she whispered.

He smiled, never so relaxed in sex.

But while he was in the middle of loving her she spoke: "I forgot to tell you I am a grandmother."

He stopped. Holy Jesus.

Then she remembered something else and tried, in fright, to raise herself.

"Roy, are you—"

But he shoved her back and went on from where he had left off.

after a hilarious celebration in the dining car (which they roused to uproar by tossing baked potatoes and ketchup bottles around) and later in the Pullman, where a wild bunch led by Roy stripped the pajamas off players already sound asleep in their berths, peeled Red Blow out of his long underwear, and totally demolished the pants of a new summer suit of Pop's, who was anyway not sold on premature celebrations, Roy slept restlessly. In his sleep he knew he was restless and blamed it (in his sleep) on all he had eaten. The Knights had come out of Sportsman's Park after trouncing the Cards in a double header and making it an even dozen in a row without a loss, and the whole club had gone gay on the train, including, mildly, Pop himself, considerably thawed out now that the team had leapfrogged over the backs of the Dodgers and Cards into third place. They were again hot on the heels of the Phils and not too distant from the Pirates, with a whole month to go before the end of the season, and about sixty per cent of their remaining games on home grounds. Roy was of course in fine fettle, the acknowledged King of Klouters, whose sensational hitting, pulverizing every kind of pitching, more than made up for his slump. Yet no matter how many bangs he collected, he was ravenously hungry for more and all he could eat besides. The Knights had boarded the train at dinner time but he had stopped off at the station to devour half a dozen franks smothered in sauerkraut and he guzzled down six bottles of pop before his meal on the train, which consisted of two oversize sirloins, at least a dozen rolls, four orders of mashed, and three (some said five) slabs of apple pie. Still that didn't do the trick, for while they were all at cards that evening, he sneaked off the train as it was being hosed and oiled and hustled up another three wieners, and later secretly arranged with the steward for a midnight snack of a long T-bone with trimmings, although that did not keep him from waking several times during the night with pangs of hunger.

When the diner opened in the morning he put away an enormous breakfast and afterwards escaped those who were up, and found himself some privacy in a half-empty coach near the engine, where nobody bothered him because he was not too recognizable in gabardine, behind dark glasses. For a while he stared at the scattered outskirts of the city they were passing through, but in reality he was wondering whether to read the fat letter from Iris Lemon he had been carrying around in his suit pocket. Roy recalled the night on the lake shore, the long swim, the fire and after. The memory of all was not unpleasant, but what for the love of mud had made her take him for a sucker who would be interested in a grandmother? He found that still terrifying to think of, and although she was a nice enough girl, it had changed her in his mind from Iris more to lemon. To do her justice he concentrated on her good looks and the pleasures of her body but when her kid's kid came to mind, despite grandma's age of only thirty-three, that was asking too much and spoiled the appetizing part of her. It was simple enough to him: if he got serious with her it could only lead to one thing—him being a grandfather. God save him from that for he personally felt as young and frisky as a colt. That was what he told himself as the train sped east, and though he had a slight bellyache he fell into a sound sleep and dreamed how on frosty mornings when he was a kid the white grass stood up prickly stiff and the frozen air deep-cleaned his insides.

He awoke with Memo on his mind. To his wonder she turned up in his room in Boston the next night. It was after supper and he was sitting in a rocker near the window reading about himself in the paper when she knocked. He opened the door and she could have thrown him with a breath, so great was his surprise (and sadness) at seeing her. Memo laughingly said she had been visiting a girl friend's summer place on the Cape, and on her way back to New York had heard the boys were in town so she stopped off to say hello, and here she was. Her face and arms were tanned and she looked better than she had in a long while. He felt too that she had changed somehow in the weeks he hadn't seen her. That made him uneasy, as if any change in her would automatically be to his hurt. He searched her face but could not uncover anything new so explained it as the five pounds she said she had put on since he had seen her last.

He felt he still held it against her for giving him very little support at a time when he could use a lot, and also for turning Pop down when he had invited her to join them on the Western trip. Yet here, alone with her in his room, she so close and inevitably desirable—this struck him with the force of an unforgettable truth: the one he had had and always wanted—he thought it wouldn't do to put on a sourpuss and make complaints. True, there was something about her, like all the food he had lately been eating, that left him, after the having of it, unsatisfied, sometimes even with a greater hunger than before. Yet she was a truly beautiful doll with a form like Miss America, and despite the bumps and bruises he had taken, he was sure that once he got an armlock on her things would go better.

His face must have shown more than he intended, because she turned moodily to the window and said, "Roy, don't bawl me out for not seeing you for a while. There are some things I just can't take and one of them is being with people who are blue. I had too much of that in my life with my mother and it really makes me desperate." More tenderly she said, "That's why I had to stand off to the side, though I didn't like to, and wait till you had worked out of it, which I knew you would do. Now here I am the first chance I got and that is the way it used to be between Bump and me."

Roy said soberly, "When are you going to find out that I ain't Bump, Memo?"

"Don't be mad," she said, lifting her face to him. "All I meant to say is that I treat all my friends the same." She was close and warm-breathed. He caught her in his arms and she snuggled tight, and let him feel the "sick" breast without complaining. But when he tried to edge her to the bed, she broke for air and said no.

"Why not?" he demanded.

"I'm not well," said Memo.

He was suspicious. "What's wrong?"

Memo laughed. "Sometimes you are very innocent, Roy. When a girl says she is not well, does she have to draw you a map?"

Then he understood and was embarrassed for being so

dimwitted. He did not insist on any more necking and thought it a good sign that she had talked to him so intimately.

The Knights took their three in Boston and the next day won a twi-night double header in Ebbets Field, making it seventeen straight wins on the comeback climb. Before Roy ended his slump they had fallen into fifth place, twelve games behind, then they slowly rose to third, and after this twin bill with Brooklyn, were within two of the Phils, who had been nip and tucking it all season with the Cards and Dodgers. The Pirates, though beaten three in a row by the Knights on their Western swing (the first Knight wins over them this season) were still in first place, two games ahead of the Phils in a tight National League race.

When the Knights returned to their home grounds for a three-game set with the cellar-dwelling Reds, the city awakened in a stampede. The fans, recovered from their stunned surprise at the brilliant progress of the team, turned out in droves. They piled into the stands with foolish smiles, for most of them had sworn off the Knights during the time of Roy's slump. Now for blocks around the field, the neighborhood was in an uproar as hordes fought their way out of subways, trolleys and buses, and along the packed streets to ticket windows that had been boarded up (to Judge Banner's heartfelt regret) from early that morning, while grunting lines of red-faced cops, reinforced by sweating mounties, tried to shove everybody back where they had come from. After many amused years at the expense of the laughingstock Knights, a scorching pennant fever blew through the city. Everywhere people were bent close to their radios or stretching their necks in bars to have a look at the miracle boys (so named by sportswriters from all over the U.S. who now crammed into the once deserted press boxes) whose every move aroused their fanatic supporters to a frenzy of excitement which whirled out of them in concentric rings around the figure of Roy Hobbs, hero and undeniable man of destiny. He, it was said by everyone, would lead the Knights to it.

The fans dearly loved Roy but Roy did not love the fans. He hadn't forgotten the dirty treatment they had dished out during the time of his trouble. Often he felt he would like to ram their cheers down their throats. Instead he took it out on the ball, pounding it to a pulp, as if the best way to get even with the fans, the pitchers who had mocked him, and the statisticians who had recorded (forever) the kind and quantity of his failures, was to smash every conceivable record. He was like a hunter stalking a bear, a whale, or maybe the sight of a single fleeing star the way he went after that ball. He gave it no rest (Wonderboy, after its long famine, chopping, chewing, devouring) and was not satisfied unless he lifted it (one eye cocked as he swung) over the roof and spinning toward the horizon. Often, for no accountable reason, he hated the pill, which represented more of himself than he was willing to give away for nothing to whoever found it one dull day in a dirty lot. Sometimes as he watched the ball soar, it seemed to him all circles, and he was mystified at his devotion to hacking at it, for he had never really liked the sight of a circle. They got you nowhere but back to the place you were to begin with, yet here he stood banging them like smoke rings out of Wonderboy and everybody cheered like crazy. The more they cheered the colder he got to them. He couldn't stop hitting and every hit made him hungry for the next (a doctor said he had no tapeworm but ate like that because he worked so hard), yet he craved no cheers from the slobs in the stands. Only once he momentarily forgave them—when reaching for a fly, he almost cracked into the wall and they gasped their fright and shrieked warnings. After he caught the ball he doffed his cap and they rocked the rafters with their thunder.

The press, generally snotty to him during his slump, also changed its tune. To a man (except one) they showered him with praise, whooped him on, and in their columns unofficially accolated him Rookie of the Year (although they agreed he resembled nothing so much as an old hand, a toughened veteran of baseball wars) and Most Valuable Player, and years before it was time talked of nominating him for a permanent niche in the Cooperstown Hall of Fame. He belonged, they wrote, with the other immortals, a giant in performance, who resembled the burly boys of the eighties and nineties more than the streamlined kids of today. He was a throwback to a time of true heroes, not of the brittle, razzle dazzle boys that had sprung up around the jack rabbit ball—a natural not seen in a dog's age, and weren't they the lucky ones he had appeared here and now to work his wonders before them? More than one writer held his aching head when he speculated on all Roy might have accomplished had he come into the game at twenty.

The exception was of course Mercy, who continued to concern himself with Roy's past rather than his accomplishments. He spent hours in the morgue, trying to dredge up possible clues to possible crimes (What's he hiding from me?), wrote for information to prison wardens, sheriffs, county truant officers, heads of orphan asylums, and semipro managers in many cities in the West and Northwest, and by offering rewards, spurred all sorts of research on Roy by small-town sportswriters. His efforts proved fruitless until one day, to his surprise, he got a letter from a man who block printed on a sheet of notebook paper that for two hundred bucks he might be tempted to tell a thing or two about the new champ. Max hastily promised the dough and got his first break. Here was an old sideshow freak who swore that Roy had worked as a clown in a small traveling carnival. For proof he sent a poster showing the clown's face—in his white and red warpaint—bursting through a paper hoop. Roy was recognizable as the snubnose Bobo, who despite the painted laugh on his pan, seemed sadeyed and unhappy. Certain the picture would create a sensation, Max had it printed on the first page above the legend, "Roy Hobbs, Clown Prince of Baseball," but most of those who bought the paper refused to believe it was Roy and those who did, didn't give a hoot.

Roy was burned about the picture and vowed to kick the blabbermouth in the teeth. But he didn't exactly do that, for when they met the next evening, in the Midtown lobby, Max made a handsome apology. He said he had to hand it to Roy for beating everybody else in the game ten different ways, and he was sorry about the picture. Roy nodded but didn't show up on time at the chophouse down the block, where he was awaited by Pop, Red, and Max—to Pop's uneasiness, because Roy was prompt for his meals these days.

The waiter, a heavyset German with a schmaltzy accent and handlebar mustaches, approached for their orders. He started the meal by spilling soup on Max's back, then serving him a steak that looked like the charcoal it had been broiled on. When Max loudly complained he brought him, after fifteen minutes, another, a bleeding beauty, but this the waiter snatched from under the columnist's knife because he had already collected Pop's and Red's finished plates and wanted the third. Max let out a yawp, the frightened waiter dropped the dishes on his lap, and while stooping to collect the pieces, lurched against the table and spilled Max's beer all over his pants.

Pop sprang up and took an angry swipe at the man but Red hauled him down. Meanwhile the waiter was trying to wipe Max's pants with a wet towel and Max was swearing bloody murder at him. This got the waiter sore. Seizing the columnist by his coat collar he shook him and said he would teach him to talk like a "shentleman und nod a slob." He laid Max across his knee, and as the customers in the chophouse looked on in disbelief, smacked his rear with a heavy hand. Max managed to twist himself free. Slapping frantically at the German's face, he knocked off his mustache. In a minute everybody in the place was shrieking with laughter, and even Pop had to smile though he said to Red he was not at all surprised it had turned out to be Roy.

Roy had a Saturday date with Memo coming up but he was lonely for her that night so he went up to the fourth floor and rang her buzzer. She opened the door, dressed in black lounging pajamas with a black ribbon tied around her horsetail of red hair, which had a stunning effect on him.

Memo's face lit in a slow blush. "Why, Roy," she said, and seemed not to know what else to say.

"Shut the door," came a man's annoyed voice from inside, "or I might catch a cold."

"Gus is here," Memo quickly explained. "Come on in."

Roy entered, greatly disappointed.

Memo lived in a large and airy one-room apartment with a kitchenette, and a Murphy bed out of sight. Gus Sands, smoking a Between-the-Acts little cigar, was sitting at a table near the curtained window, examining a hand of double solitaire he and Memo had been playing. His coat was hanging on the chair and a hand-painted tie that Roy didn't like, showing a naked lady dancing with a red

171

rose, hung like a tongue out of his unbuttoned vest, over a heavy gold watch chain.

Seeing who it was, Gus said, "Welcome home, slugger. I see you have climbed out of the hole that you were in."

"I suppose it cost you a couple of bucks," said Roy.

Gus was forced to laugh. He had extended his hand but Roy didn't shake. Memo glanced at Roy as if to say be nice to Gus.

Roy couldn't get rid of his irritation that he had found Gus here, and he felt doubly annoyed that she was still seeing him. He had heard nothing from her about Gus and had hoped the bookie was out of the picture, but here he was as shifty-eyed as ever. What she saw in this half-bald apology for a cigar store Indian had him beat, yet he was conscious of a fear in his chest that maybe Gus meant more to her than he had guessed. The thought of them sitting peacefully together playing cards gave him the uneasy feeling they might even be married or something. But that couldn't be because it didn't make sense. In the first place why would she marry a freak like Gus? Sure he had the bucks but Memo was a hot kid and she couldn't take them to bed with her. And how could she stand what he looked like in the morning without the glass eye in the slot? In the second place Gus wouldn't let *his* wife walk around without a potato-sized diamond, and the only piece of jewelry Memo wore was a ring with a small jade stone. Besides, what would they be doing here in this one-room box when Gus owned a penthouse apartment on Central Park West?

No. He blamed these fantastic thoughts on the fact that he was still not sure of her. And he kept wishing he could have her to himself tonight. Memo caught on because, when he looked at her, she shrugged.

Gus got suspicious. He stared at them with the baleful eye, the glass one frosty.

They were sitting around uncomfortably until Memo suggested they play cards. Gus cheered up at once.

"What'll it be, slugger?" he said, collecting the cards.

"Pinochle is the game for three."

"I hate pinochle," Memo said. "Let's play poker but not the open kind."

"Poker is not wise now," Gus said. "The one in the middle gets squeezed. Anybody like to shoot crap?"

He brought forth a pair of green dominoes. Roy said he was agreeable and Memo nodded. Gus wanted to roll on the table but Roy said the rug was better, with the dice bouncing against the wall.

They moved the table and squatted on the floor. Memo, kneeling, rolled first. Gus told her to fade high and in a few minutes she picked up two hundred dollars. Roy hit snake eyes right off, then sevened out after that. Gus shot, teasing Roy to cover the three one hundred dollar bills he had put down. Memo took twenty-five of it and Roy had the rest. Gus made his point and on the next roll took another two hundred from Roy. That was more than he was carrying in cash but Gus said he could play the rest of the game on credit. The bookie continued to roll passes. In no time he was twelve hundred in on Roy, not counting the cash he had lost. Roy was irritated because he didn't like to lose to Gus in front of Memo. He watched Gus's hands to make sure he wasn't palming another pair of dice. What made him suspicious was that Gus seemed to be uncomfortable. His glass eye was fastened on the dice but the good one roamed restlessly about. And he was now fading three hundred a throw and sidebetting high. Since Memo was taking only a ten spot here and there, Roy was covering the rest. By the end of Gus's second streak Roy was thirty-five hundred behind and his underwear was sweating. Gus finally went out, Memo quickly lost, then Roy, to his surprise, started off on a string of

173

passes. Now he was hot and rolled the cubes for a long haul, growing merrier by the minute as Gus grew glummer. Before Roy was through, Gus had returned the cash he had taken from him and owed him eleven hundred besides. When Roy finally hit seven, Memo got up and said she had to make coffee. Gus and Roy played on but Roy was still the lucky one. Gus said that dice ought never to be played with less than four and gave up in disgust. He dusted off his knees.

"You sure had luck in your pants tonight, slugger."

"Some call it that."

Memo added the figures. She owed Roy two ten but Gus owed him twenty-one hundred. Roy laughed out loud.

Gus wrote out a check, his eye still restless.

Memo said she would write one too.

"Forget it," Roy said.

"I have covered hers in mine," said Gus, circling his pen around before signing.

Memo flushed. "I like to pay my own way."

Gus tore up the check and wrote another. Seeing how she felt about it, Roy took Memo's, figuring he would return it in the form of some present or other.

Gus handed him a check for the twenty-one hundred. "Chicken feed," he said.

Roy gave the paper a loud smack with his lips. "I love it."

Gus dropped his guard and pinned his restless eye on Roy. "Say the word, slugger, and you can make yourself a nice pile of dough quick."

Roy wasn't sure he had heard right. Gus repeated the offer.

This time Roy was sure. "Say it again and I will spit in your good eye."

Gus's grayish complexion turned blue.

"Boys," Memo said uneasily.

Gus stalked into the bathroom.

Memo's face was pale. "Help me with the sandwiches, Roy."

"Did you hear what that bastard said to me?"

"Sometimes he talks through his hat."

"Why do you invite him here?"

She turned away. "He invited himself."

As she was slicing meat for the sandwiches Roy felt tender toward her. He slipped his arm around her waist. She looked up a little unhappily but when he kissed her she kissed back. They broke apart as Gus unlocked the bathroom door and came out glaring at them.

While they were all drinking coffee Roy was in good spirits and no longer minded that Gus was around. Memo kidded him about the way he wolfed the sandwiches, but she showed her affection by also serving him half a cold chicken which he picked to the bone. He demolished a large slab of chocolate cake and made a mental note for a hamburger or two before he went to bed. Though Gus had only had a cup of coffee he was thoughtfully picking his teeth. After a while he looked at his gold watch, buttoned his vest, and said he was going. Roy glanced at Memo but she yawned and said she had to get up very very early in the morning.

To everybody's disgust the Reds, as if contemptuous of the bums who had so long lived in the basement below them, snapped the Knights' streak at seventeen and the next day again beat them over a barrel. A great groan went up from the faithful. Stand back everybody, here they go again. Timber! As if by magic, attendance for a single game with the Phils sank to a handful. The Phils gave them another spanking. The press tipped their hats and turned their respectful attention to the Pirates, pointing out again how superb they were. It was beyond everybody how the half-baked Knights could ever hope to win the N.L. pennant. With twenty-one games left to play they were six behind the Pirates and four in back of the Phils. And to make matters worse, they'd fallen into a third-place tie with the Cards. Pop's boys still retained a mathematical chance all right but they were at best a first-rate third-place team, one writer put it, and ended his piece, "Wait till next year."

Pop held his suffering head. The players stole guilty looks at one another. Even the Great Man himself was in a rut, though not exactly a slump. Still, he was held by inferior pitching to three constipated singles in three days. Everyone on the team was conscious something drastic had to be done but none could say what. Time was after them with a bludgeon. Any game they lost was the last to lose. It was autumn almost. They saw leaves falling and shivered at the thought of the barren winds of winter.

The Pirates blew into town for their last games of the year with the Knights, a series of four. Thus far during the season they had trounced the Knights a fantastic 15-3 and despite the loss of their last three to the Knights (fool's luck) were prepared to blast them out of their field. Watching the way the Pirates cut up the pea patch with their merciless hitting and precision fielding, the New Yorkers grew more dejected. Here was a team that was really a team, not a Rube Goldberg contraption. Every man jack was a fine player and no one guy outstanding. The Knights' fans were embarrassed . . . Yet their boys managed to tease the first away from the Pirates. No one quite knew how, here a lucky bingle, there a lucky error. Opposite the first-place slickers they looked like hayseeds yet the harvest was theirs. But tomorrow was another day. Wait'll the boys from the smoky city had got the stiffness of the train ride out of their legs. Yet the Knights won again in the same inept way. Their own rooters, seeping back into the stands, whistled and cheered. By some freak of nature they took the third too. The last game was sold out before 10 A.M. Again the cops had trouble with the ticketless hordes that descended on them.

Walt Wickitt, the peerless Pirate manager, pitched his ace hurler, Dutch Vogelman, in that last game. Vogelman was a terrific pitcher, a twenty-three game winner, the only specimen in either league that season. He was poison to the Knights who had beat him only once in the past two years. Facing Roy in some six games, he had held him to a single in four, and crippled him altogether in the last two, during Roy's slump. Most everyone kissed this game goodbye, although Roy started with a homer his first time up. Schultz then gave up two runs to the Pirates. Roy hit another round tripper. Schultz made it three for the Pirates. Roy ended by slamming two more homers and that did it, 4-3. High and mighty to begin with, Vogelman looked like a drowned dog at the end, and the Pirates hurriedly packed their duffel bags and slunk out of the stadium. The Phils were now in first place by a game, the Pirates second, and the Knights were one behind them and coming up like a rocket. Again pennant fever raged through the city and there was cheering in the streets.

Now all that was left for the Knights in this nerve-racking race were four games in Brooklyn, including a Sunday double header, four with Boston and two more with the Reds, these at home. Then three away with the Phils, one of which was the playoff of the washed-out game in June when Roy had knocked the cover off the ball. Their schedule called for the wind-up in the last week of September, against the Reds in another three-game tilt at home, a soft finish, considering the fact that the Pirates and Phils had each other to contend with. If, God willing, the Knights made it (and were still functioning), the World

Series was scheduled to begin on Tuesday, October first, at the Yankee Stadium, for the Yanks had already cinched the American League pennant.

The race went touch and go. To begin with the Knights dropped a squeaker (Roy went absolutely hitless) to the Dodgers as the Pirates won and the Phils lost—both now running neck and neck for first, the Knights two behind. Just as the boys were again despairing of themselves, Roy got after the ball again. He did not let on to anyone, but he had undergone a terrible day after his slaughter of the Pirates, a day of great physical weakness, a strange draining of strength from his arms and legs, followed by a splitting headache that whooshed in his ears. However, in the second game at Ebbets Field, he took hold of himself, gripped Wonderboy, and bashed the first pitch into the clock on the right field wall. The clock spattered minutes all over the place, and after that the Dodgers never knew what time it was. All they knew was that Roy Hobbs collected a phenomenal fourteen straight hits that shot them dead three times. Carried on by the momentum, the Knights ripped the Braves and brutally trounced the Reds, taking revenge on them for having ended their recent streak of seventeen.

With only six games to play, a triple first-place tie resulted. The Knights' fans beat themselves delirious, and it became almost unbearable when the Phils lost a heartbreaker to the Cards and dropped into second place, leaving the Pirates and Knights in the tie. Before the Phils could recover, the Knights descended upon Shibe Park, followed by wild trainloads of fans who had to be there to see. They saw their loveboys take the crucial playoff (Roy was terrific), squeak through the second game (he had a poor day), and thoroughly wipe the stunned Phils off the map in the last (again stupendous). At this point of highest

178

tension the Pirate mechanism burst. To the insane cheering of the population of the City of New York, the Cubs pounded them twice, and the Reds came in with a surprise haymaker. A pall of silence descended upon Pennsylvania. Then a roar rose in Manhattan and leaped across the country. When the shouting stopped the Knights were undeniably on top by three over the Pirates, the Phils third by one more, and therefore mathematically out of the race. With three last ones to play against the lowly Reds, the Knights looked *in*. The worst that could possibly happen to them was a first-place tie with the Pirates—if the Pirates won their three from the Phils as the Knights lost theirs to the Reds—a fantastic impossibility the way Roy was mauling them.

The ride home from Philadelphia usually took a little more than an hour but it was a bughouse nightmare because of the way the fans on the train pummeled the players. Hearing that a mob had gathered at Penn Station to welcome the team, Pop ordered everyone off at Newark and into cabs. But as they approached the tunnel they were greeted by a deafening roar as every craft in the Hudson, and all the way down the bay, opened up with whistles and foghorns . . .

In their locker room after the last game at Philly, some of the boys had started chucking wet towels around but Pop, who had privately wept tears of joy, put the squelch on that.

"Cut out all that danged foolishness when we still need one more to win," he had sternly yelled.

When they protested that it looked at last that they were in, he turned lobster red and bellowed did they want to jinx themselves and cook their own gooses? As a result, despite all the attention they were receiving, the boys were a glum bunch going home. Some had secretly

179

talked of celebrating once they had ditched the old fuss-
pot but they were afraid to. Even Roy had fallen into
low spirits, only he was thinking of Memo.

His heart ached the way he yearned for her (sometimes
seeing her in a house they had bought, with a redheaded
baby on her lap, and himself going fishing in a way that
made it satisfying to fish, knowing that everything was all
right behind him, and the home-cooked meal would be
hot and plentiful, and the kid would carry the name of
Roy Hobbs into generations his old man would never
know. With this in mind he fished the stream in peace
and later, sitting around the supper table, they ate the
fish he had caught), yearning so deep that the depth ran
through ever since he could remember, remembering the
countless things he had wanted and missed out on, wondering, now that he was famous, if the intensity of his
desires would ever go down. The only way that could happen (he relived that time in bed with her) was to have her
always. That would end the dissatisfactions that ate him,
no matter how great were his triumphs, and made his life
still wanting and not having.

It later struck him that the picture he had drawn of
Memo sitting domestically home wasn't exactly the girl
she was. The kind he had in mind, though it bothered
him to admit it, was more like Iris seemed to be, only
she didn't suit him. Yet he could not help but wonder
what was in her letter and he made up his mind he would
read it once he got back in his room. Not that he would
bother to answer, but he ought at least to know what
she said.

He felt better, at the hotel, to find a note from Memo
in his mailbox, saying to come up and celebrate with a
drink. She greeted him at the door with a fresh kiss, her
face flushed with how glad she was, saying, "Well, Roy,

you've really done it. Everybody is talking about what a wonderful marvel you are."

"We still got this last one to take," he said modestly, though tickled at her praise. "I am not counting my onions till that."

"Oh, the Knights are sure to win. All the papers are saying it all depends what you do. You're the big boy, Roy."

He grabbed both her palms. "Bigger than Bump?"

Her eyelids fluttered but she said yes.

He pulled her close. She kissed for kiss with her warm wet mouth. Now is the time, he thought. Backing her against the wall, he slowly rubbed his hand up between her thighs.

She broke away, breathing heavily. He caught her and pressed his lips against her nippled blouse.

There were tears in her eyes.

He groaned, "Honey, we are the ones that are alive, not him."

"Don't say his name."

"You will forget him when I love you."

"Please let's not talk."

He lifted her in his arms and laid her down on the couch. She sat bolt upright.

"For Christ sakes, Memo, I am a grown guy and not a kid. When are you gonna be nice to me?"

"I am, Roy."

"Not the way I want it."

"I will." She was breathing quietly now.

"When?" he demanded.

She thought, distracted, then said, "Tomorrow—tomorrow night."

"That's too long."

"Later." She sighed, "Tonight."

"You are my sugar honey." He kissed her.

Her mood quickly changed. "Come on, let's celebrate."

"Celebrate what?"

"About the team."

Surprised she wanted to do that now, he said he was shaved and ready to go.

"I don't mean to go out." What she meant, she explained, was that she had prepared a snack in one of the party rooms upstairs. "They're bringing it all up from the kitchen—a buffet with cold meats and lots of other things. I thought it'd be fun to get some girls together with the boys and all enjoy ourselves."

Though he had on his mind what he was going to do to her later, and anything in between was a waste of time, still she had gone to all the trouble, and he wanted to please her. Nor was the mention of food exactly distasteful to him. He had made a double steak disappear on the train, but that was hours ago.

Memo served him a drink and finished telephoning the men she couldn't reach before. Though on the whole the players said they wanted to come, some, still remembering Pop, were doubtful they ought to, but Memo convinced them by saying that Roy and others were coming. She didn't ask the married players to bring their wives and they didn't mention the oversight to her.

At ten o'clock Memo went into the bathroom and put on a flaming yellow strapless gown. Roy got the idea that she was wearing nothing underneath and it gave him a tense pleasure. They rode up to the eighteenth floor. The party was already on. There were about a dozen men around but only four or five girls. Memo said more were coming later. Most of the players did not exactly look happy. A few were self-consciously talking to the girls, and the others were sitting on chairs gabbing among themselves. Flores stood in a corner with a melancholy expression on his phiz. Al Fowler, one of those having himself a fine time, called to him when was the wake.

Someone was pounding the keys of the upright piano against the wall. On the other side of the room, a brisk, pint-size chef with a tall puffed cap on, half again as big as him, stood behind a long, cloth-covered table, dishing out the delicatessen.

"Sure is some snack," Roy marveled. "You must've hocked your fur coat."

"Gus chipped in," Memo said absently.

He was immediately annoyed. "Is that ape coming up here?"

She looked hurt. "Don't call him dirty names. He is a fine, generous guy."

"Two bits he had the grub poisoned."

"That's not funny." Memo walked away but Roy went after her and apologized, though her concern for the bookie—even on the night they were going to sleep together—unsettled and irritated him. Furthermore, he was now worried how Pop would take it if he found out about the players at this shindig despite his warning against celebrating too soon.

He asked Memo if the manager knew what was going on.

She was sweet again. "Don't worry about him, Roy. I'd've invited him but he wouldn't fit in at all here because we are all young people. Don't get anxious about the party, because Gus said not to serve any hard liquor."

"Nice kid, Gus. Must be laying his paper on us for a change."

Memo made no reply.

Everybody was there by then. Dave Olson had a cheerful blonde on his arm. Allie, Lajong, Hinkle, and Hill were harmonizing "Down by the Old Mill Stream."

Fowler was showing some of the boys how to do a buck and wing. The cigar smoke was thick. To Roy things did still not sit just right. Everybody was watching everybody else, as if they were all waiting for a signal to get up and leave, and some of the players looked up nervously every time the door opened, as if they were expecting Doc Knobb, who used to hypnotize them before the games. Flores, from across the room, stared at Roy with black, mournful eyes, but Roy turned away. He couldn't walk out on Memo.

"Some blowout," Fowler said to him.

"Watch yourself, kid," Roy warned him in an undertone.

"Watch yourself yourself."

Roy threw him a hard look but Memo said, "Just let Roy head over to the table. He is dying for a bite."

It was true. Though the thought of having her to-night was on the top of his mind, he could not entirely forget the appetizing food. She led him to the table and he was surprised and slightly trembly at all there was of it—different kinds of delicatessen meat, appetizing fish, shrimp, crab and lobster, also caviar, salads, cheeses of all sorts, bread, rolls, and three flavors of ice cream. It made his belly ache, as if it had an existence apart from himself.

"What'll it be?" said the little chef. He had a large fork and plate poised but Roy took them from him, to his annoyance, and said he would fix what he wanted himself.

Memo helped. "Don't be stingy, Roy."

"Pile it on, honey."

"You sure are a scream the way you eat."

"I am a picnic." He kidded to ease the embarrassment his appetite caused him.

"Bump liked to shovel it down—" She caught herself.

After his plate was loaded, Memo placed a slice of ham and a roll on her own and they sat at a table in the far

184

corner of the room—away from where Flores was standing—so Roy could concentrate on the food without having to bother with anybody.

Memo watched him, fascinated. She shredded the ham
on her plate and nibbled on a roll.

"That all you're eating?" he asked.

"I guess I haven't got much appetite."

He was gobbling it down and it gave him a feeling of
both having something and wanting it the same minute
he was having it. And every mouthful seemed to have the
effect of increasing his desire for her. He thought how
satisfying it would be to lift that yellow dress over her bare
thighs.

Roy didn't realize it till she mentioned it that his plate
was empty. "Let me get you some more, hon."

"I will get it myself."

"Food is a woman's work." She took his plate to the
table and the busy little chef heaped it high with corned
beef, pastrami, turkey, potato salad, cheese, and pickles.

"You sure are nice to me," he said.

"You are a nice guy."

"Why did you get so much of it?"

"It's good for you, silly."

Roy laughed. "You sound like my grandma."

Memo was interested. "Weren't you brought up in an
orphans' home, Roy?"

"I went there after grandma died."

"Didn't you ever live with your mother?"

He was suddenly thoughtful. "Seven years."

"What was she like? Do you remember?"

"A whore. She spoiled my old man's life. He was a good
guy but died young."

A group of girls flocked through the door and Memo
hastily excused herself. They were her showgirl friends

from a Broadway musical that had just let out. She welcomed them and introduced them around. Dancing started and the party got livelier.

Roy polished his plate with a crust of bread. He felt as if he had hardly eaten anything—it was sliced so thin you could hardly chew your teeth into it.

Memo returned. "How about having something different now?" But Roy said no and got up. "Lemme say hello to some of the gals that came in."

"You are all alike." He thought she sounded jealous and it was all right if she was. The girls she brought him around to were tickled to meet him. They felt his muscles and wanted to know how he belted the ball so hard.

"Clean living," Roy told them.

The girls laughed out loud. He looked them over. The best of the bunch was a slightly chubby one with an appealing face, but in her body she did not compare to Memo.

When he told Memo she had more of what it took than the rest of them put together, she giggled nervously. He looked at her and felt she was different tonight in a way he could not figure out. He worried about Gus, but then he thought that after tonight he would be getting it steady, and then he would tell her he did not want that glass-eye monkey tailing her around.

Memo led him back to the table. She pointed out what she wanted for Roy and the chef ladled it into the plate. Her own came back with a slice of ham and a roll on it. He followed her to the corner table. He wondered if Flores was still standing in the opposite corner, watching, but he didn't look.

Gazing at the mountain of stuff Memo handed him, he said, "I am getting tired of eating."

Memo had returned to the subject of his mother. "But didn't you love her, Roy?"

He stared at her through one eye. "Who wants to know?"

"Just me."

"I don't remember." He helped himself to a forkful of food. "No."

"Didn't she love you?"

"She didn't love anybody."

Memo said, "Let's try some new combinations with the buffet. Sometimes when you eat things that you didn't know could mix together but they do, you satisfy your appetite all at once. Now let's mix this lobster meat with hidden treats of anchovies, and here we will lay it on this tasty pumpernickel and spread Greek salad over it, then smear this other slice of bread with nice sharp cheese and put it on top of the rest."

"All it needs now is a shovel of manure and a forest will grow out of it."

"Now don't be dirty, Roy."

"It looks like it could blow a man apart."

"All the food is very fresh."

After making the sandwich she went to the ladies' room. He felt depressed. Now why the hell did she have to go and ask him questions about his old lady? Thinking about her, he chewed on the sandwich. With the help of three bottles of lemon pop he downed it but had to guzzle three more of lime to get rid of the artificial lemon taste. He felt a little drunk and snickered because it was a food and pop drunk. He had the odd feeling he was down on his hands and knees searching for something that he couldn't find.

Flores stood at the table.

"If you tell them to go home," he hissed, "they weel."

Roy stared. "Tell who?"

"The players. They are afraid to stay here but they don't go because you stay."

"Go ahead and tell them to go."

"You tell them," Flores urged. "They weel leesten to your word."

"Right," said Roy.

Memo returned and Flores left him. Roy struggled to his feet, broke into a sweat, and sat down again. Fowler grabbed Memo and they whirled around. Roy didn't like them pressed so close together.

His face was damp. He reached into his pocket for a handkerchief and felt Iris' letter. For a second he thought he had found what he was looking for. More clearly than ever he remembered her pretty face and the brown eyes you could look into and see yourself as something more satisfying than you were, and he remembered telling her everything, the first time he had ever told anybody about it, and the relieved feeling he had afterward, and the long swim and Iris swimming down in the moonlit water searching for him, and the fire on the beach, she naked, and finally him banging her. For some reason this was the only thing he was ashamed of, though it couldn't be said she hadn't asked for it.

Fat girls write fat letters, he thought, and then he saw the little chef looking at him and was astonished at how hungry he felt.

Roy pushed himself up and headed for the table. The chef shined up a fast plate and with delight lifted the serving fork.

"I've had a snootful," Roy said.

The chef tittered. "It's all fresh food."

Roy looked into his button eyes. They were small pig's eyes. "Who says so?"

"It's the best there is."

"It stinks." He turned and walked stiffly to the door. Memo saw him. She waved gaily and kept on dancing.

He dragged his belly through the hall. When the elevator

came it dropped him down in the lobby. He went along the corridor into the grill room. Carefully sitting down at the table, he ordered six hamburgers and two tall glasses of milk—clean food to kill the pangs of hunger.

The waiter told the cook the order, who got six red meat patties out of the refrigerator and pressed them on the grill. They softly sputtered. He thought he oughtn't to eat any more, but then he thought I am hungry. No, I am not hungry, I am hungry, whatever that means . . . What must I do not to be hungry? He considered fasting but he hadn't fasted since he was a kid. Besides, it made him hungry. He tried hard to recapture how it felt when he was hungry after a day of fishing and was sizzling lake bass over an open fire and boiling coffee in a tin can. All around his head were the sharp-pointed stars.

He was about to lift himself out of the chair but remembered his date with Memo and stayed put. There was time to kill before that so he might as well have a bite.

A hand whacked him across the shoulders.

It was Red Blow . . . Roy slowly sat down.

"Looked for a minute like you were gonna murder me," said Red.

"I thought it was somebody else."

"Who, for instance?"

Roy thought. "I am not sure. Maybe the Mex."

"Flores?"

"Sometimes he gets on my nerves."

"He is really a nice guy."

"I guess so."

Red sat down. "Don't eat too much crap. We have a big day comin' up."

"I am just taking a bite."

"Better get to bed and have plenty of sleep."

"Yes."

Red looked glum. "Can't sleep myself. Don't know

what's the matter with me." He yawned and twitched his shoulders. "You all right?"

"Fine and dandy. Have a hamburger."

"Not for me, thanks. Guess I will go for a little walk. Best thing when you can't sleep."

Roy nodded.

"Take care of yourself, feller. Tomorrow's our day. Pop'll dance a jig after tomorrow. You'll be his hero."

Roy didn't answer.

Red smiled a little sadly. "I'm gonna be sorry when it's over."

The waiter brought the six hamburgers. Red looked at them absently. "It's all up to you." He got up and left.

Through the window Roy watched him go down the street.

"I'll be the hero."

The hamburgers looked like six dead birds. He took up the first one and gobbled it down. It was warm but dry. No more dead birds, he thought . . . not without ketch- up. He poured a blop on three of the birds. Then he shuffled them up with the other two so as not to know which three had the ketchup and which two hadn't. Eating them, he could not tell the difference except that they all tasted like dead birds. They were not satisfying but the milk was. He made a mental note to drink more milk.

He paid and left. The elevator went up like a greased shot. As it stopped he felt a ripping pain on the floor of the stomach. The wax-faced elevator man watched him with big eyes. He stared at the old scarecrow, then stumbled out. He stood alone in the hall, trying to figure it out. Something was happening that he didn't understand. He roused himself to do battle, wishing for Wonderboy, but no enemy was visible. He rested and the pain left him.

The party was quiet. Flores had disappeared. The lights were dimmed and there was some preliminary sex work going on. Olson had his blonde backed into a corner. A group near the piano were passing a secret bottle around. In the center of the darkened room one of the girls held her dress over her pink panties and was doing bumps and grinds. A silent circle watched her.

Roy buttonholed Fowler. "Stay off the rotgut, kid."

"Stay away from the stuffin's, big shot."

Roy swiped at him but Fowler was gone. He wiped his sweaty face with his sleeve and searched for Memo to tell her it was time. He couldn't find her in the fog that had blown up, so he left the party and reeled down the stairs to the fourth floor. Feeling for her buzzer, he found the key left in the lock and softly turned it.

She was lying naked in bed, chewing a turkey drumstick as she looked at the pictures in a large scrapbook. Not till he was quite close did she see him. She let out a scream.

"You frightened me, Roy." Memo shut the scrapbook.

He had caught a glimpse of Bump's face. I'll take care of that bastard. He unzipped his fly.

Her green eyes closely watched him, her belly heaving above the red flame.

Undressing caused him great distress. Inside him they were tearing up a street. The sweat dripped from his face . . . Yet there was music, the sweetest piping he had ever heard. Dropping his pants he approached for the piping fulfillment.

She drew her legs back. Her expression puzzled him. It was not—the lights were wavering, blinking on and off. A thundering locomotive roared through the mountain. As it burst out of the rock with a whistle howl he felt on the verge of an extraordinary insight, but a bolt of shuddering lightning came at him from some unknown place. He threw up his arms for protection and it socked him, yowling, in the shattered gut. He lived a pain he could not believe existed. Agonized at the extent of it, Roy thudded

191

to his knees as a picture he had long carried in his mind broke into pieces. He keeled over.

The raft with the singing green-eyed siren guarding the forbidden flame gave off into the rotting flood a scuttering one-eyed rat. In the distance though quite near, a toilet flushed, and though the hero braced himself against it, a rush of dirty water got a good grip and sucked him under.

Judge Banner had a money-saving contract with a small maternity hospital near Knights Field (it was there Bump had died) to treat all player emergencies, so that was where they had rushed Roy. The flustered obstetrician on duty decided to deliver the hero of his appendix. However, he fought them deliriously and his strength was too much for the surgeon, anesthetist, attendant, and two mild maternity nurses. They subdued him with a hypo only to uncover a scar snaking down his belly. Investigation showed he had no appendix—it had long ago been removed along with some other stuff. (All were surprised at his scarred and battered body.) The doctors considered cutting out the gall bladder or maybe part of the stomach but nobody wanted to be responsible for the effect of the operation upon the Knights and the general public. (The city was aghast. Crowds gathered outside the hospital, waiting for bulletins. The Japanese government issued an Edict of Sorrow.) So they used the stomach pump instead and dredged up unbelievable quantities of bilge. The patient moaned along with the ladies in labor on the floor, but the doctors adopted a policy of watchful waiting and held off anything drastic.

His belly racked his mind. Icy streams coursed through the fiery desert. He chattered and steamed, rarely conscious, tormented by his dreams. In them he waxed to gigantic heights then abruptly fell miles to be a little Roy dwarf (Hey, mister, you're stepping on my feet). He was caught in roaring gales amid loose, glaring lights, so bright they smothered the eyeballs. Iris' sad head topped Memo's dancing body, with Memo's vice versa upon the shimmying rest of Iris, a confused fusion that dizzied him. He hungered in nightmare for quantities of exotic food— wondrous fowl stuffed with fruit, and the multitudinous roe of tropical fish. When he bent his toothy head to devour, every last morsel vanished. So they served him a prime hunk of beef and he found it enormously delicious only to discover it was himself he was chewing. His thunderous roars sent nurses running from all directions. They were powerless before his flailing fists.

In delirium he hopped out of bed and hunted through the corridors in a nightgown—frightening the newly delivered mothers—for a mop or broom that he snatched back to his aseptic chamber and practiced vicious cuts with before the dresser mirror . . . They found him on the floor . . . At dawn he warily rose and ferreted a plumber's plunger out of the utility closet but this time he was caught by three attendants and dragged back to bed. They strapped him down and there he lay a prisoner, as the frightened Knights dropped the third of three hot potatoes to the scarred and embittered last-place Reds. Since the resurgent Pirates had scattered the brains of the Phils, three in a bloody row, the season ended in a dead heat. A single playoff game in Knights Field was arranged for Monday next, the day before the World Series.

Late that afternoon the fever abated. He returned, unstrapped, to consciousness and recognized a harried Memo at his bedside. From her he learned what had happened to the team, and groaned in anguish. When she left, with a hankie pressed to her reddened nostrils, he discovered his troubles had only just begun. The specialist in the case, a tall stoop-shouldered man with a white mustache and sad eyes, who absently hefted a heavy gold watch as he spoke, gave Roy a bill of particulars. He began almost merrily by telling him there wasn't much doubt he would participate in the Monday playoff (Roy just about leaped out of the bed but the doctor held him back with a gesture). He could play, yes, though he'd not feel at his best, nor would he be able to extend himself so far as he would like, but he would certainly be present and in the game, which, as the doctor understood it, was the big thing for both Roy and his public. (Interest in the matter was so great, he said, that he had permitted release of this news to the press.) Public clamor had compelled his reluctant yielding, though it was his considered opinion that, ideally, Roy ought to rest a good deal longer before getting back to his—ah—normal activities. But someone had explained to him that baseball players were in a way like soldiers, and since he knew that the body's response to duty sometimes achieved many of the good results of prolonged care and medication, he had agreed to let him play.

However, all good news has its counterpart of bad, he almost sadly said, and to prove the point let it come out that it would be best for Roy to say goodbye forever to baseball—if he hoped to stay alive. His blood pressure—at times amazingly high—complicated by an athlete's heart—could conceivably cause his sudden death if he were to attempt to play next season, whereas if he worked at something light and relaxing, one might say he could go on for years, as many had. The doctor slipped the gold watch into his vest pocket, and nodding to the patient, departed. Roy felt that this giant hand holding a club had broken through the clouds and with a single blow crushed his skull.

The hours that followed were the most terrifying of his life (more so than fifteen years ago). He lived in the thought of death, would not move, speak, take food or receive visitors. Yet all the while he fanatically fought the doctor's revelation, wrestled it every waking second, though something in him said the old boy with the white mustache was right. He felt he had for years suspected something wrong, and this was it. Too much pressure in the pipes— blew your conk off. (He saw it blown sky high.) He was through—finished. Only he couldn't—just couldn't believe it. Me. I. Roy Hobbs forever out of the game? Inconceivable. He thought of the fantastic hundreds of records he had broken in so short a time, which had made him a hero to the people, and he thought of the thousands—tens of thousands—that he had pledged himself to break. A moan escaped him.

Still a doubt existed. Maybe white mustache was wrong? They could misjudge them too. Maybe there was a mite less wind behind the ball than he thought, and it would hit the ground at his feet rather than land in the glove. Mistakes could happen in everything. Wouldn't be the first time a sawbones was wrong. *Maybe he was a hundred per cent dead wrong.*

The next evening, amid a procession of fathers leaving the hospital at baby-feeding time, he sneaked out of the building. A cab got him to Knights Field, and Happy

Pellers, the astonished groundskeeper, let him in. A phone call brought Dizzy to the scene. Roy changed into uniform (he almost wept to behold Wonderboy so forlorn in the locker) and Happy donned catcher's gear. Dizzy prepared to pitch. It was just to practice, Roy said, so he would have his eye and timing alert for the playoff Monday. Happy switched on the night floods to make things clearer. Dizzy practiced a few pitches and then with Roy standing at the plate, served one over the middle. As he swung, Roy felt a jet of steam blow through the center of his skull. They gathered him up, bundled him into a cab, and got him back to the hospital, where nobody had missed him.

It was a storm on and Roy out in it. Not exactly true, it was Sam Simpson who was lost and Roy outsearching him. He tracked up and down the hills, leaving his white tracks, till he come to this shack with the white on the roof.

Anybody in here? he calls.

Nope.

You don't know my friend Sam?

Nope.

He wept and try to go away.

Come on in, kiddo, I was only foolin'.

Roy dry his eyes and went in. Sam was settin' at the table under the open bulb, his collar and tie off, playing solitaire with all spades.

Roy sit by the fire till Sam finish. Sam looked up wearing his half-moon specs, glinting moonlight.

Well, son, said Sam, lightin' up on his cigar.

I swear I didn't do it, Sam.

Didn't do what?

Didn't do nothin'.

Who said you did?

Roy wouldn't answer, shut tight as a clam.

Sam stayed awhile, then he say to Roy, Take my advice, kiddo.

Yes, Sam.

Don't do it.

No, said Roy, I won't. He rose and stood headbent before Sam's chair.

Let's go back home, Sam, let's now.

Sam peered out the window.

I would like to, kiddo, honest, but we can't go out there now. Heck, it's snowin' baseballs.

When he came to, Roy made the specialist promise to tell no one about his condition just in case he had the slightest chance of improving enough to play for maybe another season. The specialist frankly said he didn't see that chance, but he was willing to keep mum because he believed in the principle of freedom of action. So he told no one and neither did Roy—not even Memo. (No one had even mentioned the subject of his playing in the Series but Roy had already privately decided to take his chances in that.)

But mostly his thoughts were dismal. That frightened feeling: bust before beginning. On the merry-go-round again about his failure to complete his mission in the game. About this he suffered most. He lay for hours staring at the window. Often the glass looked wet though it wasn't raining. A man who had been walking in bright sunshine limped away into a mist. This broke the heart . . . When the feeling passed, if it ever did, there was the necessity of making new choices. Since it was already the end of the season, he had about four months in which to cash in on testimonials, endorsements, ghost-written articles, personal appearances, and such like. But what after that, when spring training time came and he disappeared into the backwoods? He recalled a sickening procession of jobs

—as cook, well-driller, mechanic, logger, beanpicker, and for whatever odd change, semipro ballplayer. He dared not think further.

And the loneliness too, from job to job, never some place in particular for any decent length of time because of the dissatisfaction that grew, after a short while, out of anything he did . . . But supposing he could collect around twenty-five G's—could that amount, to begin with, satisfy a girl like Memo if she married him? He tried to think of ways of investing twenty-five thousand—maybe in a restaurant or tavern—to build it up to fifty, and then somehow to double that. His mind skipped from money to Memo, the only one who came to see him every day. He remembered the excitement he felt for her in that strapless yellow dress the night of the party. And bad as he felt now he couldn't help but think how desirable she had looked, waiting for him naked in bed.

Such thoughts occupied him much of the time as he sat in the armchair, thumbing through old magazines, or resting in bed. He sometimes considered suicide but the thought was too oppressive to stay long in his mind. He dozed a good deal and usually woke feeling lonely. (Except for Red, once, nobody from the team had come to see him, though small knots of fans still gathered in the street and argued whether he would really be in Monday's game.) Saturday night he awoke from an after supper nap more gloomy than ever, so he reached under his pillow for Iris' letter. But just then Memo came into the room with an armful of flowers so he gladly let it lay where it was.

Despite how attractive she usually managed to keep herself (he could appreciate that in spite of a momentary return of the nausea) she appeared worn out now, with bluish shadows under her eyes. And he noticed, as she stuffed the flowers and red autumn leaves into the vase, that she was wearing the same black dress she had worn all week, a thing she never did before, and that her hair was lusterless and not well kept. She had days ago sorrowed it was her fault that this had happened to the team. How stupid not to have waited just a day or two more. (Pop, she wept, had called her filthy names.) She had despaired every minute—really despaired—up to the time she heard he was going to be in the playoff. At least she did not have it on her conscience that he would be out of that, so she felt better now. Not better enough, he worried, or she wouldn't be so lost and lonely-looking.

After she had arranged the flowers, Memo stood mutely at the open window, gazing down into the darkening street. When he least expected it, she sobbed out in a voice full of misery, "Oh, Roy, I can't stand it any longer, I can't."

He sat up. "What's wrong?"

Her voice was choked. "I can't go on with my life as it is." Memo dropped into the armchair and began to weep. In a minute everything around her was wet.

Tossing aside the blanket he swung his legs out of bed. She looked up, attempting to smile. "Don't get up, hon. I'll be all right."

Roy sat uneasily at the edge of the bed. He never knew what to do when they cried.

"It's just that I'm fed up," she wept. "Fed up. Pop is terrible to me and I don't want to go on living off him, even if he is my uncle. I have to get a job or something, or go somewhere."

"What did that bastard shrimp say to you?"

She found a handkerchief in her purse and blew her nose.

"It isn't his words," she said sadly. "Words can't kill. It's that I'm sick of this kind of life. I want to get away."

Then she let go again and looked like a little lost bird beating around in a cage. He was moved, and hovered over her like an old maid aunt trying to stop a leak.

"Don't cry, Memo. Just say the word and I will take care of you." In a cracked voice he said, "Just marry me."

She sobbed for the longest time. So long he grew jumpy with doubts about their future relations, but then she stopped crying and said in a damp voice, "Would you have me, Roy?"

He swayed with emotion as he got out thickly, "Would I?" To keep from hitting the ground he hopped into bed and sprawled out.

She came to him, her white hands clasped, her wet eyelids like sparkling flowers. "There's one thing you have to understand, Roy, and then maybe you won't want me. That is that I am afraid to be poor." She said it with intensity, her face turning dark at her words. "Maybe I am weak or spoiled, but I am the type who has to have somebody who can support her in a decent way. I'm sick of living like a slave. I got to have a house of my own, a maid to help me with the hard work, a decent car to shop with and a fur coat for winter time when it's cold. I don't want to have to worry every time a can of beans jumps a nickel. I suppose it's wrong to want all of that but I can't help it. I've been around too long and seen too much. I saw how my mother lived and I know it killed her. I made up my mind to have certain things. You understand that, don't you, Roy?"

He nodded.

"We have to face it," she said. "You're thirty-five now and that don't give you much time left as a ball player."

"What d'ye mean?" he asked, deadpan.

But it wasn't his blood pressure she was referring to. For a minute he was afraid she had found out.

"I'm sorry to say this, Roy, but I have to be practical. Suppose the next one is your last season, or that you will have one more after that? Sure, you'll probably get a good contract till then but it costs money to live, and then what'll we do for the rest of our lives?"

It was dark in the room now. He could scarcely see her.

"Turn on the lights."

She smeared powder over her nose and under her eyes, then pressed the button.

He stared at her.

She grew restless. "Roy—"

"I was just thinking, even if I had to quit right now I could still scrounge up about twenty-five grand in the next few months. That's a lotta dough."

She seemed doubtful. "What would you do with it?"

"We'd get hitched and I would invest in a business. Everybody does that. My name is famous already. We will make out okay. You will have what you want."

"What kind of business?" Memo asked.

"I can't say for sure—maybe a restaurant."

She made a face.

"What do you have in mind?" Roy asked.

"Oh, something big, Roy. I would like you to buy into a company where you could have an executive job and won't have to go poking your nose into the stew in a smelly restaurant."

A jet of nausea shot up from his gizzard. He admitted to himself he wanted nothing to do with restaurants.

"How much dough do we need to get in on one of those big companies?"

"I should think more than twenty-five thousand."

He gulped. "Around thirty-five?"

"More like fifty."

Roy frowned. Talk of that kind of dough gave him a bellyache. But Memo was right. It had to be something big or it wouldn't pay back enough. And if it was a big company he could take it a little easy, to protect his health, without anybody kicking. He pondered where to get another twenty-five thousand, and it had to be before the start of the next baseball season because as soon as everybody saw he wasn't playing, it wouldn't be easy to cash in on his name. People had no use for a has-been. He had to be married and have the dough, both before next spring—in case he never did get to play. He thought of other means to earn some money fast—selling the story of his life to the papers, barnstorming a bit this fall and winter, not too strenuously. But neither of these things added up to much —not twenty-five grand. Roy lay back with his eyes shut.

Memo whispered something. His lids flew open. What was she doing with an old black dress on, her hair uncombed, looking like Lola, the Jersey City fortuneteller? Yet her voice was calm . . .

"Who sent you," he spoke harshly, "—that bastard Gus?"

She turned flame-faced but answered quietly, "The Judge."

"Banner?" Somebody inside of him—this nervous character lately hanging around—crashed a glass to the floor. Roy's pulses banged.

"He said he'd pay you fifteen thousand now and more next season. He says it would depend on you."

"I thought I smelled skunk."

"He asked me to deliver the message. I have nothing to do with it."

"Who else is in on this?"

"I don't know."

"Pop?"

"No."

He lay motionless for an age. She said no more, did not plead or prod. It grew late. An announcement was made for visitors to leave. She rose and tiredly put on her coat.

"I was thinking of all the years you would be out of the game."

"What does he want me to do?"

"It's something about the playoff—I don't know."

"They want me to drop it?"

She didn't answer.

"No," he said out loud.

She shrugged. "I told them you wouldn't."

She was thin and haggard-looking. Her shoulders drooped, her hands were bloodless. To refuse her just about broke his heart.

He fell into a deep slumber but had not slept very long before this rat-eyed vulture, black against the ceiling, began to flap around the room and dripping deep fat spiraled down toward his face. Wrestling together, they knocked over the tables and chairs, when the lights went on and waked him. Roy grabbed under the pillow for a gun he thought was there, only it wasn't. Awake, he saw through the glare that Judge Goodwill Banner, in dark glasses and hairy black fedora, was staring at him from the foot of the bed.

"What the hell do you want here?"

"Don't be alarmed," the Judge rumbled. "Miss Paris informed me you were not asleep, and the authorities granted me a few minutes to visit with you."

"I got nothing to say to you." The nightmare had weakened him. Not wanting the Judge to see that, he pulled himself into a sitting position.

The Judge, yellow-skinned in the electric light, and rumpled-looking, sat in the armchair with his potlike hat on. He sucked an unwilling flame into his King Oscar and tossed the burnt-out match on the floor.

"How is your health, young man?"

"Skip it. I am all right now."

The Judge scrutinized him.

"Wanna bet?" Roy said.

The Judge's rubbery lips tightened around his cigar. After a minute he removed it from his mouth and said cautiously, "I assume that Miss Paris has acquainted you with the terms of a certain proposal?"

"Leave her name out of it."

"An admirable suggestion—a proposal, you understand, made by persons unknown."

"Don't make me laugh. I got a good mind to sick the FBI on you."

The Judge examined his cigar. "I rely on your honor. You might consider, however, that there is no witness other than Miss Paris, and I assume you would be solicitous of her?"

"I said to leave her name out."

"Quite so. I believe she erred concerning the emolument offered—fifteen thousand, was it? My understanding is that twenty thousand, payable in cash in one sum, is closer to the correct amount. I'm sure you know the prevailing rate for this sort of thing is ten thousand dollars. We offer twice that. Any larger sum is unqualifiedly out of the question because it will impair the profitableness of the venture. I urge you to consider carefully. You know as well as I that you are in no condition to play."

"Then what are you offering me twenty thousand smackers for—to show your gratitude for how I have built up your bank account?"

"I see no reason for sarcasm. You were paid for your services as contracted. As for this offer, I frankly confess it is insurance. There is the possibility that you may get into the game and unexpectedly wreck it with a single blow.

I personally doubt this will occur, but we prefer to take no chances."

"Don't kid yourself that I am too weak to play. You know that the doctor himself said I'll be in there Monday."

The Judge hesitated. "Twenty-five thousand," he finally said. "Absolutely my last offer."

"I hear the bookies collect ten million a day on baseball bets."

"Ridiculous."

"That's what I hear."

"It makes no difference, I am not a bookie. What is your answer?"

"I say no."

The Judge bit his lip.

Roy said, "Ain't you ashamed that you are selling a club down the river that hasn't won a pennant in twenty-five years and now they have a chance to?"

"We'll have substantially the same team next year," the Judge answered, "and I have no doubt that we will make a better job of the entire season, supported as we shall be by new players and possibly another manager. If we take on the Yankees now—that is, if we are foolish enough to win the playoff match—they will beat us a merciless four in a row, despite your presence. You are not strong enough to withstand the strain of a World Series, and you know it. We'd be ground to pulp, made the laughingstock of organized baseball, and your foolish friend, Pop Fisher, would this time destroy himself in his humiliation."

"What about all the jack you'd miss out on, even if we only played four Series games and lost every one?"

"I have calculated the amount and am certain I can do better, on the whole, in the way I suggest. I have reason to believe that, although we are considered to be the underdogs, certain gambling interests have been betting heavily on the Knights to win. Now it is my purpose, via the un-contested—so to speak—game, to teach these parasites a lesson they will never forget. After that they will not dare to infest our stands again."

"Pardon me while I throw up."

The Judge looked hurt.

"The odds favor us," Roy said. "I saw it in tonight's paper."

"In one only. The others quote odds against us."

Roy laughed out loud.

The Judge flushed through his yellow skin. "Honi soit qui mal y pense."

"Double to you," Roy said.

"Twenty-five thousand," said the Judge with an angry gesture. "The rest is silence."

Though Roy had a splitting headache he tried to think the situation out. The way he now felt, he wouldn't be able to stand at the plate with a feather duster on his shoulder, let alone a bat. Maybe the Judge's hunch was right, and he might not be able to do a single thing to help the Knights win their game. On the other hand—maybe he'd be himself, his real self. If he helped them win the playoff—no matter if they later dropped the Series four in a row—there would still be all sorts of en-dorsement offers and maybe even a contract to do a baseball movie. Then he'd have the dough to take care of Memo in proper style. Yet suppose he played and be-cause of his weakness flopped as miserably as he had dur-ing his slump? That might sour the endorsements and everything else, and he'd end up with nothing—or very little. His mind went around in drunken circles.

All this time the Judge's voice was droning on. "I have observed," he was saying, "how one moral condition may lead to or become its opposite. I recall an occasion on the bench when out of the goodness of my heart and a warm belief in humanity I resolved to save a boy from serving a prison sentence. Though his guilt was clear, because of his age I suspended sentence and paroled him for a period of five years. That afternoon as I walked down the courthouse steps, I felt I could surely face my maker without a blush. However, not one week later the boy stood before me, arraigned as a most wicked parricide. I asked myself can any action—no matter what its origin or motive—which ends so evilly—can such an action possibly be designated as good?"

He took out a clotted handkerchief, spat into it, folded it and thrust it into his pocket. "Contrarily," he went on, "a deed of apparently evil significance may come to pure and beautiful flower. I have in mind a later case tried before me in which a physician swindled his patient, a paralytic, out of almost a quarter of a million dollars. So well did he contrive to hide the loot that it has till this day not been recovered. Nevertheless, the documentary evidence was strong enough to convict the embezzler and I sentenced him to a term of from forty to fifty years in prison, thus insuring he would not emerge from the penitentiary to enjoy his ill-gotten gains before he is eighty-three years of age. Yet, while testifying from his wheel chair at the trial, the paralytic astonished himself and all present by rising in righteous wrath against the malcontent and, indeed, tottered across the floor to wreak upon him his vengeance. Naturally the bailiff restrained him, but would you have guessed that he was, from that day on, sound in wind and limb, and as active as you or I? He wrote me afterwards that the return of his power of locomotion more than compensated him for the loss of his fortune."

Roy frowned. "Come out of the bushes."

The Judge paused. "I was trying to help you assess this action in terms of the future."

"You mean if I sell out?"

"Put it that way if you like."

"And that maybe some good might come out of it?"

"That is my assumption."

"For me, you mean?"

"For others too. It is impossible to predict who will be benefited."

"I thought you said you were doing this to get rid of the gamblers—that's good right off, ain't it?"

The Judge cleared his throat. "Indeed it is. However, one might consider, despite the difficulty of the personal situation—that is to say, within the context of one's own compunctions—that it is impossible to predict what further good may accrue to one, and others, in the future, as a result of an initially difficult decision."

Roy laughed. "You should be selling snake oil."

He had thought there might be something to the argument. He was now sure there wasn't, for as the Judge had talked he recalled an experience he had had when he was a kid. He and his dog were following an old skid road into the heart of a spooky forest when the hound suddenly let out a yelp, ran on ahead, and got lost. It was late in the afternoon and he couldn't stand the thought of leaving the dog there alone all night, so he went into the wood after it. At first he could see daylight between the trees— to this minute he remembered how still the trunks were, as the tree tops circled around in the breeze—and in sight of daylight it wasn't so bad, nor a little deeper in, despite the green gloom, but just at about the time the darkness got so thick he was conscious of having to shove against it as he hallooed for the dog, he got this scared and lonely feeling that he was impossibly lost. With his heart whamming against his ribs he looked around but could recognize no direction in the darkness, let alone discover the right one. It was cold and he shivered. Only, the payoff of it was that the mutt found him and led him out of the woods. That was good out of good.

Roy pulled the covers over his head. "Go home."

The Judge didn't move. "There is also the matter of next season's contract."

Roy listened. Would there ever be a next season? He uncovered his head. "How much?"

"I shall offer—provided we agree on the other matter —a substantial raise."

"Talk figures."

"Forty-five thousand for the season. We might also work out some small percentage on the gate."

"Twenty-five thousand for dropping the game is not enough," said Roy. As he spoke an icicle of fright punctured his spine.

The Judge scowled and drew on his half-gone cigar. "Thirty," he said, "and no more."

"Thirty-five," Roy got out. "Don't forget I stand to lose a couple of thousand on the pay I could get in the Series."

"Utterly outrageous," snapped the Judge.

"Don't slam the door on your way out."

The Judge rose, brushed his wrinkled pants and left. Roy stared at the ceiling—relieved.

The Judge returned. He removed his hat and wiped his perspiring face with his dirty handkerchief. His head was covered with a thick black wig. You never got to the bottom of that creep.

"You are impossible to deal with—but I accept." His voice was flat. He covered his head with his hat.

But Roy said he had changed his mind when the Judge was out of the room. He had thought it over and decided the boys wanted to win that game and he wanted to help them. That was good. He couldn't betray his own team and manager. That was bad.

The Judge then hissed, "You may lose Miss Paris to someone else if you are not careful."

Roy bolted up. "To who for instance?"

"A better provider."

"You mean Gus Sands?"

The Judge did not directly reply. "A word to the wise—"

"That's none of your business," said Roy. He lay back. Then he asked, "What if I couldn't lose the game by my-self? The Pirates ain't exactly world beaters. We roasted them the last seven times. The boys might do it again even if I didn't hit a thing."

The Judge rubbed his scaly hands. "The Knights are de-moralized. Without you, I doubt they can win over a sand-lot team, contrary opinion notwithstanding. As for the contingency of the flat failure of the opposing team, we have made the necessary arrangements to take care of that."

Roy was up again. "You mean there's somebody else in on this deal?"

The Judge smiled around his cigar.

"Somebody on our team?"

"A key man."

"In that case—" Roy said slowly.

"The thirty-five thousand is final. There'll be no chang-ing that."

"With forty-five for the contract—"

"Agreed. You understand you are not under any cir-cumstances to hit the ball safely?"

After a minute Roy said slowly, "I will take the pitch."

"I beg your pardon?"

"The fix is on."

The Judge caught on and said with a laugh, "I see you share my philological interests." He lit his dead King Oscar.

Through the nausea Roy remembered an old saying. He

quoted, "Woe unto him who calls evil good and good evil."

The Judge glared at him.

Memo returned and covered his face with wet kisses. She tweaked his nose, mussed his hair, and called him wonderful. After she left he couldn't sleep so he reached under his pillow and got out Iris' letter.

" . . . After my baby was born, the women of the home where my father had brought me to save himself further shame were after me to give it up. They said it would be bad for her to be brought up by an unmarried mother, and that I would have no time to myself or opportunity to take up my normal life. I tried, as they said, to be sensible and offer her for adoption, but I had been nursing her—although warned against it, nursing shrinks the breasts you know, and they were afraid for my figure—and the thought of tearing myself away from her forever was too much for me. Since Papa wouldn't have her in his house I decided to find a job and bring her up myself. That turned out to be a lot harder than I had expected, because I earned not very much and had to pay for baby's care all day, her things, the rent of course, and the clothes I had to have for work. At night I had supper to think of, bathing her, laundry, house cleaning, and preparing for the next day, which never changed from any other.

"Except for my baby I was nearly always alone, reading, mostly, to improve myself, although sometimes it was unbearable, especially before I was twenty and just after. It also took quite a while until I got rid of my guilt, or could look upon her as innocent of it, but eventually I did, and soon her loveliness and gaiety and all the tender feelings I had in my heart for her made up for a lot I had suffered. Yet I was tied to time—not so much to the past—nor to the expectations of the future, which was really too far

212

away—only to here and now, day after day, until suddenly the years unrolled and a change came—more a reward
of standing it so long than any sudden magic—and more
quickly than I could believe, she had grown into a young
woman, and almost as if I had wished it on her, fell in love
with a wonderful boy and married him. Like me she
was a mother before she was seventeen. Suddenly everywhere I looked seemed to be tomorrow, and I was at last
free to take up my life where I had left it off one summer night when I went for a walk in the park with a
stranger . . ."

He read down to the last page, where she once more
mentioned herself as a grandmother. Roy crumpled the
letter and pitched it against the wall.

on the morning of the game fist fights broke out all over the stands in Knights Field. Hats, bottles, apple cores, bananas, and the mushy contents of sack lunches were thrown around. A fan in one of the boxes had a rock bounced off his skull, opening a bleeding gash. Two special cops rushed up the steps and got hold of an innocent-looking guy with glasses, whose pockets were stuffed with odd-shaped rocks. They dragged him forth, although he was hollering he had collected them for his rock garden, and flung him headlong out of the park. He was from Pittsburgh and cursed the Knights into the ground. A disappointed truck driver who couldn't get in to see the game tackled him from behind, knocking the rock collector's head against the sidewalk and smashing his glasses. He spat out two bloody teeth and sat there sobbing till the ambulance came.

The sun hid behind the clouds for the most part. The day was chilly, football weather, but the stands were decorated with colored bunting, the flags on the grandstand roof rode high in the breeze and the crowd was raucous. The PA man tried to calm them but they were packed together too tight to be peaceful, for the Judge had sold hundreds of extra tickets and the standees raced for any seat that was vacant for a second. Besides, the Knights' fans were jumpy, their nerves ragged from following the ups and downs of the team. Some glum-face gents bitterly cursed Roy out, calling him welsher, fool, pig-horse for eating himself into that colossal bellyache. But he had his defenders, who claimed the Big Man's body burned food so fast he needed every bit he ate. They blamed the damage on ptomaine. The accusers wanted to know why no one else at the party had come down sick. They were answered where would the Knights be without Roy—at the bottom of the heap. The one who spoke got a rap on the ear for his trouble. The rapper was grabbed by a cop, run down the catwalk, and pitched into the rotunda. Yet though the fans were out of sorts and crabbing at each other, they presented a solid front when it came to laying bets. Many pessimistically shook their heads, but they counted up the seven straight wins over the Pirates, figured in that Hobbs was back, and reached into their pockets. Although there were not too many Pirate rooters around, the bets were quickly covered for every hard-earned buck.

Otto Zipp was above all this. He sat like a small mountain behind the rail in short left, reading the sports page of his newspaper. He looked neither right nor left, and if somebody tried to talk to him Otto gave him short shrift. Then when they least expected it, he would honk his horn and cry out in shrill tones, "Throw him to the hawks." After that he went back to the sports page.

When the players began drifting into the clubhouse they were surprised to see Roy there. He was wearing his uniform and slowly polishing Wonderboy. The boys said hello

215

and not much more. Flores looked at his feet. Some of them were embarrassed that they hadn't gone to see him in the hospital. Secretly they were pleased he was here. Allie Stubbs even began to kid around with Olson. Roy thought they would not act so chipper if they knew he felt weak as piss and was dreading the game. The Judge was absolutely crazy to pay him thirty-five grand not to hit when he didn't feel able to even lift a stick. He hoped Pop would guess how shaky he was and bench him. What a laugh that would be on the Judge—serve the bastard right. But when Pop came in, he didn't so much as glance in Roy's direction. He walked straight into his office and slammed the door, which suited Roy fine.

Pop had ordered everybody kept out of the clubhouse until after the game but Mercy weaseled in. All smiles, he approached Roy, asking for the true story of what went on at the party that night, but Red Blow saw him and told him to stay outside. Max had tried the same act in the hospital last week. The floor nurse caught him sneaking toward Roy's room and had him dropped out on the front steps. After leaving the clubhouse Max sent in a note, inviting Roy to come out and make a statement. People were calling him a filthy coward and what did he intend to say to that? Roy gave out a one-word unprintable reply. Mercy shot in a second note. "You'll get yours—M.M." Roy tore it up and told the usher to take no more slop from him.

Pop poked his baldy out of his door and called for Roy. The players looked around uneasily. Roy got up and finally went into the office. For an insufferable time Pop failed to speak. He was unshaven, his face exuding gray stubble that made him look eighty years old. His thin frame seemed shrunken and his left eye was a little crossed with fatigue. Pop leaned back in his creaking swivel chair, staring with tears in his eyes over his half moons at the picture of Ma on his desk. Roy examined his fingernails.

Pop sighed, "Roy, it's my own fault."

It made Roy edgy. "What is?"

"This mess that we are now in. I am not forgetting I kept you on the bench for three solid weeks in June. If I hadn't done that foolish thing we'da finished the season at least half a dozen games out in front."

Roy offered no reply.

"But your own mistake was a bad one too."

Roy nodded.

"A bad one, with the team right on top of hooking the pennant." Pop shook his head. Yet he said he wouldn't blame Roy too much because it wasn't entirely of his own doing. He then apologized for not coming to see him in the hospital. He had twice set out to but felt too grumpy to be fit company for a sick man, so he hadn't come. "It's not you that I am mad at, Roy—it's that blasted Memo. I shoulda pitched her out on her ass the first day she showed up at my door."

Roy got up.

"Sit down." Pop bent forward. "We can win today." His cold breath smelled bad. Roy drew his head back.

"Well, we can, can't we?"

He nodded.

"What's the matter with you?"

"I feel weak," Roy said, "and I am not betting how I will hit today."

Pop's voice got kindly again. "I say we can win it whichever way you feel. Once you begin to play you will feel stronger. And if the rest of those birds see you hustling they will break their backs to win. All they got to feel is there is somebody on this team who thinks they can."

Pop then related a story about a rookie third baseman

217

he once knew, a lad named Mulligan. He was a fine hitter and thrower but full of hard luck all his life. Once he was beaned at the plate and had his skull cracked. He returned for spring practice the following year and the first day out he crashed into another fielder and broke his arm. On the return from that he was on first running to second on a hit and run play and the batter smacked the ball straight at him, breaking two ribs and dislocating a disc in his spine. After that he quit baseball, to everybody's relief.

"He was just unlucky," Pop said, "and there wasn't a thing anybody could do to take the whammy off of him and change his hard luck. You know, Roy, I been lately thinking that a whole lot of people are like him, and for one reason or the other their lives will go the same way all the time, without them getting what they want, no matter what. I for one."

Then to Roy's surprise he said he never hoped to have a World Series flag. Pop swiveled his chair closer. "It ain't in the cards for me—that's all. I am wise to admit it to myself. It took a long time but I finally saw which way the arrow has been pointing." He sighed deeply. "But that don't hold true about our league pennant, Roy. That's the next best thing and I feel I am entitled to it. I feel if I win it just this once—I will be satisfied. I will be satisfied, and win or lose in the Series, I will quit baseball forever." He lowered his voice. "You see what it means to me, son?"

"I see."

"Roy, I would give my whole life to win this game and take the pennant. Promise me that you will go in there and do your damndest."

"I will go in," Roy sighed.

After the practice bell had rung, when he reluctantly climbed up out of the dugout and shoved himself toward the batting cage with his bat in his hand, as soon as the crowd got a look at him the boo birds opened up, alternating with shrill whistles and brassy catcalls. Roy hardened his jaws, but then a rumble erupted that sounded like bubbling tubfuls of people laughing and sobbing. The noise grew to a roar, boiled over, and to his astonishment, drowned out the disapprovers in an ovation of cheering. Men flung their hats into the air, scaling straws and limp felts, pounded each other's skulls, and cried themselves hoarse. Women screeched and ended up weeping. The shouting grew, piling reverberation upon reverberation, till it reached blast proportions. When it momentarily wore thin, Sadie Sutter's solemn gong could be heard, but as the roar rose again, the gonging grew faint and died in the distance. Roy felt feverish. The applause was about over when he removed his cap to clean the sweat off his brow, and once more thunder rolled across the field, continuing in waves as he entered the cage. With teeth clenched to stop the chattering, he took three swipes at the ball, driving each a decent distance. At Pop's urging he also went out onto the field to shag some flies. Again the cheers resounded, although he wished they wouldn't. He speared a few flies in his tracks, dropped his glove and walked to the dugout. The cheers trailed him in a foaming billow, but above the surflike roar and the renewed tolling of Sadie's gong, he could hear Otto Zipp's shrill curses. The dwarf drew down on his head a chorus of hisses but thumbed his cherry nose as Roy passed by. Roy paid him no heed whatsoever, infuriating Otto.

The Pirates flipped through their practice and the game began. Pop had picked Fowler to start for the Knights. Roy figured then that he knew who was in this deal with him. Leave it to the Judge to tie the bag in the most economical way—with the best hitter and pitcher. He had probably asked Pop who he was intending to pitch and then went out and bought him, though no doubt paying a good deal less than the price Roy was getting. What surprised and shocked him was that Fowler could be so corrupt though so young and in the best of health. If he only had half the promise of the future Fowler had, he would never have dirtied his paws in this business. However, as he watched Fowler pitch during the first inning he wasn't certain he was the one. His fast ball hopped today and he got rid of the first two Pirates with ease. Maybe he was playing it cagey first off, time would tell. Roy's thoughts were broken up by the sound, and echo behind him, of the crack of a bat. The third man up had taken hold of one and it was arcing into deep left. Already Flores was hot footing it in from center. It occurred to Roy that although he had promised the Judge he wouldn't hit, he had made no commitments as to catching them. Waving Flores aside, he ran several shaky steps and made a throbbing stab at the ball, spearing it on the half run for the third out. As he did so he noticed a movement up in the tower window and saw the Judge's stout figure pressed against the window. He then recollected he hadn't seen Memo since Saturday.

To nobody's surprise, Dutch Vogelman went to the mound for the Pirates. In a few minutes it was clear to all he was working with championship stuff, because he knocked the first three Knights off without half trying, including Flores, who was no easy victim. Roy had no chance to bat, for which he felt relieved. But after Fowler had also rubbed out the opposition, he was first up in the second inning. As he dragged Wonderboy up to the plate, the stands, after a short outburst, were hushed. Everybody remembered the four homers he had got off Vogelman the last time he had faced him. In the dugout Pop and the boys were peppering it up for him to give the ball a big ride, and so were Red Blow and Earl Wilson, on the baselines. What they didn't know was that Roy had been struck giddy with weakness. His heart whammed like a wheezing steam engine, his head felt nailed to a pole, his eardrums throbbed as if he were listening to the bottom of the sea, and his arms hung like dead weights. It was with the greatest effort that he raised Wonderboy. As he was slowly getting set, he sneaked a cautious glance up at the tower, and it did not exactly surprise him that Memo, still in black, was standing at the window next to the Judge, blankly gazing down at him. Anyway, he knew where she was now.

Vogelman had been taking his time. For a pitcher he was a comparatively short duck, with a long beak, powerful arms and legs, red sleeves leaking out of a battered jersey, and a nervous delivery. Despite the fact that he had ended the regular season as a twenty-five game winner, he worried to bursting beads of sweat at the thought of pitching to Roy. Every time he recalled those four gopher balls, one after the other landing in the stands, he cringed with embarrassment. And he knew, although there was nobody on base at the moment, that if he served one of them up now, it could conceivably ice the game for the Knights and louse up the very peak of his year of triumph. So Vogelman delayed by wiping the shine off the ball, inspecting the stitches, fumbling for the resin bag, scuffing his cleats in the dirt, and removing his cap to rub away the sweat he had worked up. When the boos of the crowd got good and loud, Stuffy Briggs bellowed for him to throw and Vogelman reluctantly let go with a pitch.

The ball was a whizzer but dripping lard. Weak as he felt, Roy had to smile at what he could really do to that baby if he had his heart set on it, but he swung the slightest bit too late, grunting as the ball shot past Wonderboy—which almost broke his wrists to get at it—and plunked in the pocket of the catcher's glove.

. . . Where had she been since Saturday? Sunday was the first day she hadn't come to the hospital, the day she knew he was getting out of the joint. He had left alone, followed by some reporters he wouldn't talk to, and had taken a cab to the hotel. Once in his room he got into pajamas, and wondering why she hadn't at least called him, fell asleep. He had then had this dream of her—seeing her in some city, it looked like Boston—and she didn't recognize him when they passed but walked on fast in her swaying walk. He chased after her and she was (he remembered) swallowed up in the crowd. But he saw the red hair and followed after that, only it turned out to be a dyed redhead with a mean mouth and dirty eyes. Where's Memo? he called, and woke thinking she was here in the room, but she wasn't, and he hadn't seen her till he located her up there in the tower.

Roy gazed at the empty bases. Striking out with nobody on was the least harm he could do the team, yet his fingers itched to sock it a little. He couldn't trust himself to because—who could tell?—it might go over the fence, the way Wonderboy was tugging at his muscles. Vogelman then tried a low-breaking curve that Roy had to "take" for ball one. The pitcher came back with a foolish floater that he pretended to almost break his back reaching after.

Strike two. There were only three.

. . . He was remembering the time his old lady drowned the black tom cat in the tub. It had gotten into the bathroom with her and bit at her bare ankles. She once and for all grabbed the cursed thing and dropped it into the hot tub. The cat fought to get out, but she shrilly beat it back and though it yowled mournfully, gave it no mercy. Yet it managed in its hysterical cat-way to stay afloat in the scalding water that she bathed in to cut her weight down, until she shoved its dirty biting head under, from which her hand bled all over. But when the water was drained, and the cat, all glossy wet, with its pink tongue caught between its teeth, lay there dead, the whole thing got to be too much for her and she couldn't lift it out of the tub.

He closed his eyes before the next pitch in the hope it would be quickly called against him, but it curved out for a ripe ball two. Opening his lids, he saw Mercy in a nearby seat, gazing at him with a malevolent sneer. You too, Max, Roy thought, tightening his hold on the bat. Vogelman was beginning to act more confident. You too, Vogelman, and he shut his eyes again, thinking how, after that time with Iris on the beach, when they were driving home, she rested her head against his arm. She was frightened, wanted him to comfort her but he wouldn't. "When will you grow up, Roy?" she said.

Vogelman blistered across a hot, somewhat high one, not too bad to miss, and that made it three and out. Otto Zipp held his nose and pulled the chain, and Roy, quivering, remained for a few seconds with the stick raised over his head, shriveling the dwarf into the silence and immobility that prevailed elsewhere. He threw Wonderboy aside —some in the front boxes let out a gasp—and returned empty-handed to the bench. The Judge and Memo had gone from the tower window.

As the Pirates came to bat for their half of the third (there were no Knight hits after Roy struck out) a breeze blew dust all over the place. Some of the fans with nothing better to do were shoveling the rotten fruit and slices of buttered sandwich bread into paper sacks, or kicking it under their seats. Nobody seemed to be hungry and the Stevens boys, despite all their barking, sold only a few hot coffees. Nor was there much talk of the past half inning. A few complained that Roy had never looked so bad —like a sloppy walrus. Others reminded them the game was young yet.

Neither team scored in either the third or fourth. The

way the Knights fanned made Roy wonder if they had all been bought off by the Judge. Yet it didn't seem likely. He was too stingy. In the fifth came his next turn, again first up, a small break.

The stands awoke and began a rhythmic clapping. "Lift 'at pill, Roy. Bust its guts. Make it bleed. You can do it, kid."

"You can do it," Pop hollered from the dugout steps.

With a heavy heart Roy pulled himself up to the plate. He had shooting pains in back muscles that had never bothered him before and a crick in his neck. He couldn't comfortably straighten up and the weight of Wonderboy crouched him further. But Vogelman, despite Roy's strikeout, was burdened with worry over what he still *might* do. He wiped his face with his red sleeve but failed to calm down. By wide margins his first two throws were balls. To help him out, Roy swung under the third pitch. Otto Zipp then let out a string of boos, bahs, and bums. Roy thought he better foul the next one for strike two but Vogelman wouldn't let him, throwing almost over his head. Remembering he could walk if he wanted to, Roy waited. There was no harm to anybody in that and it would look better for him. The next pitch came in too close, and that was how he got to first and the Judge again to the window. But it made no difference one way or the other, for though Lajong sacrificed him to second, Gabby slashed a high one across the diamond which the second baseman jumped for, and he tagged Roy for an unassisted double play. Nobody could blame *him* for that, Roy thought, as he headed out to the field. He stole a look back at Pop and the manager was muttering to himself out of loose lips in a bony face. It seemed to Roy he had known the old man all his life long.

He found himself thinking of maybe quitting the deal with the Judge. He could send a note up there saying the fix was off. But he couldn't think what to write Memo. He tried to imagine what it would be like living without her and couldn't stand the thought of the loneliness.

Dave Olson opened the sixth with the Knights' first hit, a thumping double. The stands sounded like a gigantic drawerful of voices that had suddenly been pulled open. But Benz went down swinging, then Fowler bunted into another quick d.p. and the drawerful of voices was shut. Roy wondered about that bunt. He had a notion Fowler would commit himself soon because time was on the go. But Fowler didn't, making it another sweep of three Pirates. He had thus far given up only two safeties. In the seventh, the Knights, sensing Vogelman was tiring, found their way to him. Allie Stubbs chopped a grass cutter through a hole in the infield for a single. Baker, attempting to lay down a bunt, was overanxious and struck out. Then Flores lifted one just above the first baseman's frantic fingers, and Stubbs, running with his head down, sprang safely into third. Roy was on deck but with two on base his heart misgave him. The crowd jumped to its feet, roaring for him to come through.

As he approached the plate, the sun, that had been plumbing the clouds since the game began, at last broke through and bathed the stadium in a golden glow that caused the crowd to murmur. As the warmth fell upon him, Roy felt a sob break in his throat. The weakness left his legs, his heart beat steadily, his giddy gut tightened, and he stood firm and strong upon the earth. Though it startled him to find it so, he had regained a sense of his own well-being. A thousand springlike thoughts crowded through his mind, blotting out the dark diagnosis of the white-mustached specialist. He felt almost happy, and that he could do anything he wanted, if he wanted. His eyes scanned the forward rows in left field but stopped at Zipp's surly face. He felt suddenly anguished at what he had promised the Judge.

On his first swing—at a bad pitch—Otto let out a stream of jeers, oaths, and horn hoots that burned Roy to his bones. I will get that little ass-faced bastard. On the next pitch he shortened his hold on Wonderboy, stepped in front of the ball, and pulled it sharply foul. The ball whizzed past Otto's nose and boomed down an entrance way. The dwarf turned into flour, then as the blood rushed back to his face, grew furious. He jumped up and down on his seat, shook his fist, and screeched curses.

"Carrion, offal, turd—flush the bowl."

Roy tried to send the next ball through his teeth. It hit the rail with a bong and bounced into the air. A fan behind Otto caught it in his straw hat. Though the crowd laughed, the boos at Roy grew louder. Red Blow held up two warning fingers. Roy chopped a third foul at the dwarf. With a shriek he covered his face with his arms and ducked.

Several rows up from Otto, a dark-haired woman in a white dress had risen and was standing alone amid the crowd. Christ, another one, Roy thought. At the last split second he had tried to hold his swing but couldn't. The ball spun like a shot at Otto, struck his hard skull with a thud, and was deflected upward. It caught the lady in the face, and to the crowd's horror, she went soundlessly down.

A commotion rose in the stands. Fans by the hundreds piled out of their seats to get at her but the cops and ushers blocked their way, warning them not to crush her to death. Stuffy Briggs called time. Roy dropped his bat, hopped into the boxes and ran up the stairs—his clacking cleats shooting sparks—and along the aisle to where she lay. Many of the fans were standing on their seats to see and there was a crowd pressed around her. Murmuring lynch threats, they let Roy through. A doctor was attending her but she was stretched out unconscious.

Roy already knew who it was. "Iris," he groaned.

Iris woke, opened her good eye and sighed, "Roy."

Lifting her in his arms, he carried her to the clubhouse. Doc Casey and Dizzy kept everybody out. Max Mercy, hot for news, jammed his foot in the door but Dizzy crushed it hard, and Max danced as he cursed.

Roy gently laid her on the trainer's table. The left side of her face was hurt, bruised and rainbow-colored. Her eye was black and the lid thick. But the right side was still calm and lovely.

What have I done, he thought, and why did I do it? And he thought of all the wrong things he had done in his life and tried to undo them but who could?

The doctor went out to call an ambulance. Roy closed the door after him.

"Oh, Roy," sighed Iris.

"Iris, I am sorry."

"Roy, you must win—"

He groaned. "Why didn't you come here before?"

"My letter—you never answered."

He bowed his head.

The doctor entered. "Contusions and lacerations. Not much to worry about, but to be on the safe side she ought to be X-rayed."

"Don't spare any expenses," Roy said.

"She'll be fine. You can go back to the game now."

"You must win, Roy," said Iris.

Seeing there was more to this than he had thought, the doctor left.

Roy turned to her trying to keep in mind that she was a grandmother but when he scanned the fine shape of her body, he couldn't. Instead there rose in him an odd disgust for Memo. It came quickly, nauseating him.

"Darling," whispered Iris, "win for our boy."

He stared at her. "What boy?"

"I am pregnant." There were tears in her eyes.

Her belly was slender . . . then the impact hit him. "Holy Jesus."

Iris smiled with quivering lips.

Bending over, he kissed her mouth and tasted blood. He kissed her breasts, they smelled of roses. He kissed her hard belly, wild with love for her and the child.

"Win for us, you were meant to."

She took his head in her hands and drew it to her bosom. How like the one who jumped me in the park that night he looks, she thought, and to drive the thought away pressed his head deeper into her breasts, thinking, this will be different. Oh, Roy, be my love and protect me. But by then the ambulance had come so they took her away.

In the dugout Pop confronted him with withering curses. "Get in there and attend to business. No more monkey shines or I will pitch you out on your banana."

Roy nodded. Climbing out of the dugout, to his dismay he found Wonderboy lying near the water fountain, in the mud. He tenderly wiped it dry. Stuffy called time in and the Pirates, furious at the long delay (Wickitt had demanded the forfeit of the game, but Pop had scared Stuffy into waiting for Roy by threatening to go to court), returned to their positions, Allie and Flores to third and first, and Roy stepped into the batter's box to face a storm of Bronx cheers. They came in wind-driven sheets until Vogelman reared and threw, then they stopped.

It was 0 and 2 on him because, except for the one he had purposely missed, Roy had turned each pitch into a foul. He watched Vogelman with burning eyes. Vogelman was almost hypnotized. He saw a different man and didn't like what he saw. His next throw was wide of the plate. Ball one. Then a quick ball two, and the pitcher was nervous again. He took a very long time with the next throw but to his horror the pellet slipped away from him and hit the dirt just short of the plate. Allie broke for home but the catcher quickly trapped it and threw to third. Flopping back, Allie made it with his fingers. Flores, in the meantime, had taken second.

And that was ball three. Roy now prayed for a decent throw.

Vogelman glanced at Allie edging into a lead again, kicked, and threw almost in desperation. Roy swung from his cleats.

Thunder crashed. The pitcher stuffed his maimed fingers into his ears. His eyes were blinded. Pop rose and crowed himself hoarse. Otto Zipp, carrying a dark lump on his noodle, cowered beneath the ledge. Some of the fans had seen lightning, thought it was going to rain, and raised their coat collars. Most of them were on their feet, raving at the flight of the ball. Allie had raced in to score, so had Flores, and Roy was heading into second, when the umpire waved them all back. The ball had landed clearly foul. The fans groaned in shuddering tones.

Wonderboy lay on the ground split lengthwise, one half pointing to first, the other to third.

The Knights' bat boy nervously collected both the pieces and thrust a Louisville Slugger into Roy's limp hand. The crowd sat in raw silence as the nerveless Vogelman delivered his next pitch. It floated in, perfect for pickling, but Roy failed to lift the bat.

Lajong, who followed, also struck out.

With the Knights back in the field, Fowler quickly gave up a whacking triple to the first Pirate hitter. This was followed by a hard double, and almost before any of the stunned fans could realize it, the first run of the game was in. Pop bounced off the bench as if electrocuted and signaled the bullpen into hot activity. Red Blow sauntered out to the mound to quiet Fowler down but Fowler said he was all right so Red left.

The next Pirate laced a long hopper to left. The shouting of the crowd woke Roy out of his grief for Wonderboy. He tore in for the ball, made a running jab for it and held it. With an effort he heaved to third, holding both runners to one bag. He knew now he was right about Fowler. The pitcher had pulled the plug. Roy signaled time and drifted in to talk to him. Both Red and Dave Olson also walked forward for a mound conference but Roy waved them back. As he approached the dark-faced Fowler, he saw the Judge up at the window, puffing his cigar.

Roy spoke in a low voice. "Watch out, kid, we don't want to lose the game."

Fowler studied him craftily. "Cut the crap, big shot. A lotta winning you been doing."

"Throw the ball good," Roy advised him.

"I will, when you start hitting it."

"Listen," Roy said patiently. "This might be my last season in the game for I am already thirty-five. You want it to be yours?"

Fowler paled. "You wouldn't dare open your trap."

"Try something funny again and you will see."

Fowler turned angrily away. The fans began to whistle and stamp. "Set 'em up," called Stuffy Briggs. Roy returned to left but after that, Fowler somehow managed to keep the next two men from connecting, and everybody said too bad that Roy hadn't given him that pep talk after the first hit. Some of the fans remarked had anybody noticed that Roy had thumbed his nose up to the tower at the end of the inning?

Every time Vogelman put Roy away, he felt infinitely better, consequently his pitching improved as the game progressed. Though he was surprised in the eighth to have Gabby Laslow touch him for a sharp single, he forced Olson to pop to short, Benz to line to him, and Fowler obliged by biting at three gamey ones for the last out. Counting up who he would have to throw to in the ninth, Vogelman discovered that if he got Stubbs, Baker, and the more difficult Flores out, there would be no Roy Hobbs to pitch to. The idea so excited him he determined to beat his brains out trying. Fowler, on the other hand, despite Roy's good advice to him, got sloppier in his throwing, although subtly, so that nobody could be sure why, only his support was a whole lot better than he had hoped for, and neither of the first two Pirates up in the ninth, though they had walloped the ball hard, could land on base. Flores, the Mexican jumping bean, had nailed both shots. The third Pirate then caught a juicy pitch and poled out a high looping beauty to left, but Roy, running back—back —back, speared it against the wall. Though he was winded and cursed Fowler through his teeth, he couldn't help but smile, picturing the pitcher's disgust. And he felt confident that the boys would hold him a turn at bat and he would destroy Vogelman and save the game, the most important thing he ever had to do in his life.

Pop, on the other hand, was losing hope. His hands trembled and his false teeth felt like rocks in his mouth, so he plucked them out and dropped them into his shirt pocket. Instead of Allie, he called Ed Simmons to pinch hit, but Vogelman, working with renewed speed and canniness, got Ed to hit a soft one to center field. Pop swayed on the bench, drooling a little out of the corners of his puckered mouth. Red was a ghost, even his freckles were pale. The stands were shrouded in darkening silence. Baker spat and approached the plate. Remembering he hadn't once hit safely today, Pop called him back and substituted Hank Kelly, another pinch hitter.

Vogelman struck him out. He dried his mouth on his sleeve, smiling faintly to himself for the first time since the game began. One more—the Mex. To finish him meant slamming the door on Hobbs, a clean shut-out, and to-morrow the World Series. The sun fell back in the sky and a hush hung like a smell in the air. Flores, with a crazed look in his eye, faced the pitcher. Fouling the first throw, he took for a ball, and swung savagely at the third pitch. He missed. Two strikes, there were only three . . . Roy felt himself slowly dying. You died alone. At least if he were up there batting . . . The Mexican's face was lit in anguish. With bulging eyes he rushed at the next throw, and cursing in Spanish, swung. The ball wobbled crazily in the air, took off, and leaped for the right field wall. Running as though death dogged him, Flores made it, sliding headlong into third. Vogelman, drained of his heart's blood, stared at him through glazed eyes.

The silence shattered into insane, raucous noise.

Roy rose from the bench. When he saw Pop searching among the other faces, his heart flopped and froze. He would gladly get down on his knees and kiss the old man's skinny, crooked feet, do anything to get up there this last time. Pop's haunted gleam settled on him, wavered, traveled down the line of grim faces . . . and came back to Roy. He called his name.

Up close he had black rings around his eyes, and when he spoke his voice broke.

"See what we have come to, Roy."

Roy stared at the dugout floor. "Let me go in."

"What would you expect to do?"

"Murder it."

"Murder which?"

"The ball—I swear."

Pop's eyes wavered to the men on the bench. Reluctantly his gaze returned to Roy. "If you weren't so damn busy gunning fouls into the stands that last time, you woulda straightened out that big one, and with three scoring, that woulda been the game."

"Now I understand why they call them fouls."

"Go on in," Pop said. He added in afterthought, "Keep us alive."

Roy selected out of the rack a bat that looked something like Wonderboy. He swung it once and advanced to the plate. Flores was dancing on the bag, beating his body as if it were burning, and jabbering in Spanish that if by the mercy of St. Christopher he was allowed to make the voyage home from third, he would forever after light candles before the saint.

The blank-faced crowd was almost hidden by the darkness crouching in the stands. Home plate lay under a deepening dusty shadow but Roy saw things with more light than he ever had before. A hit, tying up the game, would cure what ailed him. Only a homer, with himself scoring the winning run, would truly redeem him.

Vogelman was contemplating how close he had come to paradise. If the Mex had missed that pitch, the game would now be over. All night long he'd've felt eight foot tall, and when he got into bed with his wife, she'd've given it to him the way they do to heroes.

The sight of his nemesis crouched low in the brooding darkness around the plate filled him with fear.

Sighing, he brought himself, without conviction, to throw.

"Bo-ool one."

The staring faces in the stands broke into a cry that stayed till the end of the game.

Vogelman was drenched in sweat. He could have thrown a spitter without half trying but didn't know how and was afraid to monkey with them.

The next went in cap high.

"Eee bo-ool."

Wickitt, the Pirate manager, ambled out to the mound. "S'matter, Dutch?"

"Take me outa here," Vogelman moaned.

"What the hell for? You got that bastard three times so far and you can do it again."

"He gives me the shits, Walt. Look at him standing there like a goddamn gorilla. Look at his burning eyes. He ain't human."

Wickitt talked low as he studied Roy. "That ain't what I see. He looks old and beat up. Last week he had a mile-high bellyache in a ladies' hospital. They say he could drop dead any minute. Bear up and curve 'em low. I don't think he can bend to his knees. Get one strike on him and he will be your nookie."

He left the mound.

Vogelman threw the next ball with his flesh screaming.

"Bo-ool three."

He sought for Wickitt but the manager kept his face hidden.

In that case, the pitcher thought, I will walk him. They could yank him after that—he was a sick man.

Roy was also considering a walk. It would relieve him of responsibility but not make up for all the harm he had done. He discarded the idea. Vogelman made a bony steeple with his arms. Gazing at the plate, he found his eyes were misty and he couldn't read the catcher's sign. He looked again and saw Roy, in full armor, mounted on a black charger. Vogelman stared hard, his arms held high so as not to balk. Yes, there he was coming at him with a long lance as thick as a young tree. He rubbed his arm across his eyes and keeled over in a dead faint.

A roar ascended skywards.

The sun slid behind the clouds. It got cold again. Wickitt,

leaning darkly out of the dugout, raised his arm aloft to the center field bullpen. The boy who had been pitching flipped the ball to the bullpen catcher, straightened his cap, and began the long trek in. He was twenty, a scrawny youth with light eyes.

"Herman Youngberry, number sixty-six, pitching for the Pirates."

Few in the stands had heard of him, but before his long trek to the mound was finished his life was common knowledge. He was a six-footer but weighed a skinny one fifty-eight. One day about two years ago a Pirate scout watching him pitching for his home town team had written on a card, "This boy has a fluid delivery of a blinding fast ball and an exploding curve." Though he offered him a contract then and there, Youngberry refused to sign because it was his lifelong ambition to be a farmer. Everybody, including the girl he was engaged to, argued him into signing. He didn't say so but he had it in mind to earn enough money to buy a three hundred acre farm and then quit baseball forever. Sometimes when he pitched, he saw fields of golden wheat gleaming in the sun.

He had come to the Pirates on the first of September from one of their class A clubs, to help in the pennant drive. Since then he'd worked up a three won, two lost record. He'd seen what Roy had done to Vogelman the day he hit the four homers, and just now, and wasn't anxious to face him. After throwing his warm-ups he stepped off the mound and looked away as Roy got back into the box.

Despite the rest he had had, Roy's armpits were creepy with sweat. He felt a bulk of heaviness around his middle and that the individual hairs on his legs and chest were bristling.

Youngberry gazed around to see how they were playing Roy. It was straightaway and deep, with the infield pulled back too. Flores, though hopping about, was on the bag.

The pitcher took a full wind-up and became aware the Knights were yelling dirty names to rattle him.

Roy had considered and decided against a surprise bunt. As things were, it was best to take three good swings.

He felt the shadow of the Judge and Memo fouling the air around him and turned to shake his fist at them but they had left the window.

The ball lit its own path.

The speed of the pitch surprised Stuffy Briggs and it was a little time before he could work his tongue free.

"Stuh-rike."

Roy's nose was full of the dust he had raised.

"Throw him to the pigs," shrilled Otto Zipp.

If he bunted, the surprise could get him to first, and Flores home for the tying run. The only trouble was he had not much confidence in his ability to bunt. Roy stared at the kid, trying to hook his eye, but Youngberry wouldn't look at him. As Roy stared a fog blew up around the young pitcher, full of old ghosts and snowy scenes. The fog shot forth a snaky finger and Roy carefully searched under it for the ball but it was already in the catcher's mitt.

"Strike two."

"Off with his head," Otto shrieked.

It felt like winter. He wished for fire to warm his frozen fingers. Too late for the bunt now. He wished he had tried it. It would have caught them flatfooted.

Pop ran out with a rabbit's foot but Roy wouldn't take it. He would never give up, he swore. Flores had fallen to his knees on third and was imploring the sky.

Roy caught the pitcher's eye. His own had blood in them. Youngberry shuddered. He threw—a bad ball—but the batter leaped at it.

He struck out with a roar.

Bump Baily's form glowed red on the wall. There was a wail in the wind. He feared the mob would swarm all over him, tear him apart, and strew his polluted remains over the field, but they had vanished. Only O. Zipp climbed down out of his seat. He waddled to the plate, picked up the bat and took a vicious cut at something. He must've connected, because his dumpy bow legs went like pistons around the bases. Thundering down from third he slid into the plate and called himself safe.

Otto dusted himself off, lit a cigar and went home.

when it was night he dragged the two halves of the bat into left field, and with his jackknife cut a long rectangular slash into the turf and dug out the earth. With his hands he deepened the grave in the dry earth and packed the sides tight. He then placed the broken bat in it. He couldn't stand seeing it in two pieces so he removed them and tried squeezing them together in the hope they would stick but the split was smooth, as if the bat had willed its own brokenness, and the two parts would not stay together. Roy undid his shoelaces and wound one around the slender handle of the bat, and the other he tied around the hitting part of the wood, so that except for the knotted laces and the split he knew was there it looked like a whole bat. And this was the way he buried it, wishing it would take root and become a tree. He poured back the earth, carefully pressing it down, and replaced the grass. He trod on it in his stocking feet, and after a last long look around, walked off the field. At the fountain he considered whether to carry out a few handfuls of water to wet the earth above

Wonderboy but they would only leak through his fingers before he got there, and since he doubted he could find the exact spot in the dark he went down the dugout steps and into the tunnel.

He felt afraid to go in the clubhouse and so was glad the lights were left on with nobody there. From the looks of things everybody had got their clothes on and torn out. All was silence except the drip drop of the shower and he did not want to go in there. He got rid of his uniform in the soiled clothes can, then dressed in street clothes. He felt something thick against his chest and brought out a sealed envelope. Tearing it open, he discovered a package of thousand dollar bills. He had never see one before and here were thirty-five. In with the bills was a typewritten note: "The contract will have to wait. There are grave doubts that your cooperation was wholehearted." Roy burned the paper with a match. He considered burning the bills but didn't. He tried to stuff them into his wallet. The wad was too thick so he put them back in the envelope and slipped it into his pocket.

The street was chill and its swaying lights, dark. He shivered as he went to the corner. At the tower he pulled himself up the unlit stairs.

The Judge's secretary was gone but his private door was unlocked so Roy let himself in. The office was pitch black. He located the apartment door and stumbled up the narrow stairs. When he came into the Judge's overstuffed apartment, they were all sitting around a table, the red-headed Memo, the Judge with a green eyeshade over his black wig, and the Supreme Bookie, enjoying a little cigar. They were counting piles of betting slips and a mass of bills. Memo was adding the figures with an adding machine.

Gus got up quickly when he saw Roy. "Nice goin', slugger," he said softly. Smiling, he advanced with his arm extended. "That was some fine show you put on today."

Roy slugged the slug and he went down in open-mouthed wonder. His head hit the floor and the glass eye dropped out and rolled into a mousehole.

Memo was furious. "Don't touch him, you big bastard. He's worth a million of your kind."

Roy said, "You act all right, Memo, but only like a whore."

"Tut," said the Judge.

She ran to him and tried to scratch his eyes but he pushed her aside and she fell over Gus. With a cry she lifted the bookie's head on her lap and made mothering noises over him.

Roy took the envelope out of his pocket. He slapped the Judge's wig and eyeshade off and showered the thousand dollar bills on his wormy head.

The Judge raised a revolver.

"That will do, Hobbs. Another move and I shall be forced to defend myself."

Roy snatched the gun and dropped it in the wastebasket. He twisted the Judge's nose till he screamed. Then he lifted him onto the table and pounded his back with his fists. The Judge made groans and pig squeals. With his foot Roy shoved the carcass off the table. He hit the floor with a crash and had a bowel movement in his pants. He lay moaning amid the betting slips and bills.

Memo had let Gus's head fall and ran around the table to the basket. Raising the pistol, she shot at Roy's back. The bullet grazed his shoulder and broke the Judge's bathroom mirror. The glass clattered to the floor.

Roy turned to her.

"Don't come any nearer or I'll shoot."

He slowly moved forward.

"You filthy scum, I hate your guts and always have since the day you murdered Bump."

Her finger tightened on the trigger but when he came very close she sobbed aloud and thrust the muzzle into her mouth. He gently took the gun from her, opened the cylinder, and shook the cartridges into his palm. He pocketed them and again dumped the gun into the basket.

She was sobbing hysterically as he left.

Going down the tower stairs he fought his overwhelming self-hatred. In each stinking wave of it he remembered some disgusting happening of his life.

He thought, I never did learn anything out of my past life, now I have to suffer again.

When he hit the street he was exhausted. He had not shaved, and a black beard gripped his face. He felt old and grimy.

He stared into faces of people he passed along the street but nobody recognized him.

"He coulda been a king," a woman remarked to a man.

At the corner near some stores he watched the comings and goings of the night traffic. He felt the insides of him beginning to take off (chug chug choo choo . . .). Pretty soon they were in fast flight. A boy thrust a newspaper at him. He wanted to say no but had no voice. The headline screamed, "Suspicion of Hobbs's Sellout—Max Mercy." Under this was a photo Mercy had triumphantly discovered, showing Roy on his back, an obscene bullet imbedded in his gut. Around him danced a naked lady: "Hobbs at nineteen."

And there was also a statement by the baseball commissioner. "If this alleged report is true, that is the last of Roy Hobbs in organized baseball. He will be excluded from the game and all his records forever destroyed."

Roy handed the paper back to the kid.

"Say it ain't true, Roy."

When Roy looked into the boy's eyes he wanted to say it wasn't but couldn't, and he lifted his hands to his face and wept many bitter tears.

Library of Congress Cataloging in Publication Data

Malamud, Bernard.
The Natural.
(Time Reading Program)
with an introd. by Roger Angell.
I. Title.
[PS3563.A4N3 1980]   813'.54   80-20973
ISBN 0-8094-3594-2 (pbk.)
ISBN 0-8094-3593-4 (deluxe)